POACHERS

SEEKING A NEW LIFE IN TANZANIA

POACHERS

SEEKING A NEW LIFE IN TANZANIA

A Novel

Patricia Lee Sharpe

SUNSTONE PRESS

SANTA FE

Sunstone books may be purchased for educational, business, or sales promotional use.
For information please write: Special Markets Department, Sunstone Press,
P.O. Box 2321, Santa Fe, New Mexico 87504-2321.

Book and cover design › Vicki Ahl
Body typeface › Laurentian
Printed on acid-free paper
∞
eBook 978-1-61139-563-1

Library of Congress Cataloging-in-Publication Data

Names: Sharpe, Patricia Lee, 1936- author.
Title: Poachers : Seeking a new life in Tanzania : a novel / by Patricia Lee Sharpe.
Description: Santa Fe : Sunstone Press, [2018]
Identifiers: LCCN 2018032242 (print) | LCCN 2018032746 (ebook) | ISBN
  9781611395631 | ISBN 9781632932396 (softcover : alk. paper)
Classification: LCC PS3619.H356653 (ebook) | LCC PS3619.H356653 H86 2018
  (print) | DDC 813/.6--dc23
LC record available at https://lccn.loc.gov/2018032242

WWW.SUNSTONEPRESS.COM
SUNSTONE PRESS / POST OFFICE BOX 2321 / SANTA FE, NM 87504-2321 /USA
(505) 988-4418 / ORDERS ONLY (800) 243-5644 / FAX (505) 988-1025

For Nick,
best of all safari companions.

Preface

My tour as a U.S. Foreign Service Officer in Tanzania had been pretty amazing. I'd seen so much, done so much, learned so much I was anxious to share it. And so, blissfully confident of having an utterly captivating memoir completed in no time, I started writing.

Many months—and hundreds of pages later, I acknowledged the horrible truth. Such a memoir could never be published. Not because the people I'd known were uninteresting. Not because the story was boring through and through. Not because I didn't know how to string sentences together. The issue wasn't technical.

It was ethical. To the extent that I'm able to see myself clearly, I'm free to parade my own failings and imperfections. Exposing others to the same harsh spotlight is another matter. Evil or good, the movers and shakers of an era are public property. But the people I'd known in Tanzania had no reason to fear they'd be reanimated, faults and all, in anyone's memoir.

And so, a book that began as memoir became a novel, a fiction, in which the wildest thing that happens is true, in one way or another, for that time and place, although the people involved are wholly my inventions or reinventions. Call it a remix, if you will, bits and pieces culled from here and there to create a fuller, richer, more dynamic story of lives, human and non, dramatically colliding.

As for those really fine people I actually lived and worked with, I remember so many of you fondly and gratefully. Thank you for being part of my life.

—Patricia Lee Sharpe

1

Ambassador James Freeman was fed up with the Information Officer. The feeling was mutual. One or the other would have to pack up and leave Dar-es-Salaam—and it wasn't the Ambo. He demanded a competent replacement. And fast. It didn't happen. No available Foreign Service Officer would touch an assignment that looked like a suicide mission.

Then I came along.

"That's the deal." I was told. "Take it or leave it."

Having been IO at a similar post before resigning to marry a hot shot foreign correspondent, I had no qualms about facing the most combative local reporter. Jousting with a touchy ambassador was another matter. How long would I last? Irrelevant. I needed a job.

"I'll take it," I said.

Saying a cheery ciao to an ego-bruised husband in snow-bound Moscow, I celebrated Christmas in Florida with my parents, then spent a few days on paper-work and briefings in Washington, where I also did some detective work. Tanzania was a tourist Mecca for many good reasons. Climbing Mount Kilimanjaro. Going on safari to view (or hunt) the fauna. Visiting the ancestral boneyard at Olduvai Gorge. Ogling Masai in tribal regalia. Spice-shopping on exotic Zanzibar. Yet I, a renegade, had been recruited to fill a slot that should have been fought over. If Human Resources refused to supply the ugly details, old colleagues might.

One did. We'd served together in Indonesia, and—happy coincidence—my friend had worked under the reigning ambassador when Jim Freeman had occupied a top career position at the U.S. Information Agency headquarters in DC, a not unusual springboard to his current position.

"It was a clash of alpha males," my colleague told me over burger and fries (for him) and caesar salad with salmon (for me). Since then, the uppity IO had been set to learning Hangul in preparation for an assignment to Seoul, and Freeman had accepted the wild card. Me. "Now everyone's happy," my friend concluded. "For the moment, anyway."

"So what's your advice?" I asked.

"Play it straight," my friend said. "If Freeman wants your input, tell him what you think and why."

"Easy," I said. "Is that all?"

"Not quite. He may or may not agree with your brilliant analysis—and it's his call. He's the Big Enchilada."

"Remember where I'm coming from," I said, laughing. "Dealing with a Principal Officer's big fat ego beats flattering a husband's ditto."

My friend raised an eyebrow and claimed the check. "Good luck," he said. "Let me know how things work out."

Landing in Dar, I was met by Public Affairs Officer Clive Barnes, who headed the three-officer USIA post in Tanzania. He was waiting on the tarmac, a routine courtesy in the days before security got so tight, and he carried my book-heavy attaché case as we walked to his car, which was parked at the curb just outside the arrival hall. A handsome young Tanzanian was standing by the door. "Meet Juma," Clive said. "The best driver in Dar."

I had done some digging in DC, to learn what I could about my new boss. Having earned his captain's bars during the Korean War, he mustered out and became a reporter. Soon after, he joined USIA, serving in Liberia, the Philippines, Northern Ireland and Jamaica. Along the way, he won a few performance awards, but he'd yet to make the senior ranks. As for corridor reputation, the scuttlebutt that makes or breaks a Foreign Service Officer's career, I'd picked up nothing of interest. No accolades. No juicy gossip. On that level he was like a ghost.

The Clive Barnes ghost materialized in African-American form. Cap of gray hair. Trim white mustache. Impressive lack of middle-aged belly. Had bigotry stalled his promotion? Was he bitter? If so, he never revealed the hurt to me. Meanwhile, his gracious manner and good humor sped us through immigration and customs formalities. His way with Juma was similar. No smarmy faux buddy-buddy stuff, but nothing imperious either. And Clive, that day, was also an engaging tour guide, directing my gaze to landmarks, adorning them with bits of history, describing dignitaries I'd need to know, some likeable, some not, etc., etc., etc., until finally he was uttering the words I wanted to hear: "Almost there."

Straining to take in every detail of my new neighborhood, I asked Juma to slow down. Little good it did me. Most houses were obscured by high stucco walls or aggressive tangles of vegetation. All consistent with a desire for privacy. Frustrating, but understandable.

Then we came to a property with the look of a tornado touchdown.

"Here we are," Clive said.

I gasped. The house was attractive, but naked, its exterior ruthlessly stripped of anything like the normal skirt of greenery. Where shrubbery had been, I saw only stumps. Branches big and small had been thrown onto pyramids of refuse bulked up by cuttings from a bougainvillea hedge also reduced to stubble. The hack job had been recent. Leaves were withering, but green. Torn off flower petals were still vibrant with color.

"Who did this?" I demanded.

"Security wanted better sight lines," Clive explained. "Patrol cars make the rounds several times a night."

"Maybe I should leave the shades up so they can see into my bedroom, too," I said.

Clive gave me a strange look.

"Just joking," I said.

"We want you to be safe. And feel safe, too," he said. "And don't worry about the mess. It'll be gone by next week."

"Thanks," I murmured, subduing as well as I could my lack of appreciation. To be safe, evidently, I was expected to put up with terminal ugliness and total lack of privacy. No way, I decided. The hedge would grow back and quickly, too, as would the shrubs. My garden would flourish, I vowed to myself, so long as I remained in Dar. However, since the inevitable pruners were unlikely to appear in the near future, it was too soon to quarrel over landscaping. Not with Clive—and certainly not during my maiden encounter with Ambassador James Freeman, Head of Mission in Tanzania, which I put off as long as I could.

Our Mission worked like any other, back then. The Ambassador, appointed by the President, approved by the Senate, was all powerful. State Department officers handling political, economic and consular affairs fell under his direct chain of command, but always, in those Cold War days, the Embassy's press and cultural affairs were conducted by USIA, a separate entity known (confusingly) as the U.S. Information *Service* abroad. Thus USIS. Although we reported to our own superiors in Washington, we also had to please the Ambassador. How, then, to cooperate without being slavish? It was tricky, as my predecessor had discovered.

Perhaps because she'd watched that debacle unfolding, Clive's American secretary Milly Ayres played mother hen during my early days in Dar. She explained procedures, processed paperwork, introduced me to our Tanzanian staff members (known then as Foreign Service Nationals or FSNs) and ushered me to the cubbyhole that was to be my private office, for which she apologized.

"It's got a door," I said. "And a window—sort of. What more do I need?"

"You'll survive!" Milly said with a laugh.

And so, at last, she handed me off to Lily Johnson, the veteran FSN secretary I was inheriting from my predecessors, and Andrew Mweke, the even more formidable FSN Information Assistant, who doubled as post photographer. We chatted a bit, naturally, before we got down to business, at which point I plied them with questions. Were any crises brewing? Any deadlines looming? Who likes us? Who doesn't? Whom should I meet as soon as possible? And so on.

But Milly—sigh!—wasn't done with me. Two mornings later I rated a scolding. "Time to stop the dilly-dallying, Diana." Meaning: time to pay the obligatory newcomer's courtesy call on Ambassador James Freeman. "Contrary to rumors, he won't eat you up."

"Maybe not today," I conceded. "But tomorrow—or next month?"

"Depends on you," Milly said. "Personally, I like him. He doesn't sweat the small stuff." She lifted her phone. "Shall I call him?"

"Yes," I sighed. "Let's get it over with."

Milly dialed Virginia Pisa, the Ambassador's secretary, who gave me no time to agonize, no time to prepare. Her boss would expect to see me in forty-five minutes, she said.

Like many of USIA's non-FSO staff members, Milly was African-American. She turned out to be a genius at manipulating indifferent or hostile bureaucracies, and she managed to intimate, as soon as we met, that she'd keep things perking along very nicely, thank you, should her officer colleagues be simultaneously bed-bound with some bug or another.

"Why didn't you take the Foreign Service exam?" I asked, after the call to

Gina. "You could have been an officer. You could have been the boss."

"Why? Because I'm too smart." Milly snorted. "Sitting right here, I get all the benefits and none of the angst. None of the long hours either. At three thirty I'm out of here," she declared. "Remember that."

No, she wasn't skipping out early. Our work day in equator-nudging Dar began at seven thirty, before the sun got sadistic. Often, when we sponsored an evening event, we put in a twelve hour day. Or longer. Mostly we didn't mind. Thanks to our ideal location in the center of the city, albeit on the second floor of an age-blackened brickfront, a gratifyingly full house was guaranteed. We loved sending those reports back to headquarters.

Our colleagues at the Embassy enjoyed a very different ambiance, a Bauhaus-influenced box located in an upscale residential area. Approaching the property en route to my audience with the Ambo, I was astonished, even shocked, to see how tenderly its street-fronting garden had been cared for: a golf-tee lawn from which a gardener was plucking the night's sprinkling of frangipani blossoms; acacias arching over the driveway; pale purple blooms cascading from jacaranda trees; islets of flowers exploding with color like earth-bound fireworks.

That being my first visit to the Embassy, the Marine on duty at the guard post didn't recognize me. I showed my passport. He verified my appointment and clicked me through a heavy glass door into the lobby. Virginia Pisa, dark-eyed, a little chunky, aiming for an ageless image via expert highlighting, was there to greet me. She led me to her desk.

"Have a seat," she said. "Call me Gina."

I looked at my watch and apologized, "I'm a bit early."

"Not the worst sin," Gina smiled.

We chatted, getting acquainted through the usual Foreign Service preambles. Previous posts. Possible mutual friends. Post perks. Post downsides.

"How long have you been in Dar?" I asked.

"Too long," Gina replied. She'd arrived with Freeman—and at his request, an important thing to know. She could help me if she liked me.

"Are you enjoying it?" I asked.

"Can you say dull?" Gina asked, laughing. "Unless you're into the safari life. Hippos. Rhinos. The great white hunter—ha! that's a good one. Not my style."

"And the Ambassador?" I asked.

"What do you think? He's not a political appointee collecting trophies at taxpayers' expense."

I, on the other hand, was dying to go on safari, but that was no time to say so. Instead, Gina and I commiserated over a universal Foreign Service grievance: non-career ambassadors appointed as a reward for raising the monies it takes to pile up votes for a presidential candidate. As if that weren't bad enough, these political appointees usually got the plum posts. The glamorous posts. The easy, fun posts. The safari posts, for that matter.

"I'm surprised that Dar didn't go to a political appointee," I said.

Gina laughed. "Actually the politicos wanted Jim Freeman out of Washington, and Dar happened to be available. He wasn't much of a yes man."

Great! I thought. How long will I last?

Gina checked the time and picked up the phone. "Are you ready for Ms. Forrest, sir?"

Ambassador James Freeman was pushing back from his desk as I entered the room. Tall, sandy hair seriously graying, moving sinuously in a tan summer suit, he made me think of a mountain lion. He extended his hand, I met it with mine, and he gestured toward the seating area, where he took the control position, facing the door. "Welcome to Dar," he said. "I hope you've been well taken care of." He was referring to practical things. Had I been met at the airport? Had I been whisked through entry formalities? Was my house in good condition—and did I like it?

Re the house I could be honest. It was airy, cheery and comfortable. Everything else, I assured him, had gone "like clockwork."

James Freeman was satisfied. "Good," he said. "There's nothing like getting off on the right foot."

Which meant it was time to pop the question. "So tell me, Sir, how can I make your job easier?"

His reply came down to this: chauffeured around in a U.S. flag-flaunting Cadillac, he was isolated from ordinary life, but a mid-level Information Officer was free to go most anywhere anytime and speak to all kinds of people about practically everything. "So here's what I need: a weekly rundown. Interpret if you wish, but make a distinction between what you observe and what you think."

"That seems pretty straightforward," I said.

"And remember this: I don't want a lot of second guessing. Call it as you see it."

"I've been a journalist and an academic," I said. "That comes naturally."

Self-preservation comes naturally, too, I thought. Most superiors, whatever they say, tolerate very small doses of honesty from their subordinates. But so far so good. We ran out the clock by trading Foreign Service war stories.

Returning to U.S.I.S., I caught my reflection in the big brass plate that welcomed everyone to the American Center. Those were the days! No armed guards. No metal detectors. No X-ray machines scanning purses for weapons. Ignoring a balky elevator, I climbed up the stairs behind a pair of students heading for the library, the best stocked in the city. FSN Ayesha Riaz, our Chief Librarian, interrupted her due date stamping to wave at the still new IO. I waved back, then laid on some swagger as I entered Milly's domain. She responded with a thumbs up. "Whadya know! She's still alive."

"And kicking," I replied. "So watch out! Is he in?"

"He's waiting. With congrats," Milly said. "Gina called."

Clive's door was open. I stepped into an office whose book shelves actually held books. Cold war stuff. American history. Classic American literature plus Ralph Ellison, James Baldwin, Zora Neale Houston, Maya Angelou, etc., as well as the autobiography of Frederick Douglass. African works too, like Chinua Achebe's *Things Fall Apart* and Nugugi wa Thiongo's *Petals of Blood*. Even Izak Dinesen's *Out of Africa*. But no Franz Fanon. No Eldridge Cleaver. Clive was a diplomat, not a Black nationalist.

Realizing that I was eyeing the volume he'd laid on the desk as he lowered his feet to the floor, he grinned. "Keeping *au courant*," he said. "Well, actually, too good to put down." I never did make out the title, but I'd caught him at his default occupations: reading and ruminating.

Facing me across his desk, Clive defined my responsibilities based on a division of labor that suited us both. "I'll handle the Information Ministry and the politicos," he decreed, which gave me the run of the city, cultivating the working press, such as it was. For all of mainland Tanzania there was a single newspaper plus a single radio operation, each with English and Kiswahili divisions. Ditto for the island of Zanzibar, which Tanzania had absorbed at independence. As for TV, two channels sputtered along, both short on professional expertise, thus providing delicious placement possibilities for USIA materials, assuming that I—over his half glasses Clive gave me a comically stern look—assuming that I hustled to get them placed.

There were no websites back then. No Facebook. No texting. No tweeting. Even email was exotic. In our whole office, believe it or not, we had only two computers, one for Clive and Milly, the other for the rest of us, and our phones went dead from time to time for no discernible reason. Person-to-person contact still lubricates today's electronically-inundated age, but back then it was bedrock. Our messages and invitations reached their addressees in the only reliable way: on paper, handed over by our own reliable, personable couriers—like Juma, Clive's favorite driver. Or Massoud, who came to a very bad end.

Nor did we inspect those vehicles for tampering while they were parked here and there about the city. Book snitching worried us more than bombs—and there was consolation even in theft: our carefully selected titles would be handed around and read many times. Terror came twelve years later, when Al Qaeda blew up the U.S. embassies in Dar and Nairobi.

When I was in Dar, Ambassador James Freeman was the worst thief of new magazines and books. He grabbed copies of *Time* and *Newsweek* as soon as they tumbled out of the pouch. By the time he'd read them, they were too stale for our more demanding patrons. Kiki Swenson, our Cultural Affairs Officer, who oversaw the library, had complained to Clive. He nixed a confrontation with the Ambassador. "So I began ordering two copies," she told me. "I thought that was a pretty good solution." Not so. She earned a rebuke from the budget-conscious regional librarian, who circulated among posts too small to rate a resident American. This stung and was still stinging when I arrived, leading Kiki to wonder if I might broach the subject with the Ambassador. I sympathized, but not enough to jeopardize my tenuous reinstatement by flogging a lost cause.

Clive concluded our planning session with an invitation. He wanted to introduce me to our European counterparts. "How about Sunday? For dinner. Jet lag permitting," he added graciously.

"The NATO gang," I said. "I'd love to come."

As Clive ran down the list of fellow Cold Warriors, I recalled the popular corollary to a regulation requiring FSOs to report liaisons with foreigners: avoid insidious pillow talk; sleep NATO. Months would pass before my divorce was final. How lovely it would be if any of Clive's invitees were attractive—and available.

Clive's hands off approach to management was perfect for me, but Kiki Swenson, our Cultural Affairs officer, could have done with more guidance. She'd been a high school teacher in Minneapolis. The pay was low. The students were lackadaisical. Prospects for change were nil. And so, having aced a rigorous Foreign Service exam, she had endured the dreary orientation process and been reincarnated as Cultural Affairs Officer in Dar. True to USIA tradition, she attributed her success so far to the experience and good judgement of Mo (for Mohammad) Jabar and Amelia King, her two FSN cultural assistants.

"Talk about awkward," she confided as we celebrated my first TGIF in Dar. "Mo and Amelia knew the job, but the dummy was in charge."

We had secured a corner table at a popular warehouse-like hangout known for its live music. The big draw was a local combo with a repertoire heavy on the latest hits from Zaire, burbly-bubbly rhythms that kept the dance floor filled. I beat time with fingers and toes as we shared a too warm pitcher of the local beer she'd accurately described as better than the blah imports.

"Thank heaven for FSNs," I agreed. "I know the job, but not the country. What would I do without Andrew? Or Lily?"

Kiki nodded. "Tons of other people helped me, too. Tanzanians are really sweet. That's the good news."

"And the bad?"

"Inflation and the official rate of exchange. If you avoid the Black Market, like a good girl, a head of lettuce costs $10. You'll see. Hardship pay can't make up for that."

" Do you—"

"We're not supposed to, you know."

I left it at that. If Kiki was buying shillings on the black market, I'd learn soon enough.

Saturday night's dinner with Clive and his wife was a far grander affair. China. Crystal. Several courses with several wines. Conversation that was light but nuanced. Humor that ran to irony, not guffaws. On another level, the West German press attaché was single, good-looking, attentive—and overshadowed. I liked the Brit's wit (and Irish wife) better.

2

Clive was happy. I was doing most of his work as well as my own. Stressed yet bored, feeling trapped, stifled and isolated, I developed the habit of gravitating to a window, where I perched on the sill and gazed down at life on the sidewalk. Soon I was recognizing the needy regulars. Many of them were elders, knobby, wrinkled, shrunken, almost sexless, gender seeping away with life. Sadder, if possible, was a mother much too young to have lost so many teeth. She sat, leaning against the wall beneath me, sometimes nursing, sometimes flicking at flies, sometimes just cuddling her baby. Another alms-seeker was a man who'd lost a leg. He stationed himself at the corner, his powerful chest and shoulders hunched over the Y of an improvised crutch.

Very rarely did passers-by drop a coin or place a folded shilling in anyone's cup. Never the status-conscious young clerks in drip dry shirts, belted trousers and shiny leather shoes, though sometimes their sweat labor contemporaries in tee shirts, plaid sarongs and flipflops. Never the clumps of girls and boys in school uniforms, the girls linked arm in arm, giggling, the boys clowning and often scolded by self-absorbed female office workers swishing along in stylish skirts and high heels. As for the older students, they were preoccupied with their own hopes and dreams. Many of them turned into the doorway by the sign that said American Center. They were heading for the library. Kiki's responsibility, not mine.

And then there were the stout men squeezed into three piece suits and partial to heavy-looking attaché cases. They parked their cars and strode, uncharitably, into the bank across the street. What were they up to, those guys? Fencing for poachers? Laundering cash from smuggling?

Catching sight of another too prosperous-looking suspect disappearing into the bank, I put the question to Andrew, who was more interested in showing me something in the latest edition of the *News*. Kiki had invited an American economist—he'd been recommended by our Cultural Bureau in Washington—to lecture on the benefits of global free trade. The program attracted a standing room only audience, and the *News* had front-paged the story, with a photo provided by us. Meaning Andrew.

"Terrific!" I said.

"And look at this," Andrew said, turning to the editorial page. Our friends at the *News* had found the speaker to be "thoughtful," high praise given the baked-in anti-capitalist stance of the government-controlled press.

"Make sure this gets into Kiki's report," I said.

Andrew turned to go, but I drew him back toward the window. "Wait—check this out."

Ooops! My suspect had driven off while we were reveling in our coverage coup. I described him to Andrew.

"Don't jump to conclusions," he advised. "An attaché case crammed with currency might, or might not, be dicey. Tanzanians demand cash. Cash for land. Cash for houses. Cash for cars—"

"Cash for favors?" I suggested.

"You know too much," he said, smiling.

I also knew enough to refuse perfectly good fifty dollar bills when I cashed personal checks at the Embassy. Tanzania was flooded with counterfeit versions, making all fifties useless as exchange for local currency on the black market. Yes. I'd joined the dark side. The go-between was a jolly little Peace Corps volunteer. She protected her sources. We protected her—and one another. If the Ambassador knew, and surely he guessed, he took no action. Why ruin a terrific morale-booster?

Meanwhile, I coped morosely with claustrophobia and tedium, dashing off press releases, collating media reports, tendering my shards of knowledge during seances with the Ambassador, until, one glorious day, out of nowhere, the inspiration arrived. Lunching it a la brown bag at my desk, I was listening to the Voice of America, which had an enthusiastic following in Dar. As for rest of the country, I hadn't the least idea. But—this was my Great Idea!—I could find out. I could answer other questions, too. Was VOA more or less popular than the BBC, our friendly competition, and how did we stack up against our not so friendly competitors, the Soviets and the Chinese? Could any of these signals be heard out in the boonies? If so, what sorts of programs did rural people tune to? Music? News? Tips for farmers or mothers? Finally, the Biggie: what did people think about America and why?

USIA, back then, ran a respectable polling service. So did VOA. I'd worked with their reliable results at other posts. "What about Tanzania?" I asked Lily and Andrew. "Anything recent in the way of listener surveys?"

"Not in my time," Andrew replied.

I was jubilant. Since Andrew had been with USIA for ten years, there were no insuperable obstacles to an updated survey scheme.

"So how about a round trip to Mwanza?" I proposed. "Different stops coming and going. A week on the road. And I can dip my toes in Lake Victoria," I added.

Andrew laughed. "We might leave the toes out of the formal proposal."

"Pity. But that reminds me. Did you ever see *The African Queen*? I'll talk to Kiki. We can show it on movie nights."

"We've shown it. And *The Snows of Kilimanjaro*. And *Out of Africa*. And all the other White adventures in Darkest Africa—"

"So no one came?"

"Standing room only. Everyone loved them."

"And you?"

"In spite of myself."

Clive went along with my proposal, mainly to get his antsy IO off his back, I think, but the Ambassador was enthusiastic. "We don't get up country as often as we should," he mused. And then—bang! bang! bang!—he reeled off questions that, to his mind, needed answers. "Are the Russians popular? Are the Chinese having any impact at all? Is the gas shortage causing unrest? Do people look healthy? Are they glad to see you? Helpful? Above all, make a note of anyone who seems influential, anyone we should be in contact with. Keep your eyes open. Everything's grist for the mill."

But the trip almost didn't happen. Tanzania was running out of petrol. An Iranian tanker hovered at anchor just outside the harbor. Its captain refused to discharge a single drop of desperately needed cargo until the Finance Ministry cleared huge outstanding debts in foreign exchange, of which there was very little in the Treasury. Tanzania's trade balance was congenitally negative. Hence the big audience for our economist.

As the stand off continued, the gas lines grew longer. Even the Embassy's tax-free allotment of gas was rationed. Juma and Massoud compensated by spending hours in line with ordinary Tanzanian drivers. Meanwhile, up north, mangos spoiled for lack of transport. Shops in Dar ran out of corn, a staple more important than rice. Bath soap was so scarce that Mary, my newly hired maid, bent to kiss my feet when I gave her a six pack of Ivory I'd purchased at the Embassy commissary. Realizing with horror what she meant to do, I grabbed her elbows and pulled her up.

"There goes the trip," I moaned, as yet another gas short day went by. Even if we started out with Gerry cans lashed to every available square inch of roof and bumpers, we couldn't carry enough fuel to get us to Mwanza and back, without a few refills along the way.

"No problem," Andrew said. "I'll call some friends."

Despite the usual angst of elusive connections, dropped calls, crossed lines and static, Andrew's friends confirmed their access to petrol and promised to reserve some for us. I was a little uneasy about relying on black market fuel for an official trip, but restlessness and realism got the better of me.

"Can we count on them?" I asked.

"A promise beats a contract," he said. "But it won't be cheap."

"Adjust the budget," I said.

That's the way things worked in Tanzania, and Andrew was an adept. Not only was he well known and trusted in the media world, he had a network of buddies dating back to the days of his youthful athletic prowess. Andrew had shown promise as a boxer, but a sports reporter whom he idolized had convinced him that newspaper work would more fully engage his talents. When I arrived in Dar, he was nearly fifty, but he still had a boxer's build and agility. Traveling with him, I always felt safe.

Andrew's special journalistic skill was photography. Above all, he was a genius in the darkroom, having perfected a way to produce flattering images of White and Black faces in the same picture. No overexposed pale blotches. No underexposed dark blobs. He had more than earned a little perk I had no intention of ending: he could use the darkroom, chemicals included, to process his own photos, mostly of wildlife. Some had appeared in international nature and travel magazines.

And so, loaded with shillings to deal with all possible contingencies, we headed west.

3

The road, two lanes of blacktop, wound up and over the coastal hills. It sliced through the Mikumi Wildlife Preserve, then beelined across savanna and marginal farmland to the city of Mwanza on Lake Victoria. Well into the Preserve that first morning, I spotted some gray boulders thrusting through grasses I guessed to be taller than a seven foot basketball player. The rocks seemed out of place to me.

Andrew laughed. "Look again."

I did. The boulders became elephants. Farther on there was more magic. Tree trunks in a distant thicket turned into a herd of giraffes, the angle of their necks being the giveaway. Soon wilderness yielded to agriculture, and I met my first ever guinea fowl. Andrew braked so hard I thought my seat belt would crack my ribs. A guinea hen was conducting five little fluffballs across the asphalt. Black on black—except for mama's crimson comb and her white speckled feathers.

Cattle with xylophone ribs grazed by fences that were mostly symbolic, and some goats wandered about. Guinea corn, the favored crop, made room every so often for mustard plots standing out as yellow patches on a green quilt. Other fields were devoted to ground nuts or to a leafy green whose name I forget. It was destined for stews I never enjoyed as much as the Arab-influenced cuisine of the Swahili coast, which extended to the North and South of Dar.

Around noon Andrew pulled off the road and parked alongside a collection of fuel drums adjacent to a little shop, a mere shack with a broad counter, the local equivalent of a 7-11. The proprietor looked up from his seat on a crate, threw his cigarette aside and rushed over to the Land Rover. "Mzee!" he called. "Mzee!" That's Kiswahili for "Old Man," a term of respect and affection.

The title didn't bother Andrew, whose shaved head was occasionally guilty of stubble that was gray as well as black. After the two of them had collided in a hearty embrace, Andrew uncoiled a siphon from the Land Rover's tool kit. He thrust one end into a drum, placed the other end between his lips and began sucking. Imagining myself gargling gas, I couldn't bear to watch.

I turned away, bought soda and some snacks from a young girl who should have been in school, not making change for her father, and stood there, munching on cashews, scanning the horizon and watching an occasional car go by. His siphoning done, Andrew cleansed his palate with cola while chatting with his buddy, in Kiswahili. Traces of English hinted at marriages, funerals, kids, politics. A matter of good manners, Andrew explained. Except for the sly, extra queries about radio programs.

"Good show," I said.

It began to feel like a comedy routine. As soon as we pulled up to a petrol pump or collection of drums, someone would shout "Bwana!" or "Mzee!" Andrew would hop down, perform the greeting ritual, report on family affairs, shake his head over the state of the country—and append the radio quiz. After the umpteenth re-enactment, Andrew chuckled ruefully. "Even out here I have to behave. There's always someone to tell the tale."

"Aha!" I said. "Not good, just prudent. But I'm not free either. Whether I like it or not, I'm always representing the U.S."

"Not sincere, just well paid," said Andrew.

"That's a little extreme," I said.

Sometimes the road took us through the center of a small town. We'd pass a school, a clinic, a police station and, strung out along the highway, all the facilities truckers and travelers might need. Liquor shops. Rooming houses. Eateries. Cycle and motor repair. Tire patching. It was strip commercial, African style. Sometimes we bought gum we'd never chew or cigarettes we'd never smoke. As we paid, we'd chat about this and that, including a great program on VOA last night. "Did you hear it? No? So, what *do* you listen to?" Lunch stops were productive, too. Was our method scientific? Of course not. But anecdotes beat total ignorance.

The Land Rover had a radio, but we also tested reception via my own little AM/FM/shortwave transistor and a more powerful set from the office. When road noise obliterated talk shows, we listened to music—and what a selection we had!

Western classical. American jazz, pop and country. African sound from all over the continent—Nigerian high life, vocals with clicks à la Miriam Makeba, those burbly bubbly Congolese rhythms, arrangements for stringed instruments with a Middle Eastern twang, even some radically eclectic music from Mali, Andrew's favorite, which I'd never heard before, but liked very much. "I'll buy you some cassettes," he promised. And so we learned that VOA was audible everywhere. As was the competition. The playing field was level.

During the first afternoon on the road my transistor went dead. Not wishing to waste time by asking Andrew to stop, I contrived some contortions that allowed me to reach into the back seat to rummage about for fresh batteries. As I shoved things around, a flap on Andrew's camera bag fell open. Sun glinted on his always-ready Nikon—and on something else. A revolver. I asked Andrew to pull over.

"Guess what I found," I said.

Andrew placed the revolver in my palm, where it nestled as if it had been custom-designed for me. I'd never held a gun before.

"Is it loaded?" I asked.

"Yes."

"And the safety's on?"

"Of course."

"You should have told me," I said. "This is a business trip. Not a safari."

"You never know."

"Guns don't make me feel safer. They make me nervous."

"I'll teach you to shoot."

"I don't want to shoot."

"Sometimes there's no choice. On the road, in the bush, it's good to be prepared."

I was well aware that poachers slaughtered park rangers as well as horn-heavy rhinos and massive tuskers. I knew that drivers had been robbed at night on the sea drive in Dar—and that a shadowy crime ring had broken into some foreigners' homes, which explained the over-pruning of my own garden. Andrew's rationale had validity, but we were on a business trip. "I should have been consulted," I insisted. "I should have been informed."

Sliding the revolver into the glove compartment, Andrew shifted from neutral into first gear. "Better get going," he said. "We're expected for dinner."

Thank goodness for music! The next hour was the most strained, most awkward that Andrew and I ever spent together. Deliverance came only when we parked next to a truck with a USAID logo on its door. We spent that night in a hostel with a team of dairy specialists dedicated to improving milk yields. Before we left, I visited cows in their barns and pastures, got educated by dairy experts and posed for Andrew's Nikon with said cows and experts. The reward for USAID? A project-friendly feature story in the *News.* We slept well, we ate well, we enjoyed good company, but we weren't moochers. And we also had a chance to quiz Tanzanian biologists and workers about their favorite radio programs.

Eventually we reached Mwanza, where I did indeed dip my toe into Lake Victoria, whose shallows were so clogged with water hyacinth that fishermen struggled to get their boats in and out. Long before that, however, we'd learned that VOA's non-propagandistic approach was paying off. VOA news was valued everywhere for its objectivity and trustworthiness. BBC news might win more ears in this ex-British colony, but VOA's message was thereby strengthened, not canceled out. We were allies. When it came to music, however, no international service could beat VOA, and those music lovers loved America, too. American popular culture had conquered the world, a fact that undermined Congressional enthusiasm for a tax-supported information agency after the Berlin wall fell.

But dissolution was inconceivable when I was in Tanzania. The Cold War was largely an information war, and USIA waged it ingeniously, using every available medium to tell America's story "warts and all," as we proudly put it. Looking back from these more troubled times, I see, as I didn't then, how easy the job was. Compared to the Soviet Union, a police state with a floundering economy, how could a rich, free, strong, stable, creative America not look good? Meanwhile, our trip report was going to be unequivocal: don't mess with success. VOA makes friends for America.

So did Andrew and I. We watched water gush from new village water pumps, admired embroidery produced by rural women seeking extra income and watched protein sources aka fish swimming around in ponds created on a dry plateau—all USAID or Peace Corps beneficiaries. And, yes, I dipped my toe in Lake Victoria, whose shoreline was so clogged with water hyacinth that local fishermen were struggling to make a living.

Determined to make the most of every mile and every hour, we planned a final morning of delivering several boxes of American books (selected by Kiki) to a school library and visiting a well baby clinic. We'd lunch with the latter's staff and arrive in Dar before sundown.

Life refused to follow schedule.

At the school, for instance, the ceremonies (recorded stage by stage by Andrew's Nikon) should have gone like this: I would present a dramatic-looking stack of books to the head teacher; the assembled children would sing a charming song; the principal, having thanked USIS, would conduct us to the Land Rover. What actually happened was this: a first grader waved his hand and shouted, "I want a picture, too!" Every child in the school, it turned out, wanted a picture with the nice lady from Dar. The principal sputtered, scolded, protested and, inevitably, gave in. Numbers dictated separate photos for each grade, pupils arranged by height and flanked by teachers, easy enough to do, but our schedule was in ruins.

An hour later, Tanzanian road etiquette dictated that we assist a driver who had raised the hood of old sedan so that he could stare haplessly at the engine. Andrew took a look. "It's overheated," he declared. No wonder! The water reservoir was empty. In addition, the dipstick showed a dangerously low oil level.

Andrew rolled his eyes. "Maybe I should check the gas tank, too." Surprise! It was half full.

The driver, who'd said little during the diagnosis, wondered if we might supply him with water—and maybe some oil, too. He was willing to pay and pulled out his wallet. I waved the wallet aside. With Dar so close, we had more of everything than we needed. "Will two quarts do?" I asked. He got some gas, too.

By the time our Good Samaritan moment was over, we were even further behind schedule.

"You should have charged him and charged him double," muttered Andrew. "For stupidity."

"I was tempted," I confessed.

The visit to a well baby clinic produced its own delays. Lunch lasted forever. Then I had to watch babies being weighed, babies being measured, babies being inoculated, pregnant women getting advice on prenatal care, non-pregnant women being counseled on how to stay that way, followed, naturally, by sessions with lady doctors rapturously in love with their work and desperate for funds to keep the clinic open. I opened my purse and out flew some shillings. Mine.

All the while, Andrew's Nikon was busy. Dozens of heart-warming photos.

I loved every moment at the clinic, but the sun was flirting with the hills we had to cross, and the hills themselves were barely visible on the horizon. Andrew guesstimated a post midnight arrival in Dar.

I groaned.

"There's an alternative," he said. He had friends in residence at the Mikumi Wildlife Preserve, an American couple doing research on baboons. "We can spend the night with them. They won't let us starve either."

4

Highway behind us, we plunged into muggy spooky darkness, pushing through branches and undergrowth that would have made a bloody mess of my bare arm, if I hadn't rolled the window up. Potholes threw us around like thrill seekers on a carnival ride.

"Sorry," Andrew said. "Can't avoid them."

"You're sure we're on the right track?"

"It's always like this. Keeps out the tourists. "

"We're not tourists, but still. Barging in. Without warning—"

"Not to worry. It's lonely out here. Phil and Eileen love company, and sometimes the camp's pretty lively. Last time I turned up, some primatologists from Australia were visiting. I had to sleep in the kitchen hut. No big deal. I can sleep anywhere. The problem was the elephant."

"The elephant?" I echoed.

"The elephant. We sat around talking, singing, drinking beer—and more beer. Which is why, probably, I overlooked a bowl of bananas."

The drift was clear. Where I come from, the danger is bears. Don't keep food in your tent. Not even toothpaste.

"So," I guessed, "the bananas were shouting come hither, and the message was picked up by—"

"The elephant."

Strange noises woke him. The creature was feeling around with its trunk, looking for a way in.

"The moon was full. I could see—I can still see—those white tusks on the other side of the screen—and me in a hut as strong as cardboard. Fortunately the elephant didn't know that."

"What about your trusty revolver?"

Andrew snorted. "Against an elephant?"

"So what happened?" I asked.

"He walked away."

"That's it?"

"Well, I like the story. It's got suspense and a happy ending. You should like it, too."

"Meaning relax?"

"Something like that."

"You've got to be kidding," I said.

Eventually we broke into a clearing. On its periphery stood several small structures, only one with lights on. As we turned into what Andrew called the usual parking spot, a screened door opened. I saw two people, one tall, one much shorter, silhouetted against the brightness inside.

"Phil and Eileen," Andrew said.

Our welcome was all that car weary travelers might hope for. Hugs for Andrew. Big smiles and warm handshakes for me. Affectionate insults. Absurd compliments. A hint in the air of good food waiting.

"Andrew, you old bastard, who is this beautiful woman?" That was Phil.

As for Eileen: "What a wonderful surprise! You're just in time to eat."

They drew us out of the mosquito zone into the kitchen hut, where the table was quickly reset for four. Minutes later Eileen was ladling spicy beans over hillocks of rice. Phil's job was prying caps off beer bottles. An oil lamp suspended over the table united us in a circle of light, a fellowship of humans surrounded by wilderness and darkness.

Phil handed me a beer, wondrously cold, thanks to a gas-powered fridge. "Welcome to the Baboon Camp," he said.

"Thank you," I said. "I'm glad to be here."

Phil's thinning hairline suggested that he was edging into middle age. Eileen was considerably younger. They both had ponytails. Phil was the one with the beard. Their story wasn't unusual. He'd been a young assistant professor. She'd been a smart, ambitious grad student. Their research overlapped, and romance had crept up on them. "We were colleagues," Eileen said. "Working together on these really interesting projects. And then suddenly—oh wow!—we were more."

"So we legalized it," Phil said.

I raised my bottle. "Congratulations," I said.

Phil and Eileen were studying baboons, yellow baboons, which seemed odd to me. Who loves a baboon, after all? Lots of people, I learned—and for the same reason that researchers attach their lives to chimps or mountain gorillas: a fascinating similarity to humans. But baboon territory is also elephant territory, and Phil and Eileen were preoccupied, that night, with a recently announced, fearfully low elephant count.

Helicopter hunting was an unrealized nightmare in those days. China had yet to become a global economic power. Even so, providing Asian ivory carvers with raw material was depleting the elephant population. Big, strong and smart as they are, elephants were no match for human poachers. Ruthless, heavily-armed, able to afford fast new vehicles, the ivory mafia outgunned and outran a devoted and largely honest, but underpaid and poorly-equipped Tanzanian park ranger service.

"It's all these new roads," Phil grumbled. "Grubbing for oil, the multinationals make it too easy for poachers to get in and out."

Andrew agreed. With Rafiq Khan, a Pakistani friend who owned a trucking company, he conducted a modest safari business in the Selous Game Preserve, where hunting by permit was allowed. Their safaris weren't for hedonists, I'd been told. No fancy camp furniture. No vintage wine served in claret glasses with a pretty ping. But clients went home with the photos or trophies they'd dreamed of. Faced with bidders for the same date, Andrew favored photographers, or so he claimed. Rafiq stressed the bottom line: big game hunters had deeper pockets. Meanwhile, around the table in Mikumi, there was agreement: uncontrolled road building would funnel hoards of tourists into previously pristine terrain, jeopardizing the wildlife, diluting the mystique of the bush.

A little less mystique would have been fine with me that night. Phil, Eileen and Andrew were completely at home, completely at ease, but I felt like bait in a well lit trap. Flimsy was the obvious word for the hut. Its walls, sheeted waist-high in thin corrugated metal, were topped by an even less substantial strip of screening. Old-style air conditioning. Its roof, of the same corrugated material, extended verandah-like to shield occupants from harsh sunlight and wind-blown rain. The other huts differed only in function, two for sleeping, one serving as work space.

There was, supposedly, a ranger station a mile or so away, but the unrelieved blackness that pressed in upon us made me feel as if we were the only humans on the entire planet. We'd be in serious trouble, or dead, before a radioed SOS brought aid in case of emergency or threat. Yet darkness had its brighter side. Away from the sooty air and never quenched lights of Dar, the stars seemed bigger and amazingly close, as if I could pluck them, like Christmas ornaments. And the soft hum, thrum and chirruping of insects so resembled the sweet sound of summer at home that I forgot, for long moments, to be alert for signs of impending danger.

The sound of a bottle cap hitting the table top brought me out of my reverie. Phil had replaced my empty bottle with a full one, and the subject had changed to practical matters. Research funding was drying up, evidently. Phil and Eileen feared that the era of automatic grant renewals might be ending.

"Every year you worry," Andrew said with a smile. "Every year the money comes through."

"I hope you're right," Eileen said. "But this year it's worse. Cuts even for the Baboon Camp. That's going to hurt a lot of researchers."

"What the Camp really needs is an increase," Phil said. "The huts are rusting—and the Suzuki's a joke. Almost as bad as your Land Rover."

Meaning Andrew's. Every year the Embassy auctioned off items deemed surplus for one reason or another. A vintage Land Rover had been relinquished by one of Clive's predecessors, and Andrew had bought it. My colleagues in Dar joked that only Andrew's special juju kept the rattletrap running after all these years.

"The consortium meets next month, and we'll know our fate." Phil uncapped his third bottle of beer. "Consolation, celebration—either way let's throw a party, a beach party. We need a break."

Eileen turned to me. "Including you, Diana."

"I'll be there," I promised.

Phil and Eileen had other problems, too. Tanzanian customs authorities had been unusually obstructive of late; it was taking longer and longer to clear vehicle parts—the Suzuki was in desperate need of a new muffler, for instance—and lab materials. Old friends in the bureaucracy, while essentially sympathetic, had been suggesting that a little more tea, the polite term for bribery, might solve the problem.

"The Embassy won't play the tea game," I said. "But the pressure never lets up, as Andrew knows."

Andrew, long-standing point man for USIS import complications, nodded in weary confirmation. "Same game. Every time. Our stuff's duty free. But papers get lost, items get misplaced, key people are on endless leave. So we play a waiting game, and eventually lost things get found. Every so often, though, the Ambassador has to lean on someone."

"At least you don't have to worry about renewing residence permits," Phil said. "Or gun permits. That's got trickier, too."

"I don't suppose you could help us," Eileen ventured.

"If cultural agreements are being violated, we could probably do some nudging. But I can't make promises," I explained. "That's Kiki's territory."

Phil shook his head. "What a way to treat a new friend—whining and begging. So tell us about your trip. First time up country. How did you like it?"

"Wonderful!" I said, but I couldn't elaborate, because Andrew waggled his fingers for silence. "Shhhh!" he whispered. "Elephant."

We hushed. My eyes followed his pointing finger.

It was no more than fifty feet away, an enormous gray shape visible only because of reflected lamplight on a moonless night, an honest-to-god untrained, unchained elephant strolling calmly through the camp. It was so close I could hear the faint swish swish of dry grass brushing against its ankles. My heart was thud thudding. My muscles went twitchy trembly. My fingertips, my lips, every part of me tingled with alertness. The elephant kept on walking.

After a reasonable interval, Andrew stood. He opened the screen door, switched on his flashlight and swept its strong white beam from left to right, right to left.

"Nothing," he reported and strode toward the outhouse on the other side of the fire pit at the hub of the clearing.

"Andrew's not looking for elephants," Eileen explained. "He's looking for lions. Their eyes reflect light."

"Don't move around at night without being super alert," Phil said.

"Right," said Eileen. "This isn't suburbia, and hurrah for that—except when the pump goes out. Or the generator breaks down. Or gas is hard to get—like now."

"The perfect cure for neurosis." Phil laughed. "Too many real worries."

I was only half listening, because I was focused on Andrew's progress toward the loo. His sun-bleached khakis grew fainter and fainter until all I could follow was the play of his flashlight. When he got back, I would have to make that trip, and the prospect was generating sweet memories of Holiday Inns, all rooms with bath, phone and TV. No mosquitoes. No flies. No elephants. No lions.

"We were so noisy," I said. "How could Andrew hear the elephant?"

"He's a hunter," said Phil.

"Unfortunately," Eileen sighed. "But he's into ecology. He cares about wildlife."

Andrew and I had bickered about that on the road. Animal killers as animal lovers? It made no sense to me.

"You can't hunt animals that don't exist," Andrew said.

"I've heard that one before, " I retorted. "Every deer season back home. I still think hunters like the killing most."

"Don't forget the skill element. Tracking. Marksmanship. I used to shoot more, but bloodthirsty? I don't think so."

We'd left it at that.

Once Andrew was out of sight, Phil asked about our plans for the morning. "If you've got a little flexibility, tag along with us."

"The routine is simple," Eileen said. "We follow baboons and take notes. You won't be in the way. And don't worry about safety." Park rules prohibited foot safaris (or researchers on foot) unless accompanied by a ranger, she explained. "A ranger with a gun," she added. That made it easier for a coward to sign on, assuming Andrew was agreeable.

"He has a family to get home to," I said.

"Don't worry about him," Eileen said with a laugh. "He hates Dar."

It was hard to keep my mind on the conversation. My bladder was reminding me of a little girl who generated endless excuses to stay up a little longer so she wouldn't have to climb the stairs into darkness. Now those imaginary monsters had turned into real elephants and highly possible lions.

Andrew rejoined us. I relieved him of the flashlight. "My turn, I'm sorry to say."

"Newcomers are always nervous," Phil said. "But we haven't lost anyone yet."

"I can keep you company," Eileen offered.

"Just watch," I said.

Talk about minutes dragging! Hardly breathing from fear, I swept my path with light, as instructed. Away from the door. Past the Land Rover. Beyond the fire pit. Through some grass—swish! swish! And then I was shut, safely, in the outhouse, which was slightly smelly. The return trip was worse. Hostile darkness now behind me, I imagined claws digging into my shoulders, which isn't to say I'd lost all traces of pride and ego. As soon as I dared, a few meters from the hut, I switched off the flashlight.

"Well, that wasn't so bad," I said, placing the torch on the counter by the sink, hoping no one would see my hand shaking.

"Congrats! Some people never get used to it," said Eileen.

Andrew raised his beer bottle. "To friends," he proposed.

"To friends," I echoed. "You've made me feel as if I belong."

"You do," said Eileen. "Andrew always brings okay people."

We clinked our bottles, and then it was time to call it a night, with Andrew, once again, relegated to the kitchen hut. "Check for bananas," I teased, after he'd carried my gear to the guest hut, where Eileen was tucking blankets over fresh sheets. I offered to help, but there was nothing more to do.

"I'd like to say, 'Don't worry,' but you will," Eileen said, as she prepared to leave me to my doom. "I won't bother to say, 'Sleep well' either. No one does, the first night. What I will say is, 'See you in the morning.' For sure."

Were Eileen's assurances as good as a sleeping pill? Of course not. I worried about lions. I worried about elephants. Above all, I worried about stampeding cape buffalo. Day or night, according to Andrew, you could never tell what would spook a buffalo, and a herd on the rampage would flatten the flimsy hut, and me, in no time.

The terror began in earnest when I heard the snorting and breathing. Between my pillow and the unknown beasts there was only a laughable sheet of metal and utterly useless mesh. Did I do my wildly-beating heart a favor by creeping over to the screen to see if the midnight munchers were harmless impala rather than powerful hut stompers? Of course not. I huddled there in goose bumpy terror, wondering when I should scream and who would come if I did.

Andrew would come. With his gun. So would Phil and Eileen.

Clasping that certainty to me, I tried to enjoy the cool air that was feathering over my cheeks while the rest of me was heaped with blankets. Even through the screen's mesh, I could see the Milky Way, whose stars were so bright I could almost believe the story about the cosmic klutz who'd tipped over a jug of milk, or the one about the mythic DeBeers who'd seeded the vastness with a zillion zillion sparklers. From time to time, meanwhile, I registered sounds I was getting inured to, heavy breathing, a hoof kicking at hard dirt. Then came the whomp. From a well-muscled tail, I supposed, later. The hut shuddered.

Instantly I was up on my elbows and screaming—or trying to scream, since I produced no sound, just a constriction of muscles that hurt my throat. If only I had a gun, I thought, I could protect myself. I could summon Andrew. Or Phil. But a welcome silence told me that the beasts had departed. I didn't need help. I needed sleep.

5

Dawn was misty and chillier than I expected. Did I really want to abandon my cocoon in order to traipse around the savanna all morning? As prey for lions or venomous mambas? As collateral damage for mindlessly stampeding Cape buffalo? Following baboons, no less. I'd been on the road for six days. I wanted to get home.

Propping myself on my elbows to peer through the screen, I saw that a fire had been kindled in the fire pit. Phil and Andrew appeared to be loading things into the Suzuki. Eileen was talking to a young Tanzanian. Khaki uniform. Rifle slung on shoulder. A park ranger assigned to protect the baboon people, I decided. Seeing the ranger reminded me that Phil had been adamant about getting an early start. "If the baboons drop out of their sleeping tree before we reach it, we'll waste a day or more trying to find them," he'd said.

Eileen had backed him up. "No kidding. It's happened."

I fell back on my pillow, defeated. I had to get up, and quickly, if only to say thanks and good bye. Moments later, dressed and shivering, I had a mug of coffee in hand.

"Just what I needed," I said.

"It rained last night. That's why it's so cold," Eileen said. "Didn't you hear it?"

"I didn't hear a thing," I said.

"So you did sleep. Good." She pointed me toward a pan of leftover rice and beans that shared the grill with the coffee pot. "Help yourself," she said. "But first, meet John Mwinyi, indispensable member of the team and a very good friend."

We shook hands. "I'm so glad you're here," I said, eying John's rifle. Only then did I realize that my brain's baboon-watching switch had moved to "on."

John had walked over from the ranger station. Son of a farmer who culti-vated a nearby shamba, he'd graduated from the local agricultural university. He wasn't following in his father's footsteps, he joked, because he was too lazy for a farmer's hard life. Actually, he explained, he wanted to find a way for people to thrive—and for wildlife to survive. "Too many people. Not enough land. Animals ruin farms and hurt people. People slaughter animals. A vicious cycle. So here I am." Not merely as a guard either. Like Phil and Eileen, he would be collecting data.

"On what?" I asked.

"Everything under the sun—or not," he grinned, acknowledging a sky as gray as elephant hide. "This morning's low temperature. The look of the vegeta-tion. Every animal I see. Anything odd."

Phil climbed down from the roof of the Suzuki and banged on a fender to get our attention. "Hey, you guys! Time to go!"

Leaving Andrew contentedly cracking eggs to scramble and savor with his rice and beans— "I've followed baboons once and that's enough!" he said—we headed out. Eileen rode up front next to Phil. Thrown against one another in the back seat, our heads often coming concussion-close to the Suzuki's roof ribs, John and I had the formality knocked out of our relationship well before we reached the main road, along which the Suzuki's tires traveled sweetly, smoothly and much too briefly.

Driving cross country did not slow Phil down. "We're way behind sched-ule," he muttered, swerving around stumps and termite mounds and sinkholes and chalk-white buffalo skulls as if he were negotiating slalom gates.

"Yikes!" I exclaimed, without meaning to.

"Don't worry!" Phil shouted, above the roar of the muffler, which would be history as soon as its replacement was released from the clutches of the Customs mafia. "I know this terrain better than I know myself!"

Here and there the ground fog persisted, like a dingy white sheet propped up by acacias whose umbrellas were lost in the mist. For the most part, however, the sun had burnt through, and I could see the chain of low hills on the far side of the highway.

"Think of those hills as a compass," Eileen said. "When you can't see the sun, look for the hills."

Aside from those acacias and the occasional towering baobab with seed pods dangling like sausages in a butcher shop, vegetation was low, prickly and too sparse to cover the ground, whose surface was already drying to crust. Zigging, zagging, detouring around gullies, often coming close, yet always missing, axle-threatening rocks, we reached the troupe's sleeping tree, an isolated giant with no low branches. The whole troupe was still in occupation.

"I see Zsa Zsa," said Eileen.

"There's Dogo," said Phil.

John Mwinyi was also taking attendance, but soundlessly, eyes scanning the tree, head bobbing in recognition.

"There's Habari," Eileen was saying.

"There's Amigo!" said Phil.

Cutie, Lulu, Njema, Bub and thirteen other baboons were also present. The baboon-counters relaxed. None of the troupe had been lost to predators overnight. They were lingering in the tree because they didn't intend to succumb now.

What the baboons feared, however, was an unexpected treat for the city mouse who had slept well in spite of her terrors: two big, beautiful, straw-colored lionesses had installed themselves at the foot of the tree. The ladies looked so companionable, so relaxed, so benign, that I confessed an impulse to jump out of the Suzuki and fling my arms around them, as if I were a child in a toy store.

"Don't be a fool!" exclaimed Eileen, grabbing my arm and locking the door.

"I'm sorry," I said. "I was just kidding."

"Forget it," Eileen said. "I overreacted. But some people are really stupid."

"For sure," Phil agreed. "Last year some German tried for a close up of a lioness and her cubs. She mauled him badly."

"He died," said John. "And the lion had to be shot."

"By you?" I asked.

"No. Another ranger."

Lions avoid adult elephants, and a kick in the head from a mother giraffe can be fatal. Otherwise, game park lions have nothing to fear, not even people, assuming they're smart enough to forgo human snacks. These lady lions seemed to know the rules. They'd got to their feet to observe our approach, but they resumed their vigil as soon as Phil cut the engine, the hope doubtless being that a hunger-ravaged baboon would forget the danger and drop down to the wrong kind of breakfast.

Trapped in the little Suzuki, we sat and sat and sat. The last wisps of fog dissipated. The sun rose higher.

"How about some coffee," Phil suggested.

I opened a knapsack containing, in addition to a large thermos of coffee, boiled eggs, peanut butter and jelly sandwiches, and bananas. Also on hand: first aid items, extra ammunition for John and lots of water. We sipped tepid coffee. We nibbled. We talked. Fully unveiling itself, the sun had me feeling like a pot in a super heated kiln, despite the fully rolled down windows. The lions moved so little they might have been cardboard cutouts in a photographer's studio.

Waiting was hard on Phil. He squirmed He sighed. He grimaced. He tapped his thumbs on the wheel.

I, true to character, generated a menagerie of worries. "Say the lions do move off," I speculated. "The baboons drop out of the tree, and we're on our way, trailing right behind them. Meanwhile, two hungry cats are slinking around, perfectly camouflaged by tall dry grass—"

"Stay cool!" Eileen advised. "The baboons are super aware. They listen to the birds, too. At the least sign of danger, a baboon gives a warning bark and everyone's on guard. One day the troupe was stalked by a leopard. The females grabbed their babies. The males strutted back and forth, displaying their teeth. Very scary. You'll see. The leopard slunk away."

"Leopards, too!" I exclaimed. "Thanks a whole lot for the reassurance, Eileen."

"Eileen's right," Phil said. "John's rifle is a kind of a prop. A security blanket. He's used it only once."

I stared at John. "You actually had to shoot?"

John nodded.

"It was only a small herd of buffalo," Phil explained, as if that would console me. "About twelve of them. They'd stopped grazing and they were facing us, as if they were trying to decide what to do. They looked pretty belligerent, but then buffalos always look belligerent. The situation could have gone either way."

"We shouted, which usually does the trick," said Eileen. "But not this time. They were edging forward—"

"So John fired a warning shot—"

"And they ran away," said Eileen.

"Lions, buffalo, leopards, elephants—what else do I have to watch out for if these baboons ever start moving?"

"Snakes," said John, naming the one creature Tanzanians themselves hated and feared. Except for people living in posh neighborhoods like mine, Tanzanian landscaping featured much bare packed earth. Not pretty. But no snake could approach a house unseen.

"Tsetses!" shouted Eileen, slapping at the back of her neck. "Roll up the windows!"

I'd just swatted something, too, and five or six flies were buzzing around the margins of the windshield. Eileen set to squashing them with the rag she'd used earlier to mop up condensation from the fog. Already a red blotch had risen on my arm. It was hot to the touch and very itchy.
"Tsetse flies?" I asked. "As in sleeping sickness?"

"Tsetse aren't carriers here," Phil said. "But don't scratch. The bites can get badly infected. Check out Eileen's legs."

Eileen wore shorts—"It's cooler!" she said—and her legs were speckled with sores I hadn't noticed before, little red volcanos of infection.

"Be fair to the tsetses!" Eileen laughed. "Some of these are tick bites."

Ticks, too! What on earth was I doing there? Breakfast had been gluey leftovers. The coffee had been hot, but instant is always dreadful. Where the savanna wasn't blotched with tattered, dried out vegetation, it was scarred with stubble and ash from brush fires, some spontaneous, some set by poachers. Not quite the seductive terrain of safari legend—although, according to Andrew, the whole savanna would soon be green and stay so for a few weeks, matching the perennial lushness of the gentle hills that felt a touch of dew most nights. Already I could see tender blades of new grass pushing up through straw.

Meanwhile, even for me, lion-watching had lost its charm.

"Phil," Eileen said, at last. "It's time."

Phil glanced at John, whose nod made it unanimous. "We're researchers," he explained. "We're supposed to be observing animals, not pushing them around. But we have to be practical."

At the first revving of the engine, the ladies regarded us haughtily, as if we were snapping gum during a chamber music concert. Phil kept at it. Vroom! Vroom! Loud rasping jolts of sound. Joint by reluctant joint, the lions got up, tails twitching, yellow eyes glaring. Phil leaned on the horn, adding beeps to to the engine's snarl. I covered my ears, as did Eileen. Even John had a pained look. Finally the ladies padded off, though very slowly. Dignity was preserved.

Once the lions were out of sight, famished baboons began dropping out of the tree, a shower of very strange fruit. Each set to foraging as soon as he or she hit the ground, but cautiously, submitting most morsels to a quick sniff or taste test. What tempted, I observed, could be just about anything those leathery little hands could reach. They stripped seeds from old dry grass; they excavated little roots that looked like white carrots; they trapped insects on the ground and on the wing; they dug for grubs. If a low-ranking baboon crowded a VIP, the elite specimen glowered, bared its canines and growled. Females generally deferred to males. Young males respected their elders, so long as age hadn't compromised strength. Between power-hungry equals there might be a tussle.

"If a skirmish looks likely," Eileen warned, "keep your distance."

The young baboons, like their parents, filled their stomachs first. But soon the urge to play was paramount. They weren't *like* children. They were children. They played follow the leader right up to the tree tops where they leaped from branch to branch one after the other, the smallest lagging, but ready to give every maneuver a try. Springing toward a distant branch, a little one would seem to be perilously short of momentum and then, almost too late, tiny fingers would grasp a twig I'd have thought too weak to support a small bird. I could breathe again.

Eileen, Phil and John moved at troupe speed, making notes. From time to time Eileen paused to brush at flies attacking her legs. Since she was the most generous with spontaneous commentary, I mostly followed her, mindful not to ask too many stupid questions.

"See those dark shapes," she said, pointing her pencil toward a slight rise.

"Bushes?" I asked, hopefully.

"Buffalo," she replied, clapping her hands and hooting.

The bushes moved over the rise and out of sight.

The baboons foraged as a loose pack, grouping and regrouping. Individuals might break ranks, often with a rollicking sort of gallop, but they never went far on their own. Unlike my companions, I couldn't begin to read baboon emotions, but their eyes spoke to me of curiosity, intelligence, even humor, as well as watchfulness. My distant cousins.

Participating in this world as anthropologists and primatologists, Phil and Eileen never touched a baboon, not even to treat a sickly baby, which was heart-breaking, Eileen confessed. The depth of their bonding was equally evident when a fight occurred. They flinched at each bite or slash they recorded. And when a young male taunted the alpha, they got really worried. Sooner or later the contest for dominance would be for real.

"The loser, you see, has to leave the troupe," Eileen explained. "It might be some time before he can join—or take over—another troupe. That leaves him all alone and very vulnerable."

Once that morning we sighted a solitary male. Even John got excited.

"It could be Groucho," he said.

But it wasn't.

"How can you tell?" I asked. "They all look alike to me."

"Groucho had a really evil temper," said Phil. "He was always fighting, but he seldom won, so he's all scarred up. We know every scar."

I could tell adults from the immature, of course. And only boys had little black hoses dangling between their legs. Females as well as males had leathery black rumps, except when the feminine model swelled up and got bubble gum pink with seductive receptivity. Some rosy rumps dribbled viscous white semen. Others were subsiding into the paler pink of pregnancy.

"Look at their tails," Phil advised. "The crooks have different angles. That's what helped me at first."

"These are yellow baboons," added Eileen. "But some are more yellow than others."

"After a while you know their personalities, too," said Phil. "Habari's name means news—he's always on the alert. Zsa Zsa's always presenting herself, even when she's not in heat. Dogo's an adult, but he's a runt and he behaves like one, so he won't get driven out. Bub's kinda dumb. Njema's God's gift to women, or so he thinks."

"He never gives up!" Eileen said. "But Cutie can't stand him."

"Actually," Phil confessed, "only John knows them all. He knows every blessed animal in at least five troupes."

John smiled, ever so discreetly, over his clipboard. A well brought up East African would never crow about himself, but there's nothing unmannerly about quietly appreciating appreciation.

Phil and Eileen weren't competing with one another. Their projects were utterly distinct. Phil was studying the effect of the estrous cycle on behavior. He was also recording who mounted whom for a genetic study. Eileen had begun by charting maternal care patterns for her PhD dissertation. The behavior she'd observed had opened some radical new possibilities that her advisors had refused to endorse. No problem. She did a little deleting. Now, with her doctorate safely recorded, she was free to explore those interesting avenues.

"I've met some pushy, competitive human mothers," Eileen said. "But look at that! See the big female trying to grab a baby away from its mother? See how rough she is? It's a tug of war, and Lulu, the mother, has to let go. Does Big Mama want to cuddle the baby? Or does she want to smother it? How much pulling and hauling can a baby take? If Lulu's infant dies, could that be good for Big Mama's kids? So what do we have here? Incipient infanticide maybe? Some very important people don't want to see it that way. But how else can I explain such behavior?"

Eileen's question reminded me of what I'd read about Jane Goodall. Senior primatologists had been unwilling to accept her contention that chimpanzees were capable of murderous behavior.

"But Jane had done the watching," Eileen said. "She had the data. And she's made it easier for a new generation."

With Phil and Eileen keeping tabs on different baboons, they often drifted apart. Little by little I was doing the same, following individuals who intrigued me, often the kiddies. Occasionally I strayed after jewel-bright butterflies, hoping for a better look at their markings. But always I was aware of my distance from John and his protective rifle.

Until I wasn't, because I was falling under the spell of the savanna. I reveled in its spaciousness, its silence, the way an unbounded land bled into a blue and nearly cloudless sky. Hawks were circling up there—or maybe vultures looking for corpses. That was okay, too. Leaning against the giant finger of an apparently abandoned termite mound, I felt relaxed and free and unafraid. Buoyant. Bodiless. A vessel of energy. Whitman's improbable daughter, I was part and parcel of it all.

And then Eileen was calling and waving. It was time to go.

6

The plan was this: Phil and John would continue their data-collecting. Eileen and I would retrieve the Suzuki. As soon as we reached the Baboon Camp, Andrew and I would jump into the Land Rover and head off for Dar. Eileen would stay put until Phil radioed the location of the baboons' choice of sleeping tree. He and John would be waiting nearby. Eileen would collect them.

It was a simple, sensible plan, but not quite perfect, from my point of view. Eileen and I would be weaponless during our little trek back to the Suzuki.

"It's a question of exposure," Eileen explained.

"If I'd known I'd be so much trouble—"

"Don't feel guilty. We invited you."

I did feel a twinge of guilt, but mostly I felt like helpless tasty tempting prey. My mystical bonding with the savanna was gone, gone, gone.

"Let's go," I said. "Hills on the right?"

Eileen nodded, looking at her watch. "Right on schedule, too. We'll reach the Suzuki in no time."

"I just hope we reach it."

Eileen laid her hand on my arm. "It's natural to feel vulnerable, Diana, but believe me! If John were the tiniest bit worried, he'd have vetoed this plan."

"Oh?"

"Animals hate the heat," she explained. "By noon their bellies are full, and they're dozing in the shade. It's absolutely the best time for us to move around. Except for the sun." She pulled a tube out of the canvas shoulder bag that held her notes, applied some white goo to her nose and forearms and handed the tube to me. "Sun block. You should use it, too."

Trailing behind Eileen, protected from ultra violet rays, if not from lions, I recognized nothing from the morning's trek. Not a single crazy baobab. Not one termite mound. Unlike the baboons who had been following their normal foraging strategy, whatever that was, Eileen deviated as little as possible from a beeline, and she didn't walk. She strode. I struggled to keep up. We crunched through the first layer of dirt, stomped on low vegetation, got scratched by thorns and took every gully head on. Some of these mini ravines were still mucky at the bottom. Sliding in was easy. Crawling out wasn't. We'd been sweaty and dusty before. Soon were muddy, too. As for fearsome animals, I saw none. Just lizards and insects.

Sooner than I expected, Eileen pointed to a flickering of brightness in the distance. "The Suzuki's windshield," she said. Next came a glimpse of white paint. We'd made it! Or so I thought, briefly. The dark areas just beyond the car *weren't* pools of welcome shade. They were elephants. Five of them: three adults equipped with serious tusks; one adolescent; one small enough to make an elephant mother super protective.

I froze. I gasped.

Eileen laid a finger to her lips and whispered. "Elephants have very bad vision. We're downwind, too. They may not have noticed us. Follow me. Do exactly what I do."

Hunched over to take advantage of the largely illusory cover of discontinuous vegetation, we approached the Suzuki as quietly as we could. Soon there was only the vehicle between us and oblivion. Eileen readied her car key. She slipped it soundlessly into the lock, turned it and—click! A very tiny click, but Eileen hadn't said that elephants were hard of hearing.

"Quick!" she hissed. Get in!"

I'd hardly drawn my door shut when the engine started. That, not the click, commanded the elephants' attention. They shuffled about until they were positioned shoulder to shoulder, all eyes focused on us. And what else were they doing? Fanning their ears, whatever that meant.

We backed, we turned, we moved away, but slowly. It was no time to snag an axle or tumble into a gully.

"What are they doing?" Eileen demanded.

"Just standing there," I reported. "Isn't that odd? Where's the trumpeting? Where's the terrifying charge?"

"They've probably experienced cars and people before," she said. "But complacency kills. Never threaten or startle or tease them. A few months ago a tourist at the Mikumi guest house decided to show off by feeding bananas to a tame-looking elephant. The elephant was not grateful. He stomped the man—or gored him. I forget which."

"And?"

"The man survived. So did the elephant. It wasn't a rogue. Just provoked."

Shortly after we were back on the highway we encountered a mountainous bull elephant with mile long tusks. He was straddling the white line in the middle of the road, and he was not in a hurry to move. Eileen cut the engine and we waited.

"No wonder poachers kill so many elephants!" I exclaimed.

"We're still in the park," said Eileen. "Elephants know they're safe. Or would be, if not for poachers. Ever heard about poisoned melons scattered along game trails? The whole herd dies. Infants as well as adults."

"What does John think about all this?"

"What do you think?"

"How about his colleagues?"

"Mostly they don't like it. But the ones on the take seldom get punished. Not even when tons of tusks stuffed into bales of cotton marked for export are somehow confiscated and burnt," Eileen said. "It's a sham. All for show. Politics."

"I believe you," I said. "The domestic market isn't exactly invisible."

Shortly after I arrived in Tanzania, I visited the ivory market with a new friend. Kiki had introduced me to Agnes Beaulieu, who worked for a French NGO concentrating on women's health. Agnes offered to show me around. I accepted. Among our stops was the outdoor market. I found carvings in rosewood and ebony there, as well as ivory. Catholic Madonnas. Buddhist goddesses. Tribal beauties. Animals from antelope to zebra. Chess pieces. Jewelry. Trays. Bowls. Wooden fruit to display in those wooden bowls. I wasn't in a buying mood that day, and I would never be in the mood to buy ivory, but I fell in love with *makonde*, a distinctive Tanzanian genre often depicting ordinary people at work, though some carvers also produced massive abstract pieces from tree roots. "I'll be back," I promised one vender. Agnes, meanwhile, had bought a painting that illustrated a folk tale about a bird unable to protect her precious eggs from predators. Sad subject notwithstanding, the execution, involving a crocodile in a tree, was delightful.

Eventually the road hog elephant moved aside. We were underway again, humming along the highway, humming songs we both knew. When we bounced into Camp, we found Andrew lounging in a hammock. He was reading a detective novel by Agatha Christie.

"Welcome back," he called. "How'd it go?"

"Wonderful!" I said, with a twirl of joy. "What have you been up to, besides Dame Agatha?"

"Well, you could admire our shiny clean Land Rover."

"You didn't have to do that," I said.

"No," he said. "But it was dusty and full of footprints."

Eileen laughed. "Of course," she said. "The Mahoneys."

"The Mahoneys?" I echoed.

"Our uninvited resident baboons," she explained. "The Mahoneys have learned that people leave food in vehicles. They do their darnedest to get at it."

"Tracks on the hood. Tracks on the roof. Tracks on the windscreen. You see," Andrew said, "I've been studying baboons, too. Mr. Mahoney tried to steal my rice and beans but settled for a banana peel. Mrs. Mahoney picked nits out of Milly's head, but lacks the skill to do a decent job of cornrows. Malloy got swatted for trying to grab a share of the banana peel. All of them informed the observer that they are forming a committee to protest the burning of garbage."

I laughed and turned to Eileen. "Andrew's on to something. Your next study. A whole family of volunteers existing by their wits. Not only surviving, but reproducing."

"And what clever kids they are!" Eileen agreed, as we watched Malloy and Milly playing hide-and-seek among the empty gerry cans on the Land Rover's roof, in the process making dirty prints on a clean car. She clapped her hands. The young baboons jumped down and scampered into the bush. Eileen sighed. "We create an ecological niche. It gets filled. Are we delighted? Not a bit. Still, annoying as they are, the Mahoneys keep a certain distance, and they've never hurt anyone. So we adapt. After all, we're the real intruders around here, trespassers poaching data from baboons."

"Well, these two intruders are leaving," I said, as Andrew loaded our things into the Land Rover. "Thank you for everything, especially this morning."

"Any time," said Eileen. "I mean it."

During the hour it took to escape the borders of the preserve, Andrew and I played the game of who'll-be-first-to-spot-the-well-camouflaged-animal. I was doing better and better. Or was I? According to Andrew, the competition wasn't fair. He was driving. He had to pay attention to the road.

"Which gives you an excuse for letting me feel good. Like now," I said, pointing toward a hyena skulking in the brush alongside the highway.

Andrew grinned. "You'll never know."

Little by little, as elephants and giraffes began to seem commonplace, I found myself intrigued by intermingled herds of zebra and—"What are they?" I asked

"Wildebeest," said Andrew. "Gnus in English."

Strange creatures, those wildebeeste, antelopes supposedly, but they looked as if they'd been assembled by jamming together odd parts from other animals. Down-sloping spine thanks to seemingly mismatched front and back legs. Tufted tail. Incurving, bison-like horns. Stringy goatee. Random tufts of body hair. Grazing among the zebra, the wildebeeste behaved pretty much like their boring and more beautiful cousins, but every so often a loner broke into a wild and crazy routine, tossing its head, twisting its torso, leaping into the air like a bronco bucking for no apparent reason.

"Is that a mating dance?" I asked. "Or what?"

"They have parasites," Andrew replied. "Worms inside the skull. I've seen them."

Some months later I mentioned Andrew's hypothesis to an American biologist killing time between the end of a safari and the late night departure of his flight home. He'd dropped by to see what USIS was doing about wildlife conservation, which was little, Kiki confessed. "I'm no expert on wildebeeste," he told me, "but I've never heard of such parasites."

Once Mikumi was behind us, we had the fun of swerving around batches of coffee beans spread out to dry on the highway. Our tires smashed not a one, but I shuddered to think of coffee brewed from such contaminated beans. Meanwhile, we were constantly making room for cyclists and pedestrians, the usual rural people, of course, but also, during one stretch, pairs and threesomes of tall, slender young men garbed in shockingly short, tightly belted, toga-like costumes created by draping a length of cloth over one shoulder. Very revealing when cars sped by.

"Masai warriors," Andrew said. "There's a resettlement project around here."

Necks adorned with bead necklaces, ears pierced by beaded hoops, they marched along, spears balanced on their shoulders as if at any moment lions might threaten their non-existent cattle. Another warrior came cycling by. His spear bridged shoulder and handle bars. I smiled at that. The classically handsome Masai had been admired by British military men, who romanticized them as descendants of Africa-based Roman legions, but modern Tanzania was less nostalgic about the pastoral way of life. As we passed yet another beautiful specimen of young manhood, I found myself wondering. Which was worse? To market oneself as a tourist attraction or to languish, like an endangered species, on a reservation?

Amusing, minus the pathos, was the Chicago Bar Disco and Hotel a few miles farther on. It featured a street-facing wall spray painted with a frieze of dancers. Men in bell bottoms. Women in miniskirts. Three powerful-looking motorcycles parked in front of the mural suggested that the place might be open. "Let's stop," I said. "I'm hungry.

"Soon," Andrew promised. "There's a better place."

The road forsook savanna and began winding up the hills that lay between us and home. Foot traffic ceased. Farmland gave way to natural vegetation. Thickets of trees snaked up troughs that drained the hill tops. Behind and below lay Tanzania's share of the vast African interior, and soon, from the crest, we'd be looking down on the Arab-influenced Swahili coastline. I found it hard to imagine a restaurant on that lightly trafficked road.

"Just wait," said Andrew

A few curves later Andrew parked along the shoulder of the highway. I saw no welcoming sign, no parking lot, no building, just wood fires licking at huge vats tended by women in the nearly universal rural costume. Tee shirt. Hip-hugging wrap known as a *kanga.* Colorful head tie. Their offerings were substantial. Spicy stewed beans. Rice pilaf. Lamb kebabs. Boiled corn on the cob. We found some reasonably flat boulders, and there we relaxed, prying lamb from skewers, spooning up stew, gnawing kernels from corn cobs. Happy with my dinner, happily contemplating our week on the road, I observed that the trip had been successful beyond my highest hopes.

Andrew agreed. "It went well."

"Thanks to you," I said. "You paved the way. You made it easy for me."

"That's my job. Besides you made it easy for me."

"How so?"

"You took everything in stride. The heat. The pot holes. The uncomfortable beds. The flies. The food."

"Speak for yourself," I said. "And speaking of food, these ladies deserve a real restaurant. But that wouldn't be half as much fun."

"That's what I mean," Andrew said. "So how about a real weekend in the bush? Nothing posh. But Rafiq and I haven't lost a client or a friend yet."

"I thought you'd never ask," I said.

Traffic increased as we approached Dar, which reminded me of the Iranian tanker that had been hovering so enticingly off shore. Was petrol still in short supply? Had we been foolish, supplying so much fuel to the stranded motorist? As we penetrated the straggling outskirts of the capital, Andrew observed that we'd pass within a block of his house en route to mine. Might we let his wife know that all was well? No cell phones back then.

"Mind? Don't be silly," I said. "We're a day late. She must be worried."

A short sandy drive led to an unpainted concrete shoe box with unglazed windows barred and fitted with shutters, which is to say, a comfortable middle class home in Dar. On the way out of town Andrew had told me why house exteriors in Dar were generally so shabby-looking. "The nail that sticks up," he said, "gets pounded down." Andrew's front yard was consistent with that aesthetic—and unmown grass in need indicated that he did not share the national snake phobia.

A woman and a boy emerged from the house.

"My wife, Lucille," Andrew said. "My son, Peter."

Lucille was a friendly, plump. still pretty woman, who wore a citified, ruffled blouse with her *kanga*. She had a shy way of using English, which explained her reluctance to attend Embassy parties or receptions where everybody chattered fluently in the old colonial tongue. As for Peter, he was nearly as tall as his father, but thinner, as young men usually are. Nodding politely, he unloaded Andrew's things and carried them into the house.

I'd expected to pour a glass of wine, put on some music and flop contentedly into my favorite chair with a book when I got home, but the formula didn't work. It was Sunday, Mary's day off, and the place felt depressingly empty. The solution was obvious. I called Agnes Beaulieu.

The phone range and rang, and only because I was so desperate did it let it keep ringing. Finally, out of breath, she answered, having run in from the garden, where she'd been hosing down her much-beloved but mischievous standard poodle, whose name was Mamzelle.

"Did you ever try to get mud off a black dog when it's dark?" she asked.

"What made you wait 'til after dark?" I asked.

"I didn't wait to clean her. She waited to get dirty."

Agnes needed some time to towel Mamzelle and change into dry clean clothes. "Unless you'd rather come here," she offered.

"I'm bushed," I said. "I can't move."

Agnes arrived. Her short curly hair was wet, her face *au natural*. She wore shorts and a too large tee shirt, but she was French. Nothing about her ever lacked an aura of elegance that would fail me even if I could afford a designer wardrobe. No matter. We'd become friends who loved to curl up at opposite ends of my sofa and talk the night away. That night she sipped at a gin and tonic, while I delivered a comic version of my adventures. I also mentioned Andrew's safari offer.

"You're really tempted?" She laughed. "You're crazy!"

"Why?"

"An elephant's an elephant. See one and you've seen them all."

"You don't know—"

"Oh yes I do. I've been here for five years now. I've seen leopards and wild dogs, too. Most people don't. I've been to all the parks. Up and grouchy at five a.m. Sweaty and thirsty at five p.m. Time for sundowners. So, *ma cherie*, I'm glad you had a good time. These days I seldom have to leave Dar, and that suits me just fine. As for safaris, didn't you know that everyone's after Andrew? He's picky about clients. If he invites you, it's a compliment."

"But he works for me. Won't that complicate things?"

Agnes hit her head with the palm of her hand. "Oh, you Anglo-Saxons! Loosen up. Have another drink, and I'll tell you who's been asking around about you."

"I don't get loose. I get drunk."

"That's okay, too. So guess who? The German press attache. You know. Dieter. I saw him at a party while you were away. He remembered you from dinner at Clive's. Expect a call."

7

Gas lines were non-existent when Andrew and I got back to Dar, but the hunt for foreign exchange was on again, this time to replace a faulty turbine. Until the normally sympathetic cadre of aid donors stopped preaching about fiscal discipline and coughed up financing, we'd have to put up with a power shedding regime intended to equalize the inconvenience. So, every day at noon, our office lights stopped lighting, our office machinery took a break, our air conditioning died and the elevator went on strike.

And people got short tempered.

Although the electricity usually surged back by mid afternoon, some of us went home to power cuts in the evening, too. Worst hit were the working mothers, like my secretary Lily and our librarian Aisha, whose homes got water from rooftop tanks kept full by electric pumps. Night after night, they fought the darkness with candles and oil lamps, bathed their children in skimpy buckets of water, left dirty dishes in the sink and watched the laundry pile up. Dealing with the backlog turned weekends into unrelieved drudgery. Wishing to alleviate the burden for Lily, I allowed her to slip out early a few times. Clive, citing precedent and fair play, intervened. I had to stop. Lily, after all, wasn't the only victim of power shedding. Meanwhile, some of us were luckier—or should I say more privileged? My house had a generator, a noisy gas guzzler. So did Kiki's. And Clive's. And Milly's. When the power failed, our generators switched on. Automatically.

At work Clive suffered the least. Venetian blinds deflected the heat while admitting plenty of light through windows that occupied much of his wall space. So there he sat, book on lap, feet on desk, shed of coat and tie, ever primed to philosophize. The rest of us, meanwhile, were starved for illumination. Fluorescent lighting was unpleasant enough, its cold spectrum, the way it flickered and hummed, but the alternative was gloom, and our few, small windows were also hopeless for ventilation because ocean breezes never reached our side of the building. Result? We worked at normal intensity until noon, then slipped into torpor, waiting for the juice of modern life to return.

Kiki found it impossible to suffer silently. She envisioned herself in Scandinavia. She wanted to know about Moscow winters, which I had thoroughly enjoyed, aside from the husband part, especially the cross country skiing through spruce and birch forests ringing the city. Daily she stormed into my office to sound off. "Can't type. Can't read. Can't play Swahili tapes. Can't use the coffee maker. Can't do anything. Is this ridiculous or what?"

Usually I happily agreed. It was ridiculous. But not always, especially if she caught me after a tense session with the Ambo.

One day I was at my desk, angling the *News* toward my little window, the only way I could skim the small type below the headlines. The lead story described a generous aid package from socialist Sweden, whose policies made perfect sense to me, as I had unwisely confided to the Ambassador during one of our weekly sessions. "The Nordics lean left," I'd conceded. "But freely. Shouldn't we applaud their support for Tanzanian development, if only because it takes the pressure off us? Socialist or not, Nyerere's not corrupt. Or so it's said." Meanwhile, I continued recklessly, the U.S. had embraced a kleptomaniac in Zaire. Cost to us: millions of dollars stolen. Rejecting my logic, Freeman treated me to a little lecture about holding our noses in pursuit of Cold War allies. That was self-defeating, so far as I was concerned, but I pulled back from the brink. Taking the coward's—or the wise underling's—way out, I'd nodded thoughtfully and changed the subject.

With Kiki, however, I could push back, as I did one day when she was expecting a bitch session à deux. "Look at it this way," I suggested. "Can't fight over computer time either."

Uncomfortable with gearing down to survive the daily dose of power shedding, Andrew and I did our best to escape it altogether, our destination depending on which sectors of the city were functioning normally. Most newsrooms had never been air conditioned, but we reveled in strengthening our ties with journalists above whom ceiling fans whirled so fast that paperweights were essential equipment. And oh! did we envy the reporters able to pound away all day on the very manual typewriters that my predecessors had given away, a few years before, when USIS switched over to electricity-dependent Selectrics.

Other powerless afternoons I gave talks on free speech to journalism students, with whom I also shared reporters' tricks-of-the-trade. University classrooms could be oven-hot. My compensation took the form of long round trips with the car's AC on high. I also accepted, at short or no notice, invitations to address Rotarians and other groups at their luncheon meetings. The Scotch came on the rocks, and facilities in hotels equipped with back up generators could be downright chilly. Have script. Will perform.

If local reporters were present, even the most ordinary luncheon talks could have a significant impact. The day after I'd responded to a hostile question about Ronald Reagan's bombing of Libya's capital Tripoli, my parents phoned me from Florida. A Palm Beach daily had printed a news service story in which I'd been quoted. "Read it to me," I begged. "I need to know: is it accurate?" Happily, it was. My parents had objected to my husband-dumping, but they regarded my job with respect after that.

Knowing I hated Dar's steamy heat, Andrew teased me. Maybe he'd overestimated my ability to cope with the climate, he said.

"There's a difference," I replied.

"Hot is hot," he said.

"No. It's a matter of expectation. Leaving Dar, we turned our backs on the—ha! ha!—comforts of city life. We entered a different reality. But this office, right now, is a lot hotter than the huts at the Baboon Camp ever are. Speaking of which, you promised me a safari."

"Rafiq's been out of town. Big Pakistani wedding in Nairobi. Some business to take care of, too. I don't know when he'll be back."

While we sweltered, the Embassy purred along sweat-free. At the first sputter of failing power, a powerful generator started up. Once when I went to see the Ambassador, I found Gini wearing a sweater. "I'm freezing," she complained.

"Lucky you," I said.

Up to a point we envied our colleagues at the embassy. Their equipment worked. They could see what they were doing. Above all, they were cool. On the other hand, stoically meeting the challenge of power shedding gave the USIA team one more reason to feel superior about the insight we gained from our greater immersion in local life, whether we were posted to Delhi, Dakar or Dar. State Department officers, we believed, were office-bound, rule-ridden and absurdly susceptible to scare stories about their foreign surroundings. Meanwhile, a good number of State officers looked down on us. We weren't "real" FSOs, they sneered. Not always behind our backs.

None of this sometimes good natured mutual sniping prevented me from taking advantage of the Embassy's air conditioning when I could. I'd prolong my sessions with the Ambassador by offering baroque responses to simple questions. After each debriefing, I joined embassy colleagues for shop talk and gossip at the embassy snack bar. Who's up for promotion? Who's backstabbing whom? Who's sleeping around? Nor was I the only one seeking relief. Clive grumbled less about attending mandatory Country Team meetings. Kiki devoured classified cables we couldn't keep on our unsecured premises. Milly's daily errands consumed more time.

Actually, even had Washington agreed to grace our budget with a high-capacity back up generator, the obstacles to installation would have been hard to overcome. Like much real estate in Dar, our building was government-owned. Call it tea and bureaucracy. Since we'd never pay the former, the paper pushers were lethargic at best—and our unimpressive aid program gave us little political leverage, as I told the Ambassador one day, when he was in an especially good mood.

Power-shedding did have a surprising plus side. Minus electricity, light just barely penetrated the interior space that housed the library. The stacks were so dark that it was hard to locate material without a flashlight. Clive had a look, made a decision and decreed during a staff meeting that the library would close at noon for the duration. "Can you live with that?" he asked, turning to Aisha.

Aisha sighed. Her mantra as a librarian was "more, more, more." More hours. More patrons. More service. More impact. "Do I have a choice?" she asked.

"Safety first," Clive said.

And so our statistics showed fewer young men hanging around to bask in the glorious coolness of the library's AC (if, indeed, that's all they were doing) to the annoyance of our superiors in Washington, who—believe it or not!—had suggested chair removal as a solution.

Looking back, I can see with embarrassing clarity how we Americans cast ourselves in ego-pleasing scenarios when the lights went out. Kiki raged. She wanted to change the world by tomorrow at the latest. I saw the situation as something of an adventure, a challenge to pass with brio. Clive philosophized: "Tides rise and fall. The power comes and goes."

Milly, characteristically, was more interested in practical consequences, too many of which were not to her liking. As an unapologetic elevator addict, she resented the need to feel her way down a dark stairwell at the end of the day. Anyone wearing her fashionable high heeled sandals would have felt wobbly and insecure, but she'd worked as PAO secretary in Paris and she refused to dress down for Dar. It would show lack of respect, she contended. And she'd feel dowdy.

Clive laughed at her scruples. "Wear Adidas," he suggested.

"Maybe I should wear hot pants, too."

"Better yet," he said.

Poor Milly. Although she had spent most of her Foreign Service career very contentedly in Europe, she had been seized by a roots mania that caused her to jump at the Dar assignment despite the reduction in status. She, like many others, would reconnect and experience a proud new Africa taking its proper place in the post-colonial world. Unfortunately, while the Asian Tigers raced ahead, churning out exports, creating an ever-expanding middle class, Africa was on another trajectory. Month after month, Milly's dreams were dashed. "Tea! Tea! Tea!" she'd explode. "Little guys! Big men! They're all on the take!"

To compensate for the pain of disillusionment, perhaps, Milly developed a lust for ivory. She trolled the outdoor market every Sunday, then boasted about her finds and bargains on Monday, as if we weren't living in a city surrounded by dwindling herds and vanishing species. Seated at her dinner table, savoring her fine rendition of French cuisine, we'd be surrounded by a collection of ivories whose natural luster was enhanced by candlelight. Sometimes, during a lull in the conversation, my eyes would fall on a carving, and I'd hear elephants weeping in the shadows.

To give Milly her due, she cared passionately about people. Undernourished children feverish with malaria. Water-toting village women raped on their way back from the river. Widows deprived of property by in-laws. She contributed generously to the NGO Agnes directed.

And maybe we were all poachers in Tanzania. Milly's ivory mania was fed not only by ruthless gangs in the bush but also by corrupt officials and amoral businessmen. Clive kept us all working hard, often after hours, poaching on our time to make his own life easier. The U.S. and the Soviets pursued the Cold War even in this African backwater, just as the wealthy everywhere extort the powerless poor. Men, universally, exploit women while pretending to protect them. Mosquitoes and tsetse flies suck blood from every creature they land on. As for the food chain on the savanna—herbivores beware! Lions rule. And vultures clean up the mess.

On whom, then, was I preying, since I could hardly be an exception? Well, I pushed policy for the U.S. government, which offered me a decent income and a chance to travel. Also, USIA had thrown me a lifeline and I was grateful. In Tanzania I worked hard and imaginatively, and I would continue to do so, unless my conscience screamed louder than it had so far—or I found something more congenial to do. Meanwhile, I also intended to enjoy myself, if only Andrew would organize that safari he'd promised.

Further re Milly: by the time I arrived in Dar, she was well on her way to a shamelessly liberated stage of political incorrectness. "Roots schmoots," she snorted one day, mopping sweat from her forehead, her upper lip and her modest cleavage. "I just thank the good Lord my ancestors caught the one way economy passage to America."

Having sent Juma out to buy us some ice cream, Milly, Kiki and I were trying to spoon up our shares of chocolate swirl before soft turned to soupiness.

"Excuse me," I said. "Did I hear you right?"

"Let me put it this way," Milly said. "Where would I be if they hadn't?"

"Not sitting in that seat," I said.

"No indeedy," said Milly, slurping up her last spoonful. "Now let's get some work done."

"Or pretend to," Kiki said, and we all laughed.

Kiki had earned Clive's admiration by studying Kiswahili, a Bantu language with a huge Arabic vocabulary. Not only was Kiswahili the official language of Tanzania, it was also the lingua franca for East Africa, but FSOs posted to Dar weren't required to learn it because educated Tanzanians were articulate English speakers. Even so, who could deny the public relations boost from showing cultural respect? Or the value of gleaning information directly from non-English speakers? So language loving FSOs were reimbursed for fees they paid to qualified Kiswahili tutors.

Kiki's motivation, however, was neither professional nor intellectual. As the in-country director of the Fulbright program, an array of U.S.-funded educational exchanges, she'd recently chaired a panel charged with interviewing

Tanzanians hoping to study or conduct research in the U.S., including a linguist specializing in Black English. He was very smart, Kiki reported. And good-looking. And sexy. Funny, too.

And so—click!

The attraction was mutual, but discretion was essential, to avoid the appearance of favoritism. Only after the largely autonomous Fulbright Board had voted unanimously to support David's project, was Kiki free to accept his invitation. "To help me celebrate," he said. They spent the evening at a night club, drinking beer, dancing to those burbly-bubbly Congolese rhythms, talking, talking, talking. Soon Kiki was looking for a Swahili teacher.

Learning of her quest, I raised an eyebrow. "Oh?"

"A good Cultural Affairs Officer shows a sincere interest in Tanzanian culture."

"Very noble," I said. "If David isn't a cultural contact, who is?"

Kiki was Norwegian, from Minnesota, a blue-eyed blond. David was Nilotic, tall, thin, blue-black, as handsome as the Masai warriors I'd seen on the road back from Mikumi. Posing together for a photo, they presented the toughest possible challenge to Andrew's brilliant darkroom technique.

My own love life was nil. The German press attaché hadn't called, which had bruised my ego, but only a little, I told Agnes, because I was deeply ambivalent about dating anyone at all. "I'm not ready," I explained, as we laid out our contributions to a no-host beach party. "I'm still in recovery."

We were escaping Dar's heat by spending a Sunday with a mob of other foreigners on a glorious stretch of white sand to the north of the city. Ocean breezes. Palm groves within whose bowers local boys beheaded green coconuts, inserted straws and offered them for sale. Waves impressive but not vicious, an invitation to body surfing at its best: long glides through frothy foam all the way to the high water mark. A few of the younger men put on a show of surf boarding, blaming their unimpressive performance on the angle of the waves, the inconstant wind, the slope of the shelf, the people who got in their way. Everything but their own ineptness. Emboldened by the fact that I wasn't the only person confronting the ocean, I threw myself into wave after wave.

"It's unnatural," Agnes decreed, after I'd dried off and stretched out next to her on my blanket under her beach umbrella. "All this time without a man."

"Meaning I'm not like you?" I retorted.

Agnes was an exception to my men-prey-on-women generalization. Every male acquaintance was a candidate for her bed. Many actually got there. I should refine that. She had standards that had to do with intelligence, good taste and guaranteed freedom from HIV or AIDS. And even she had her monogamous interludes. Recently she'd been involved with a French doctor working for Médécins sans Frontières. His name was Martin. But Martin had been reassigned, she told me, to Francophone Mali.

"It's better for him," she said. "His English was as bad as your French."

"I'm so sorry," I said.

"C'est la vie," she said, not very convincingly. "Let's eat. Let's join the party."

8

The phone rang. The doorbell rang. Pointing Andrew and Rafiq toward the patio, where Mary would serve them coffee, I gave my attention, reluctantly, to Clive, on the phone.

"What luck!" he exclaimed. "I thought you might be half way to the Selous by now."

"We were just about to leave," I said.

"Just give me an hour," he pleaded. He'd toiled through much of the night, revising and polishing the Country Plan, but prudence demanded a final scan by my "keen eyes" before it was sent off in the diplomatic pouch on Monday. That's when the courier would leave for Washington via Nairobi.

"Of course, Clive. Send it over." What else could I say?

The Country Plan was the bedrock USIA planning document in those years. Each post had to envision a well integrated program to advance U.S. policy imperatives, then specify the resources needed to carry out the plan. Speakers on this or that subject. Books and other materials for the library. Exchange program slots—David's Fulbright, for example. Visiting poets or pianists. Support for exhibits, festivals and conferences. Supplies for the darkroom. Audio-visual equipment. Funds for staff travel and for entertaining key contacts. (Even in Muslim countries decent Scotch was a diplomatic necessity.) In sum, everything we'd need to make friends and gain support in the bipolar world of the Cold War. If we did it right, we'd get what we wanted. If we were sloppy, we'd be sorry.

The doorbell rang again. It was Juma, envelope in hand. Invited in, he declined. He would wait, as drivers do, slumped behind the wheel, dozing, daydreaming, listening to music, until he could, as directed, deliver the draft to

Milly, who had a magical way with formatting documents. I could imagine her reaction. Clive's deadline nudging was a recurrent irritant.

To go or not to go? Once Juma had been sent off and I'd been introduced, at long last, to Andrew's partner Rafiq, we debated. He and Andrew had planned a whirlwind introduction to the bush for me, just one night, but authentic, a matter of tents and real exposure, but Clive's request for an hour of my time had turned into a trip-threatening theft of three. Still, if we stopped debating and started moving—and everything went smoothly, Andrew insisted, we'd be on the other side of the Rufiji River, with camp set up, well before dark.

"Just barely before dark, even if all goes well," Rafiq muttered.

"Which it seldom does," Andrew admitted.

"I'm sorry," I said.

"It wasn't your fault," said Andrew.

"No, it wasn't," Rafiq agreed. "And, as for smooth going, this baby will do her part." Rapping his knuckles on the unscratched, undented body of his brand new Land Rover, he invited me to climb aboard, which I did, taking full possession of the back seat.

"Let's go," I said.

We'd hardly left my driveway before the comradely bantering up front began. "Nice car," Andrew said. "But how do you repair an automatic shift in the bush?"

"You don't," Rafiq shot back "It doesn't break down."

"Dream on," Andrew said. He turned around to look at me. "Actually Rafiq can fix anything on wheels. So far, anyway. That's why I put up with him in the bush."

"I'm also a better shot—"

"He just likes to kill more."

"And a better cook."

"If you don't mind waiting until midnight."

"You'll see," said Rafiq, his eyes meeting mine in the rear view mirror. "My curries are worth waiting for."

"I'm hungry already," I said.

"Better have a banana," Andrew advised.

"So, Rafiq, why can't you repair Andrew's Land Rover properly?" I asked.

"That's no Land Rover," Rafiq objected. "It's an incomplete collection of spare parts."

"So find the parts he needs."

"Aye—there's the rub," said Rafiq. Like Andrew, he'd attended good English medium schools.

"True," Andrew nodded.

"Everything I get—if I get it—I pay through the nose for. And sometimes even that doesn't work," Rafiq complained. "I'm an Asian, they say. I don't belong. But, hey! Who gets the food on the shelves in this country? The Central Committee? Don't make me laugh. We own the stores. We run the trucks. And we're treated like scum, like milk cows."

"Careful," said Andrew. "She's still a believer—or wants to be."

"If you're so unhappy, why don't you leave?" I asked.

"Easier said than done. The Tanzanians don't want me. The Paks say I'm Tanzanian." He gave a short bitter laugh. "I'm working on something better for my kids, though. My son's at Suffolk University. My daughter's at Cambridge. If they're smart, they'll find a way to stay in the U.K. And the little ones will follow."

"At least you can afford to send them to the U.K.," Andrew said. "What am I going to do with Peter?"

"What's wrong with the U.S.?" I asked. "Talk to Kiki—or Aisha."

"Assuming he'll qualify," snorted Andrew. "Which isn't likely. Peter's English teacher is barely literate, so far as I can tell. Peter shrugs. English is a colonial language, he says. Africans don't need it. I tell him no one speaks Swahili in Nigeria. They speak their own languages—plus English. So what, he says. He'll go to university here. Some university! No books. No labs. No water in the loo. But he'll get in. Plenty of seats and reserved for Africans, as if Asians care—"

"They do," said Rafiq. "On principle, anyway."

Absorbed in the back and forth, I hadn't noticed time and miles flying by. We were well into the countryside south of Dar when Rafiq veered onto the shoulder of the highway and stopped.

"Sorry," he said. He got out and headed for a tree.

I decided to stretch my legs, as did Andrew, who was hot and thirsty. Opening the tailgate, he dragged out the cooler. "Beer, coke or water?" he asked. I took two bottles of water, one for me, one for Rafiq. Andrew climbed into the back of the Land Rover then. "Looking for something," he said.

Back on the highway, rolling along, Rafiq passed a couple of slowpoke vehicles, then swung around an oil tanker, inviting (and avoiding by the tiniest margin) a collision with an onrushing bus as he darted back into the proper lane.

"We've got a problem," Andrew said.

Hurrah! I thought. I wouldn't be the killjoy begging for caution.

But Andrew's concern had nothing to do with Rafiq's driving. "We're missing a tent," he said.

"You're kidding," Rafiq said.

"No question about it," Andrew said.

"How can that be?" I asked.

Andrew sighed. "Lucille. She's the family packer. But she wasn't feeling well. Fever."

In other words, a malaria attack—and he'd left her to suffer alone. "How could you?" I demanded. "Well, Peter's there, I suppose."

"No," said Andrew. "He's up North, on a Youth Corps tree-planting project."

"How nice for him," I said.

"She'll be all right," Andrew insisted, with a long guilt-ridden sigh. "But—I should have told her not to get up. I should have done my own packing and made my own breakfast."

Recurrent malaria attacks were a fact of life in Tanzania. We Americans took anti-malarials daily, but most Tanzanians didn't, including Lucille, evident-ly. On top of that, windows weren't screened, bed nets weren't used religiously and stagnant water bred mosquitoes. The fortunate, like Lucille, suffered in comfort. The unlucky dragged around, doing anything to earn a few shillings. The truly unlucky succumbed, as did an FSO in Nairobi. She'd adhered too strict-ly to Christian Science doctrine. Although we tried to persuade our Tanzanian colleagues to protect themselves, it was not unusual for someone to lean, listless and glassy-eyed, on Milly's desk. Milly would look up and say, "Go home. Go to bed."

In fact, Andrew seemed to be unusually considerate for a Tanzanian hus-band. He didn't gamble or womanize. He didn't get drunk and beat his wife. Nor did he flaunt his virility by making her pregnant every year. Cholera had ended Andrew's first marriage, leaving him a widower with two daughters, now married. That gave him three offspring, counting Peter. Enough, he'd decided, making him a hero to my friend Agnes. African women would be better off—and so would Africa, she said, if more men were like Andrew. Agnes had a point. But Andrew's scruples had left Lucille with only one child. I wondered how she felt about that.

I felt guilty, too. We could have cancelled the trip.

The sun was lower than we'd hoped by the time we reached the top of a hill overlooking the Rufiji River and I saw the ferry, miniaturized by distance, laboring toward our side of the river. The drive from Dar had not gone smoothly. At one point the road had been washed out. The detour cost us a half hour. Further on, a collision between a truck and a van had blocked the highway, which was also the primary route between Kenya and Mozambique. Traffic backed up, and it was an hour before we got to see what the problem was.

None of that seemed important as I beheld a broad, muddy, fast-flowing river, into whose waters the black strip we were driving on appeared to vanish. Looking down, I thought of Joseph Conrad's mighty Congo and of the Zambezi cascading over Victoria Falls. I thought of the bend in V.S. Naipal's unnamed river and felt myself smiling as I remembered the funny-sounding Limpopo in the *Jungle Tales* I'd loved as a child. The search for the sources of the Nile and tales of the fabled city of Timbuktu just north of the Niger—those I remembered, too, as I waited to be overcome by my own profound reaction to magnificence. But I was only me. Looking down at the silt-stained Rufiji, all that came to mind was hot cocoa streaming from a saucepan into a cup, which, ludicrous or not, would have to stand for the Indian Ocean, just a few miles down river.

Meanwhile, Andrew and Rafiq were doing some calculations. It would take an hour, more or less, for the ferry to reach our side of the river, then dock, unload, reload, cast off and haul us to the other side, where the highway appeared to be crawling out of the river. From that point, they estimated, it would take, maybe, two hours to pick up a warden at the ranger station, hunt down some bush meat and reach their customary camp site, by which time it would be very dark indeed, close to midnight instead of noon, our too optimistically anticipated arrival time.

"I have an idea," Andrew said.

Having heard that before, I liked the sound of it.

"Turn right," Andrew said.

"Turn right?" I echoed. No ferry? No river crossing?

"It's the only solution," Andrew replied. "We'll stay with Alice."

Rafiq agreed. "That takes care of the tent problem, too."

"We'll try again, on a longer weekend," Andrew promised.

"Or take some time off," I suggested. I was his boss, after all, and I could manage Clive.

Leaving the highway, we followed a narrow dirt road that began by paralleling the river then angled inland. Soon we emerged from riverine forest onto broad, open savanna, flat and dry. By that time Rafiq had turned on the headlights.

"Who's Alice?" I asked.

"She's a district nurse," Andrew said. "In Alipolaka."

"Never heard of it," I said.

"It's a new village," Rafiq said. "Actually, an old village in a new place. Not on the map yet."

"There's only one problem," Andrew said. "She may not be home."

Having heard that before, too, I took it calmly.

In due time, we were passing a house here, a house there, with snatches of light visible through windows and doorways, until, finally, there were buildings on either side of the road, which had acquired light poles without streetlights. Kerosine lanterns lit the few tiny shops that hadn't shut for the night. Through open doors I saw women, cooking perhaps, while men, naturally, lounged on verandahs, drinking beer, playing games, killing time before dinner. Children ran about in the relative coolness of early evening.

Rafiq drove very slowly. He and Andrew were examining every house. "It's been a while," Rafiq explained.

"No. No. No. No," Andrew muttered. And then came a triumphal, "This is it!"

A tall woman in standard tee shirt and *kanga* stood on the verandah of a small house much like its neighbors. She appeared to be comforting a good-sized baby.

Andrew called out. "Alice!"

Rafiq turned into a space beside the house. As headlights struck her face, Alice raised a hand to shield her eyes. When she could see again, puzzlement became delight. "Andrew! Rafiq! *Jambo! Jambo!* You are welcome!"

Andrew folded Alice into a bear hug that engulfed the baby as well. Rafiq wrapped an arm around her shoulder, a warm half hug by a lapsed Muslim still shy about touching women. Feeling like an alien, an intruder, I held back, but Alice put an end to that. "Come in! Come in!" she said.

And so we did, through an unscreened doorway, I noted, although nurse Alice should have known better. But that's all the mental carping I could do. Not only the parlor and the kitchen, but also (as I would discover) the outhouse and the bath—everything was as clean and shipshape as a hospital operating room. And I did see mosquito nets thrown back over T-shaped supports when I peeked into bedrooms. But no one wanted to stay inside. It was cooler on the verandah, although we could hardly see one another.

"I have an idea," Andrew said. He rose from his place in our chat circle and made for the Land Rover, followed by Rafiq, who seemed to have read his mind.

Andrew returned with a tangle of Christmas lights. They'd be plugged into a portable generator, against whose activation I protested. "Too noisy," I said.

"Not this one," Andrew said, as he looped the lights wherever he could around the verandah. When he was done, he shouted, "Let there be light!" the signal for Rafiq to get the contraption started. I covered my ears.

But the generator didn't roar. It murmured. Maybe Andrew and Rafiq didn't offer luxurious safaris, I thought, but their clients weren't roughing it either. Meanwhile, the rainbow on a string was so bright, so gay, so unexpected, that every kid in the village come running, including two little girls who joined us on the verandah. "My daughters," Alice said. "Sally and Phyllis." Her baby, now stirring and showing signs of sleepy time crossness, was Rose.

It was entertaining, at first, to watch a bunch of scrappy, boisterous kids clowning around as if a carnival had come to town, but how would Alice get rid of them—and when? Quickly and easily, I learned. Alice was a figure of respect in Alipolaka. When she held up her hand and announced that it was time to leave us in peace, the capering around ceased. The children, except for two boys and Sally and Phyllis, melted into the darkness.

"We've come for the beer, ma'am," said one of the boys, in Swahili. Andrew translated. If I were Kiki, I thought, I wouldn't need an intermediary.

Gently, but firmly, Alice handed a protesting baby to a surprised, but not unwilling Andrew. "Come with me," she told the boys. "Sally, Phyllis, you, too." She led them around to the back of the house. When they reappeared, a few minutes later, all of them were carrying beer. The two boys struggled with a heavy case. I hoped they didn't have to lug it too far. Sally and Phyllis had it easy.

Just two large bottles each. Placing them on the little table around which we'd arranged our seats, they dropped me a charming little curtsey and scampered off to join their friends.

"I'll get some glasses," Alice said.

Rafiq jumped to his feet. "Please, please, Alice, put the beer away. We've got plenty in the cooler."

"He's right, Alice," Andrew said. "You didn't exactly invite us."

Alice folded her arms in full authority figure mode. "You are always welcome," she said. "And you are my guests."

Andrew and Rafiq exchanged glances and began laughing. "This is strictly in honor of you, Diana," Andrew explained. "Usually we pay or provide."

Opening a bottle before she left the verandah, thus emphasizing her determination, Alice fetched glasses, then gave us an expert pour. Foam met rims and went no further.

"Cheers," said Andrew.

"So, how was your trip?" Alice asked.

Rafiq began at the beginning, playing our frustrations for laughs, but he'd hardly got us out of Dar before an old man carrying a jute shopping bag approached the verandah. Alice excused herself. The old man followed. When the two returned, the bag was full and very heavy.

"I hope that's the last one." Alice sighed and sank into a chair for the first time since we'd arrived. She closed her eyes for a moment, breathing deeply, savored a few swallows of beer, then held out her arms for baby Rose, whom Andrew had coaxed back to sleep.

"For a nurse," I said, "you have a very interesting dispensary."

"Yes," Alice confessed. "I'm also in the beer business. Not legally, as Rafiq knows, but what can I do? I'm supposed to be running a clinic, but there's no medicine, and I hardly ever get paid. Still, I do what I can. I make rehydration fluid with plain old sugar and salt. I nag about boiling water. I clean wounds and set uncomplicated fractures. It's not enough—"

"Better than nothing," I said.

"That's why I stay," she said. "And now, you must be hungry."

"Do you have a chicken?" Rafiq asked. "I promised Diana a curry."

"Do I have a chicken!" Alice hooted.

"Good. You won't drink our beer, but I can make a curry."

"Be my guest," Alice said, getting up and handing little Rose to me this time, a peaceful and easy-to-handle Rose, I'm happy to report. Once again, Alice disappeared into the darkness behind the house.

Andrew raided the Land Rover's safari cache for pots, a portable gas stove, a bottle of cooking oil and a bag containing tomatoes and onions, which Rafiq set to chopping and frying. That alone smelled good, but when he added the turmeric, the cumin, the coriander (and later the garam masala), the aroma of an authentic korma promised a day redeemed. Andrew, playing waiter to Rafiq's chef, topped up our glasses. Between pours, he looked at his watch. "Right on time," he said. "We'll eat at ten thirty."

Suddenly: a loud squawk.

"The chicken?" I asked.

Rafiq grinned.

Alice returned with a plucked carcass and a sack of rice. "Boil plenty," she advised. "I need to put this child to bed."

"She's precious," I said, giving little Rose a good night kiss. "A little darling. Not so little, actually, but she weighs practically nothing."

"Yes, poor thing. I thought I'd lost her."

"Fever?"

"Malaria. Or maybe not. Only a doctor could say—and we haven't seen a doctor in Alipolaka for months." Kissing little Rose on the forehead, she sighed. "Sometimes I get so discouraged. They burned our old village and gave us this. Efficiency would provide a better life, they said. Piped water. Electricity. A real clinic. A high school." She smiled, wanly.

"I've read about consolidating villages," I said. "It seemed like a good idea. But the burning and coercion—that's news to me."

"African socialism," Rafiq snorted.

"It *was* a nice idea," Alice retorted. "But where's the water? Where's the electricity? And tomorrow morning, Diana, you'll see all the dead cashew trees. The farmers can't tend their orchards anymore. Too far to go on foot."

Rafiq amplified. "Cashews used to be a big source of foreign exchange. No more."

A slender young man dressed in well-creased trousers and bush shirt called greetings from the street. He was looking for Andrew, not beer. "*Jambo, mzee*," he said. "I'm happy to find you here."

"*Jambo*, Charles. Join us. Have some beer," Andrew replied. "I hope you're planning to help us out this year. Suleiman will be with us, as usual, but we need you, too."

"I would be honored, Sir."

"Good. We'll be stopping by. Soon. Now, have a beer, and join us for supper, too."

"I'm sorry, Sir, but I cannot."

Alice emerged from the house in time to see Charles retreating. "A girl friend," she said. "He's a good boy though."

"Yes, he is," said Andrew. "He'd have done well in high school."

"Don't get me going," Alice said. "Have some more beer."

Which we did, lots of it, along with Rafiq's chicken korma and rice.

"You could open a restaurant in the U.S.," I said.

"I may have to," Rafiq said.

The bed that night was narrow but comfortable. I heard mosquitoes buzzing. They couldn't reach me, but they kept me awake. So did the low murmur of voices audible from the verandah where, just outside my unscreened, unglazed, wide open window, Andrew and Rafiq had spread their sleeping bags. And then, after an interlude of sleep, or maybe I was dreaming, I began to hear whispering again, a different kind of whisper, intimate even. Alice had been married twice, I'd learned that evening. Her first husband, drowned in a river accident, had given her a son and a daughter, both grown. Phyllis, Sally and Rose were the products of a second marriage, to a man who worked in Dar, returning infrequently to Alipolaka. Was Alice lonely? How lonely?

Morning came with the aroma of coffee and a call to breakfast, eggs from Alice's chicken coop, toast from bread Andrew had purchased in Dar, and just two of us at table, Alice and me. Baby Rose lay on a blanket, struggling mightily to roll over and get into crawling position. Phyllis and Sally were in school. One room. One teacher. Elementary instruction only. Andrew and Rafiq had driven to the river for water. In the rainy season, Alice said, she used water barrels to collect every drop of rainwater from the roof, but most of the year she depended on the kindness of her neighbors to keep her supplied.

"It's their way of thanking me," she explained, "for the little I can do."

"Well, you've been very kind to me," I said. "Thank you."

"You are welcome," she replied. "Friends help friends."

"It was so frustrating," I said. "Seeing the river and then not crossing it."

"You will. One day," Alice said. She smiled then, as if she were remembering something pleasant. "The old village was on the river bank," she recalled. "Sometimes it flooded, and we complained. But we had trees, and shade all year round. And now!" Alice shook her head. "No trees. No water. Welcome to the revolution!"

9

Alipolaka by day was as charming as a tic-tac-toe grid, an ideologue's imposition that the guinea pigs forced to live there hadn't had time (or money enough) to humanize. Adding to the bleakness were the orchards that Alice had told me about. Acres and acres of dead or dying cashew trees, once the basis of a lucrative export industry, and some idle cashew processing facilities, too, all lost to a country greatly in need of income.

Long after we left that ghost land, I was haunted by those ruined orchards, a tragedy so sad, so unnecessary and, quite possibly, totally unanticipated by the ideologues in power. And then came a thought that made me feel better. At least I could do something to help Alice. I'd start by calling Agnes when I got home. She could join me for dinner that very night, hopefully at the harborside Nzuri Café, where we'd do a little scheming.

Agnes, I discovered, hadn't returned from a family planning conference in Kampala, where she'd expected to see Martin. Kiki was committed to an evening with David. Milly declared that dinners at Nzuri came inevitably with a serving of blood-thirsty mosquitoes, which she could do without. So I went on my own. Since it was Sunday, not Friday or Saturday, when the place was always jammed and jiving, I rated a perfect little table under the stars.

The Nzuri Café lived up to its name in every way, *nzuri* meaning good in Swahili, because its proprietress, known to everyone as Mama, presided, not naggingly, but good-naturedly, over every detail, beginning at dawn, when she was on the beach to greet the fishing boats as they arrived with the night's catch. Her entrepreneurship wasn't quite legal in Tanzania, but the fishermen liked her and she paid well for the fish, so she got what she wanted before the rest was carted off to the controlled pricing of the central market. Most likely Mama also distributed tea to the right people from time to time. Furthermore, for all her attention to the caliber of her cuisine and the friendly competence of her servers, she was smart enough to keep her restaurant looking so ramshackle and temporary that no comrade would see it as a serious threat to a planned economy.

I ordered the calamari, plus hummus, baba ganouj and pita as starters, with beer.

Little waves slished in and out. Palm fronds clacked in a light breeze that blended the oddly compatible scents of frangipani and fishy mud flats. Gazing seaward I saw the lights of a freighter anchored in the harbor. To the south, red and white lights blinked unrelentingly to warn low-flying planes of an antenna rising from the site of an army installation. So there I was, more or less in harmony with the universe, when a male voice behind me said, "May I join you?"

It was the West German press attaché whom I'd met at Clive's welcoming party, the one who was going to phone me, according to Agnes, but hadn't. What was his name? Dieter—very German.

"What a surprise!" I said, with a parsimonious nod. "I heard you'd been sent to Ghana."

"I was," he said, taking the empty chair. "For a few months. They needed some help."

The waiter stopped by, offering to bring me another beer. "And the gentleman?" he inquired.

"Something for the gentleman, too," I said. What else could I say?

"It's nice here, isn't it?" he said.

"Yes, but I've heard that Accra is much more interesting than Dar."

"It's bigger," he said. "And West Africa is very different from East Africa. More vibrant. Especially Nigeria. You should visit Lagos sometime."

"Yes, I should."

And so it went, tediously, until I could plead, without a hint of rudeness, that I was desperately in need of a good night's sleep, so would he excuse me—as, naturally, he would. He rose, thanked me for the beer and took his leave. I should mention the vestigial Teutonic bow, which reminded me of Alice's daughters, curtseying. What would he make of that? I wondered.

Not until Thursday did I catch up with Agnes. Hoping that her professional experience would generate more pros than cons for helping Alice, I suggested sundowners at my place. Early evening was never very cool on my patio, but there was perfumed compensation. We were surrounded by flowering shrubs that had grown back so vigorously that I feared a visit, any day, from the security officer's minions. Mary had instructions to phone instantly should anyone with pruning shears set foot on the property. Meanwhile, she greeted Agnes and poured our wine, a California chenin blanc, icy cold, which my dear French friend judged, ever so delicately, to be "quite nice." We more than nibbled on peanuts and freshly fried plantain chips.

"Some of the villagers were hauling water on bicycles," I observed, as I described the situation in Alipolaka. "Imagine how many trips that took."

"They're the lucky ones," Agnes shrugged. "The Rufiji never dries up. Wells do. And I guess they weren't carrying pots on their heads either."

Her reaction started me. "That's pretty unsympathetic," I said.

Admitting to borderline insensitivity, Agnes blamed spill-over from the conference, which had left her seething with anger. "You Americans!" she said. "You and the Africans! When I wasn't guilty of infanticide, I was guilty of genocide. Your bunch, Diana, they don't want contraception, but they don't want abortion either. Utterly illogical. As for the Africans, family planning may sound good, they say, but it's really a plot to suppress black populations." Agnes paused to thank Mary for replenishing her wine glass, then resumed her tirade. "Meanwhile, the world's population is spiraling out of control, and African life expectancy is pathetically short. For God's sake, Diana, I'm here to keep mothers and children healthy, not to fight race wars or religious wars."

"Don't blame me," I pleaded. "I agree with you."

"But you support the policy," she retorted.

"I don't support it," I protested. "I explain it."

"Hair-splitting," Agnes retorted. "And the Pope! 'The act of love must be open to life.' Right! Half the sex in this world is rape or semi-rape. So, too many women have too many pregnancies, and babies die because starving women don't have enough milk. Not to mention women who die having babies they don't want."

"Look, Agnes, I support family planning, and as for rape, marital or otherwise—"

"That reminds me," Agnes said, changing gears, at last. "I'm worried about Hasina. Sheik's getting impatient. He wants a son."

Agnes had introduced me to Hasina, a full professor at the university, whose speciality was economic history, a sensitive subject in socialist Tanzania. Hasina had met and married her husband Sheikh in the U.S., where both had received their doctorates, his in the politically neutral arena of organic chemistry. He was director of a hospital lab in Dar. Their daughter Noor, now six, had been born while they were still in Ohio.

I stared at Agnes, whose horrified expression suggested she was thinking the same thing. "What if he discovers she's on the pill—"

"He could throw her out and keep Noor, too."

"He could," I agreed, "under Sharia law."

"That would kill Hasina, but Sheikh's probably under pressure from his parents," Agnes said. "You know how it is. Hasina walks in the door, and right away they're looking at her waistline and asking, 'When are we going to have another grandchild?' Then, when Hasina's out of hearing, they're saying, 'Divorce her. Take another wife.'"

"Sheikh needs some backbone," I said.

"And yet, with all that, Hasina manages to be so—if you'll pardon the expression—productive," Agnes said. "She's giving another paper in Nairobi next month. Maybe she should take Noor along and not come back."

"Actually, if Noor was born in the U.S., she'd be a U.S. citizen," I said. "That could make a difference."

"*Mon dieu!* this is depressing," groaned Agnes. "Let's cut the chatter and look at the stars and smell the jasmine."

"And have something to eat. Stay. There's plenty."

I went inside to discover that Mary had already set the table for two. The stew, chicken with a West African peanut sauce, was ready to serve. Talked out, we ate silently, not inside, but on the patio, which would have been lovely, if Agnes hadn't looked so somber. Troubled even.

"Is something the matter?" I asked.

"Martin," she said.

"Oh no! He's found someone else?"

"Worse. He was working with AIDS patients, and he got a little sloppy about the blood work. He pricked himself. But the odds were good, he decided, and besides he was too busy to worry about himself—"

"Oh no!" I said, again.

"Wait!" she said. "There's more."

She and Martin had spent the night together, waking predictably with shared sweet memories and ghastly hangovers, both quickly neutralized when Martin said he need to know her thinking on something that was beginning to trouble him. He'd felt so tired, so exhausted, recently. Maybe he should get tested—

"Maybe! And he hadn't warned me!" Agnes voice was rising. She was almost shouting. "I'm furious, Diana. And scared. How can a doctor be so stupid? So irresponsible?"

Sharing her disbelief, I shook my head.

"I *liked* Martin. I *trusted* him." Agnes continued, staring into her wine glass as if she were reading someone's tragic fortune, that someone being herself. "It's not fair. AIDS. HIV. Why now? Why us? When *we're* young."

"Fair or not," I said, "I'll be worried sick until you get the results—and you have to call me, instantly. But—for me, personally? Well, it doesn't touch me."

"Diana," said Agnes. "You can't say you don't like sex."

"Depends."

"How about your Kraut?"

"Boring," I said.

"What about Andrew?

"Agnes, I'm his supervisor. And he's married."

"He's tall. He's built. He's very nice, very intelligent. What did you *really* think that night when you heard the voices?"

"I was disappointed."

"That he didn't come to you?"

"Don't be absurd! I'd thought there was at least one African male who wasn't promiscuous. If he was with Alice, I was wrong—"

"I'm sorry," Agnes said. "I'm feeling low. I guess I want everyone else to be miserable, too. Tell me more about your weekend."

In fact, there was something I wanted to run by her.

Some kilometers beyond Alipolaka, Rafiq had spotted paw prints in the road. He stopped the Land Rover, got out and studied the tracks. "Lion," he said.

"Big one," Andrew agreed.

I joined Rafiq, for a really good look at my first lion tracks. Alice had mentioned that the people in the village were on the alert for a man-eater. He'd been driven off, but only after a little boy had been mauled. Were these his tracks? Was a lion actually following us? Scary! And exciting.

Examination over, Rafiq had handed me the car keys. "Your turn," he said. "You drive."

"Me?"

"You know how to shift, don't you?"

By the time we'd reached my house, Rafiq and Andrew had decided that I had the makings of a fine driver during the hunting season. If I took the wheel, they'd be free to shoot. With gun or camera, as the case might be. So—would I?

"And should I?" I put the question to Agnes. "I don't know what to do. My conscience resists. Yet, driving or not, I'll be eating bush meat, so what's the difference?"

Agnes laughed at my scruples. "If you like the bush, do it. If you don't, don't."

10

Elliot Babson, the controversial American anthropologist who may (or may not) have discovered an unanticipated link between humans and apes, burst into the office with a copy of his latest book. It was a gift for Milly, who liked to flirt with visiting professors. U.S. government-funded scholars got USIS services as part of the deal, but the savviest of us cultivated any academic who walked in the door. Familiar with remote areas, moving in rarified, close to people we needed to know, spotting trends oftentimes before we did, academics were very useful to their country, even when they had no such conscious intentions. We, in return, lit fires when officials put roadblocks in the way of legitimate research. Above all, when American students or scholars got sick or hurt, we did everything possible, in Tanzania and elsewhere, to get them cared for. Often we saved lives.

"For services rendered," Babson said, presenting the book to Milly. "What do you think of the title?"

I read the dust cover as Milly held it up: *By George! The New Man from Olduvai.*

By then, everyone in the office, all of whom had met Babson or knew him by reputation, had congregated around Milly's desk. The chorus of chuckles suggested that the title was a winner, George being the name that Babson had given to his collection of bones.

Visiting Olduvai Gorge had long been one of the major tourist objectives in Tanzania, right up there with climbing Mount Kilimanjaro and going on safari. I'd yet to pay my respects to the ancestors. Mostly for lack of time, but I'd also been deterred by Milly's account of her own excursion, which had taken place since she'd last seen Babson. She was no enthusiast.

"You may call it a gorge, Elliot," she scoffed. "I call it a gully, the world's most famous gravel pit. Lizard heaven. With goat droppings. Whooo-ee! Everyone's out of the bus and scrabbling around, stuffing pockets and purses with Stone Age artifacts. Talk about wishful thinking! On the road back to Dar, I thought, 'Oh boy, if this is evolution and we're the final fruits—what a hoot!'"

Clive picked up a piece of chert, allegedly from Olduvai. Milly used it as a paperweight. "What about this, Elliot? Hand axe or wishful thinking?"

Babson hefted it. He studied its facets with comic seriousness. "Well, it would make a good weapon—"

Milly snatched it back. "You don't have to be delicate. I keep it for laughs. And," she added, looking at Clive, "if I weren't such a nice person, it would have become a murder weapon long ago."

"It's smart to keep your eyes peeled at Olduvai," Babson said. "Especially during the rainy season. How do you think I found George?"

Kiki supplied the prompt. "How?" she asked.

"We had some pretty good hunches," Babson said, "but we love Lady Luck. And *we,*" he added, focusing an exaggerated frown on Milly, "didn't sneak away with material of assumed anthropological value."

"You said it wasn't an axe," Milly protested.

"But you hoped it was."

"You *would* have walked off with George, if you could have."

Babson rolled his eyes. "That's *so* nineteenth century."

"Speaking of authenticity," Clive said, "some of your colleagues claim that George is as authentic as Milly's paperweight."

Babson tapped the cover of his book. "It's all here. Read it for yourself. But first—" He searched in his backpack, found a Cross pen with a 24 carat gleam, opened *By George* to the title page and scrawled an inscription: "For Milly. Superwoman lives! Best wishes wherever you go. Elliot."

Recapping his pen, Babson consulted his watch and said, "I've got to go. Appointment at the Ministry of Culture—which reminds me of a great inscription story."

It had happened in Kenya, where an incumbent Minister of Culture had been replaced, overnight, for obscure political reasons, leaving Babson with a presentation book inscribed to the wrong man.

"So what did you do?" Milly asked.

Babson laughed. "I whipped it out, readdressed the dedication and said, 'If you're good enough to fill his shoes, you deserve his book.' And then I prayed. The new guy had a sense of humor. He approved our project."

It was a good anecdote, apt and well-told. I decided to invite Babson to dinner, "Tonight," I said. "If you're free."

Babson was available, but Clive was busy. So was Milly, but Kiki would bring David, whose studies of pre-literate languages would surely interest Babson. Andrew agreed to corral some journalists, providing them with transportation, if needed, and I invited Bruce Virgilio, an officer in the Consular section, who might be useful to Babson. Having sent his pregnant wife back to the States to gestate at a safe distance from the malaria menace, Virgilio would come alone. With no effort at all, I snagged Agnes, who had phoned to tell me about a seminar on women's health that might interest the people at USAID, in which case, she suggested, USIS might cooperate on publicity. She went into more detail, but there was only one thing I wanted to know. As soon as I could interrupt, I asked about Martin. "Any news about the test yet?"

"Nothing," she said. "I can't sleep."

"Stay strong," I said. "He's probably okay."

Having commissioned Agnes to invite Hasina and Sheik, I rushed home to see what kind of dinner Mary could put together on such short notice, a challenge that would, I knew, delight her. Employed by a single woman determined to stay slim, which means I ate well, but healthfully, she was a frustrated culinary artist. Parties allowed her to go wild with carbs and calories. Kiki, meanwhile, had volunteered the services of her cook as bartender. He was agreeable to making a few extra shillings.

Juggling menu ideas in my head, I rushed home at lunchtime, opened my front door and found Phil Cheyney in the living room. Slumped in a wing chair, he looked so bereft and miserable I forgot to be annoyed that Mary hadn't called to tell me of his unexpected arrival.

"Phil!" I exclaimed.

Making a largely symbolic effort to rise, he spoke in a lifeless tone that frightened me. "Sorry about crashing in," he said, "but our usual support system's out of town."

"You're welcome any time," I replied. "Now what on earth has happened?"

Phil, hands on face, sank deeper into the nest-like chair. "Njema," he whimpered. "I think he's going to die."

Kneeling by the chair, I placed a hand on his knee and waited.

"He's confused and uncoordinated," Phil continued. "Concussion, probably. Even if he survives, he may never be himself again."

"That's terrible."

"The whole troupe's ruined. Years of trust destroyed. Years of data shot to pot. Years of my life down the drain—"

Once we'd been summoned to lunch on the patio, I consigned Phil to the therapy of tuna fish sandwiches made with homemade mayonnaise on home baked bread in order to join Mary in the kitchen and work out the dinner menu. When I got back to the table, Phil was up to telling a tale of once-trusted colleagues, close friends actually, whose research efforts had targeted the wrong troupe of baboons.

"It's partly our own fault," he confessed. "We were stuck in camp, writing grant proposals, and John was down with fever. So another ranger was assigned. The guy swore up and down that he knew our troupe. He promised to steer clear."

But he didn't. And so the wrong baboons were lured into cages and darted with an anesthetic that worked too slowly on Big Mama, Habari, Dogo and Njema, who fought furiously to escape. "They were a bloody mess, especially Njema," Phil said. "It took a second dart to subdue him."

Although other members of the troupe had lost consciousness too quickly to injure themselves, even they, Phil feared, would never trust a human being again. At any rate, blood drawn, vials of blood sealed and labeled, the uninjured baboons had been released as soon as they were alert. The still-caged, bloody victims of science were driven back to camp, where all hell broke loose.

"You can imagine the scene," Phil said. "I was fit to kill."

"Was he ever!" Eileen confirmed. She shrugged out of her backpack and wrapped her arms around Phil. "He was ranting and raving and declaring that those bungling bastards sure as hell weren't welcome to spend another night with us. He'd get them thrown out of the country, too. I thought he was going to start bashing his own head against something."

"After all that," I observed, "I'm surprised you're here today."

"No choice, so we radioed John, who was feeling much better," Eileen said.

"He agreed to play vet—he's qualified—while we picked up supplies, including the damned muffler that should have arrived months ago. Rafiq's guys took forever, but finally it's installed. That's what took me so long. And all the time I was thinking about Njema. He could be dead by the time we get back."

"If not," Phil moaned, "he'll be a cripple, a retard, hanging around camp, nothing but a pet, worse than the Mahoneys—if they'll put up with him. I'd just love to get those visas revoked—"

"Whoa!" I said. "Play that game and you'll be out of the country as fast as they are."

"Well, those fuckers better have their gear packed by the time we get back. They can analyze their samples somewhere else," Phil declared. And then his head was cradled in his hands again. "Oh god, we should have known—"

"Trust John," said Eileen. "And, meanwhile, Diana, we're hoping you might have a spare room—"

Warning them of the impending dinner, to which they were invited, although they were free to boycott, I urged them to shower and relax, while I returned to work, where I discovered that the electricity had quit for no good reason. Up the stairs I trudged, with less than my usual energy. I, too, was worried about the baboons. I also had a boring press release to write. USAID had recruited an American dairy specialist to advise Tanzania's Department of Agriculture on maximizing milk production, and Kiki had arranged for him to lecture about something bovine, which meant publicity was needed. More cows, I sighed, and got to work. I was still trying to translate statistics into English, when Andrew appeared, waving the *News*. He glanced at my clumsy first draft.

"Does this mean we're going to be clearing livestock through customs?"

"The bulls stay home," I said. "Their contributions come freeze dried or deep frozen or something."

"That should keep the freight costs down," said Andrew. "No objection so long as they confine it to cattle."

"Don't be archaic," I said. "Where do you think test tube babies come from?"

"Speaking of cattle," Andrew said, "listen to this, from the *News*. Two cattle geneticists from Colorado—your state. The same guys we're getting? I hope not. Anyway, they arrived in Kenya to see about improving cattle for the Masai. And now I quote: 'We knew that owning a large herd of cattle was highly prestigious and assumed that the cattle were prized for their color or markings. Our field studies revealed that the tribe were actually breeding stock for milk yield and disease resistance—'"

"Surprise! Surprise!" Mo sneered. Kiki had tasked him with recruiting some Tanzanian discussants for the dairy talk. "As if the Masai were some kind of half wits."

"I have news that's not so funny," Andrew said. "Peter's been offered a chance to study in the Soviet Union. Five years, including one to learn Russian."

"Is Peter happy?"

Andrew reproached me. "Let's be serious. Can't the Americans match it?"

"Ask Kiki," I advised, not for the first time. "And cross your fingers. Competition for study in the U.S. is a whole lot stiffer."

I told him about the baboons, expressing my hope that Phil and Eileen would join us for dinner. "And Andrew—do bring Lucille," I added.

"She won't come. She never does."

She didn't come, but everyone else did, including Agnes, with an array of French cheeses mere hours from Paris via an Air France flight.

"I know the pilot," Agnes said, with a wink, which didn't surprise me. Also not surprising: after an unsuccessful attempt to beguile the happily married Phil, she concentrated on Elliot Babson, who turned out to be more susceptible. Watch out, Martin, I thought. Not sympathetically. He deserved to be dumped. Agnes, I hoped, would restrain herself, sticking to flirting so long as her own HIV status was uncertain.

Andrew spent much of the evening shepherding the bright, but relatively unsophisticated reporters he'd invited, one of them a young woman, to whom I introduced Hasina, as a kind of big sister. Different professions. Same need to break down gender barriers. As for the young male reporter, after politely asking me how I liked Tanzania and learning that I did, very much, let me know what he thought about U.S. foreign policy. He was pretty negative, which was normal for passionate young Leftists. I invited him to drop by the office. We could have a deeper discussion, I promised, and I had a book that might interest him. Meanwhile, I suggested that he interview Elliott Babson, whose discovery of George was rocking the world of anthropology. The reporter cornered Virgilio instead, to grill him about—what else?—visas.

Poor Virgilio. Every other week he declared his intention to become a hermit. Practically everyone he met wanted a U.S. visa, but very few applicants qualified, especially when it came to students, like Andrew's son Peter. Speaking of Peter, Virgilio was regretful, since everyone liked Andrew. "But rules are rules," he sighed. "Show me a letter of acceptance from any reputable college or university," he added, "and Peter's on his way. I'll guarantee the visa."

Virgilio, naturally, had his own agenda for the evening. It had to do with procuring an invitation to visit the Baboon camp, which he got, since Phil and Eileen were eager for good relations with the Consular section, whose American contingent kept changing. (Tanzania was a hardship post. Two year assignments were the norm.)

Meanwhile, the exodus of guests had begun. Babson left with Agnes, I noted. Having persuaded Virgilio to chauffeur the young reporters wherever they wished, I invited Andrew to stay behind. As for Phil and Eileen, they had bowed out long before, pleading exhaustion.

"We could be in for some trouble," I said, as I closed the door behind Vigilio and the young reporters, who had thoroughly enjoyed all the free booze.

"Trouble? In that case, these glasses need refilling." By then a veteran of many such parties at my house, Andrew did the honors and joined me on the sofa. "What kind of trouble?"

"More Fort Dietrich nonsense," I said.

"Meaning?"

Mary appeared then, to collect the last of the glasses and other party debris. Thanking her, I said she was free to finish the washing up in the morning, if she wished.

"It's a matter of being proactive," I said. "Those researchers were supposedly drawing blood for some sort of genetic test. But who's to say they weren't injecting baboons with the AIDS virus?"

"Custom-made in the good old U.S.A.?"

"Exactly."

We and our colleagues around the world had been working for some time to counter one of the more egregious Soviet disinformation campaigns of the day: the idea that the AIDS virus had been concocted in Frederick, Maryland, at the sadly not fictional biological warfare laboratories at Fort Dietrich, from which the virus had escaped—or from which, in the nastiest version of the smear, the scourge had been disseminated. Reputable scientists were theorizing that the virus had leaped, most likely via the food chain, from chimpanzees to humans, but conjecture wasn't proof at that early date. Africa, meanwhile, was reeling from a catastrophic AIDS epidemic. People were fearful, angry and desperate for answers. Scapegoats were welcome. Enter the Soviets with their Fort Dietrich story.

"So what's the plan?" Andrew asked.

"Fight fiction with facts," I said. It was our usual antidote, and it usually worked. I'd already requested from Eileen a complete description of the offending baboon project and its source of funding. We'd also needed the names of scientists able to vouch for the project as honest science. "I had to ask Eileen," I observed. "Phil's going bonkers.'

Andrew agreed. "He's taking it hard."

"Question: will he be able to control himself if some diligent reporter shows up at the Baboon Camp?" I asked. "And what if the government decides to close the place down?"

Andrew shook his head.

I poured some more wine to ease the pain.

"Should I alert other posts?" Andrew asked. "Nairobi? Lilongwe?"

"Hopefully we won't have to," I said. "Clive needs to know, but he won't panic."

"How about Freeman?"

"I'll handle him."

"It seems almost obscene to change the subject," Andrew said, "But Rafiq and I were wondering if you'd like to do a little driving this weekend."

"Oh?"

"We'll be hunting. With Luke Kupinga. He heads a bureau in the Finance Ministry."

"That's four—plus helpers and rangers and all the gear. Won't it be rather crowded?"

"Two Land Rovers. Rafiq's and Luke's."

"The answer is yes," I said.

11

A single Land Rover idled in the driveway.

"Where's Luke?" I asked, climbing into the passenger seat next to Rafiq, who wouldn't be relinquishing the wheel until we reached the other side of the Rufiji. That was fine with me. Let him negotiate the lose-lose game of dealing with Tanzania's two lane highways: risk our lives with repeated close-call passing or take all day to get to the river.

"His minister called last night," Rafiq explained. "An ivory shipment got intercepted. Some comrades are implicated."

"Is Luke involved?"

"Well, Customs is. That's Finance."

"That's not what I meant."

"I know," Rafiq said.

"It wasn't your truck, was it?"

"Would I be here if ivory had been found in one of my lorries?"

"Knowing our dear country," said Andrew, who'd settled himself in the center of the back seat, "quite possibly."

I supplied the scenario. "The phone rings. Your wife, ever so politely, replies, 'Oh, I'm very sorry my husband's not home.' And it's true, you're not—"

"*My* wife would go to pieces if she had to manage that kind of thing." Rafiq said. "And *you've* got mighty cynical!"

"A line's been crossed," I said.

The day before I'd had to pay off a policeman. I'd given a gardener the shillings he needed to keep from being arrested for lacking a document another policeman had just confiscated. The original crime? Who knew? Imaginary deficiencies relating to his bicycle? The supposedly erratic way the poor fellow rode? Lack of respect for authority? Looking poor and helpless? "Were the cops colluding?" I asked. "Looks like. So, if I were really cynical, Rafiq, I'd ask why you have a friend in the Finance Ministry."

Forgoing a reply, but not a brief disgusted look, Rafiq started the Land Rover and released the parking brake.

We went nowhere. Andrew had shouted, "Wait! Wait!"

He jumped out and disappeared behind the house, seeking the victimized gardener, I assumed. In the office Andrew was unofficial ombudsman. He'd do his best for the gardener, too. The payoff had averted arrest, but the all important document had not been restored.

I got out. Why sit in the car before I had to? Rafiq lounged against a dusty fender and addressed my question. The deep vee of his unbuttoned shirt revealed a gold chain and a distracting mat of dark hair. "You could also ask why Andrew's my friend," he said. "It's simple. I have a vehicle that's reliable. He's a genius with people. Both of us hate Dar. Mutual benefit. Luke's a good guy. He works hard. He deserves a break. So we make it a threesome. But say we were up to something. In that case, how do you fit in? At a certain point, everyone's suspect. That means you, too."

"Me?"

"What rate are you getting for your dollars these days? What happens to your car when you leave?"

"I've just got here," I protested.

"Don't tell me you're not playing the black market. Only fools don't. So we're all vulnerable, which is good, actually. When you know your accuser's weakness, he goes down if you do."

"Insurance."

"But this isn't Zaire," Rafiq continued. "It's not Nigeria."

"Not yet," agreed Andrew, who'd returned, coffee mug in hand, Mary in tow. She bore a tray with coffee for me and Rafiq. "But we're learning fast." Rapidly downing his own brew, Andrew thanked Mary and reclaimed his commodious back seat. "Let's change the subject. Aren't we supposed to be getting away from all this?"

"If smuggling's the subject," I persisted, "maybe you two *are* involved—and I make a convenient front. Not that you'd tell me."

"Sometimes, here, it's better not to know," Andrew said.

"Rafiq says the more you know the safer you are."

"I don't smuggle ivory," said Rafiq.

"He doesn't," Andrew said. "We don't. End of story."

"Well, there's one thing I do need to know." I laughed. "What's the tent situation?"

"One for each of us," Andrew said. "And if you can't get yours up, you sleep by the fire, with Charles and Suleiman."

"So long as I don't have to wash sooty pots and pans."

"That's Suleiman's job." Rafiq said. "But Charles is usually willing to help."

Our first stop was the ice house, located in a section of the city where finicky distinctions between public and private, residential and commercial, did not apply. Butchers, tailors, electricians, cloth sellers, chemists—they worked where they lived. Shops occupied front rooms. Sewing machines whirred on porches. Lesser venders had taken over the walkways, diverting pedestrians into the street, where they begrudged the right of way to vehicles. Rafiq was inclined to lean on the horn. I suggested patience, partly to be considerate, but also because I wanted to take everything in. I seldom got to such parts of the city.

The ice house shared a block with auto body shops and iron works that confronted pedestrians with a steeplechase of cast iron gates, window grills, bedsteads, plant holders, dining sets—and piles of iron rods awaiting their fate. Squinting into dark work spaces, I saw flying sparks and welders' blue flames. The hissing and crackling of acetylene torches competed for attention with the thump thumping of rubber hammers on fenders that looked, to me, crumpled beyond redemption. Work was going full blast. It was seven o'clock in the morning.

As Rafiq edged the Land Rover toward the curb in front of the ice house, a thin-to-wraith-like old man in a shabby black overcoat rose and came toward us. He'd been sitting on Andrew's mammoth ice chest. His beard, mostly white, was closely trimmed, and a lacy little cap played peek-a-boo with his baldness. This was Suleiman, and his trademark was that coat, which lent him the look of a *qadi* or Muslim judge, although he'd found it, Andrew confided, in a used clothing bin. By midday, it might be unbuttoned, but Suleiman took it off only at night, and then only to draw it over his shoulders as a blanket.

Leaving Dar, we didn't stop again until we reached Alipolaka, where we picked up Charles and delivered a box of medical supplies to Alice, who rued our arrival an hour too late. With ordinary soap for antiseptic and no antibiotic cream to prevent infection, she'd just stitched up a villager's deep panga wound. Parting cardboard flaps, she peered inside the box and saw the ointment she needed, several tubes of it. "I'll call him back," she said, words far more gratifying than any formal thank you note. In the future, I decided, there would be more boxes.

And then we turned our attention to little Rose, who'd been standing, wobbly but determined, on her own reassuringly chubby little feet. "She's getting strong," I observed, keeping to myself the fear that she, like too many children in Africa, might not make it to school age.

"She's walking, too," Alice said. "Just a few steps. But she's on her way."

She was, in fact, tottering toward Andrew, who picked her up and gave her a kiss.

I excused myself to take advantage of the world's cleanest outhouse. When I returned, Charles scrambled to the roof of the Land Rover, joining Suleiman, who'd refused to share the back seat with Andrew, not for religious reasons, but in deference to some long ingrained caste system.

We reached the river in good time—and at just the right time. Foot passengers enough to populate a village had accumulated, but the queue of vehicles was reassuringly short, and the ferry was closing in on its primitive landing spot just below us. The ferry, for that matter, was nothing more than a huge raft urged along by flanking tugs that seemed to be struggling. What if one of those tugs, soon to be pushing me and my companions against that very same, very insistent current, all of a sudden stalled, midstream? As for the huge dead trees that hurtled by every so often, they reminded me of battering rams. Or torpedoes. How disastrous would a collision be?

But Rafiq wasn't worried. Nor was Andrew. And the boatmen knew their job. The ferry glided into position. Hawsers were quickly secured. Vehicles and pedestrians streamed ashore, making room for us.

There's a bridge over the Rufiji now, but standing in the bow just a few feet above the water, my hair blown back, my clothes pressed against me, the ferry laboring against that fearsomely strong current, I felt the power of the river more intensely than anyone glancing over a parapet could begin to imagine. It was thrilling—and over too soon. The ferry kissed the far bank, ever so gently, and I gave myself to the throng of foot passengers as they picked up their bundles, took their children in hand and waited for the crew to lower the chain that hemmed us in.

The moment for driver switching came when we stopped at the park border to add a ranger to our crew. His name was Malik, and he was delighted to be working with Andrew and Rafiq again. Greetings over, Malik joined Charles and Suleiman on the roof. I took the wheel. "Where to?" I asked.

Andrew laughed. "Not so fast!"

It was instruction time. The first thing I needed to know was the meaning of the rapping. Charles on the right and Malik on the left were the lookouts. A rapping on either side of the roof would signal game sighted in the corresponding direction. The driver would have to react appropriately, moderating speed, turning as needed, stopping at the right time—and, always, keeping noise to a minimum. My mentors promised to coach me until I got the hang of it.

My bush driving career began with following a pair of ruts on the perimeter of the park, and yet, if I had heard correctly, not all the rapping would be coming from the *non* park side of the track, an expectation that invited a discussion about law and ethics, I thought. That evening, for sure. Meanwhile, I was much too busy to engage in brain-taxing debate.

The track cut through light forest, for the most part, but sometimes the trees receded, making room for dwellings and their garden plots. Often, in such hamlets, with yapping dogs attacking our tires and me trying not to run over chickens, the road itself turned into the equivalent of a sand box. The Land Rover's handling got mushy. We lost momentum. No problem. I shifted into four wheel drive and kept going, however slowly.

Black cotton soil was more hazardous. I'd never heard of it, until Rafiq forced me to halt just short of some muck I'd taken to be the last stage of an ordinary puddle. "When you see that stuff, don't drive through it," he said.

"Why?" I asked.

"If it's wet, you'll bog down. Dry, it's like steel." He pointed to a grayish patch that had hardened while imprinted with a herd's worth of goat or cow tracks. "Drive across that and you'll end up with shredded tires."

I smelled exaggeration, but let it go.

"Tell her the winch story," Andrew prompted. His grin, visible in the rear view mirror, was mischievous—or maybe even malicious.

"Later," Rafiq said, a bit sharply. "Time to get us a hog."

A warthog is a stubby, short-legged creature whose sooty coloring is hard to distinguish from black cotton soil, wet or dry. Add tufts of grass or tangles of undergrowth, and a motionless wart hog is well nigh invisible, unless a ray of sunlight strikes his up-curving tusks. On the run, however, he's at the mercy of two foolish habits. Halfway to cover, he'll pause and glance back, to gauge how he's doing. Bam! That's it! But only if the hunter has a split second reaction time. When the hog takes off again, his angle of retreat is unpredictable. There's also the matter of the flag, his tufted tail, which points skyward when he's startled into flight. First comes the lifted muzzle, giving, ever so briefly, a glimpse of that lumpy, bumpy face, its bulging eyes and bold nostrils, its curvaceous tusks, and then he's off, zigzagging through the vegetation, flag fluttering provocatively. Shoot me if you can!

But I knew zero about the behavior of warthogs—or hunters—that first day behind the wheel. Nor had I anticipated the physical and mental demands of handling a vehicle that bucked like a rodeo bull as I coped with hazard-strewn terrain of the sort that Phil had (apparently) navigated with such ease. In no time at all, my knuckles ached from gripping the wheel, and the tension in my face and shoulders had reached serious pain level. Far from being one with the universe, I was trying to be one with the Land Rover.

Then, suddenly, I was aware of Andrew joggling my shoulder. "Stooooop!" he said, in a raspy whisper. "Stop!"

I stopped, but too abruptly. Screeching brakes alarmed the hog, who sped off, flag jauntily waving.

"Sorry," I said, feeling stupid. I'd processed the roof tap as the sound of a dislodged rock thunking against the Land Rover. "I'm really sorry. I'll do better."

"That's all right," Andrew said. "It always takes a while."

Rafiq was silent. He was the one who'd shot wide and lost the hog.

I drove on, listening, listening, listening, for the next tap, which came from Charles on the left. Andrew's feet were touching ground the instant the Land Rover had come to an exquisitely soundless halt. The hog had noticed nothing. Then a bird sounded the alarm.

Andrew was annoyed, but not with me. "Good job," he said. "Keep it up."

"She'll do," Rafiq grunted. "Let's go."

My lips were cracking, my throat was dry, every part of me that touched the seat was soggy with trapped perspiration, and my arms and shoulders strained at the effort to control a steering mechanism in thrall to the wheels' preference for the easy and usually wrong direction. But it was fun. Best of all, my conscience wasn't nagging me about the ethics of chauffeuring hunters any more. I was too darn busy keeping us safe and—yes!—making us successful.

And so I was ready for the next tap, from Malik, on the right.

Slowly, smoothly, perfectly, I applied the brake, and oh wow! A whole litter of warthogs was rooting around in a patch of guinea corn sprouts. The mother raised her grotesque black head to check us out, and the feast was over. One big flag followed by seven little ones trotted rapidly toward cover that wouldn't be needed.

"Drive on!" Andrew commanded. "I won't shoot a mother."

"Easy shot," Rafiq muttered. "It's getting late."

As we gained distance from the river, easily arable terrain gave way to higher, dryer, flatter, more open savanna, its panoramas punctuated mostly by lonely-looking acacia trees. Here and there a crazy looking baobab performed its contortions against the boundless sky that had sent me into ecstasies during my morning with the baboons in Mikumi.

A tap from Charles. Hogs on the right—and no glitches of any kind. Two ran for it. One went down.

"Camp meat," said Rafiq.

But not for Malik and Suleiman, which made me wonder why we'd gone after a hog in the first place, but I said nothing. With help from Malik, Charles slung the bloody carcass onto a tarp in the back of the Land Rover, and Suleiman would soon be butchering and grilling it. Unlike Rafiq, however, both Suleiman and Malik would starve before eating pork. Or so they claimed. Meanwhile, some refreshment was in order: beer for everyone, including the non-pork eaters, whose religion called for spurning alcohol, too. I smiled to myself, thinking of how frequently principles get massaged. However, there was one rule I couldn't bend.

"The driver had better stick to something soft," I said.

"Your choice," Andrew shrugged. "How's it going?"

"I love it," I said. "It's tiring, though. Especially the bushwhacking."

"You'll harden up," Andrew promised. "I could take over, but we're pretty close to our camp site. It shouldn't take us long to bring down an impala."

"An impala? Do we have a permit?"

"No. But they aren't endangered."

"They're so beautiful—and graceful."

"Meaning the right to life depends on how you look?"

"Touché!" I grinned. "But why not go for impala in the first place?

"A service to farmers," Andrew said. "They hate hogs."

Charles gathered up the empty cans, tossing them into the back of the Land Rover, more or less on top of the hog. I climbed, stiffly, into position behind the wheel.

"All aboard," I called.

Even on the savanna there were occasional thickets of trees and bushes. This was impala habitat, providing camouflage from predators and tender leaves to nibble on. And so we found them, a harem of does, plus, not far away, the presiding buck, whose rack was so impressive I was amazed he'd avoided collection by trophy hunters. Noticing our approach, one of the does gave a little bark. Immediately the corps de ballet was vaulting, in fluid arcs, over rocks and fallen trees, with Prince Charming quickly overtaking his slower concubines. Andrew and Rafiq fired rapidly, not aiming, it seemed, so much as hoping for a lucky shot. Sure enough, one creature collapsed mid-leap. The buck was down. Those prodigious antlers were up for grabs.

I set the Land Rover's parking brake and reached the scene in time to see the thrashing and trembling, the body heaving up and falling back, the eyes wide with something that looked like terror. I watched as Malik darted in with his knife. He grabbed an antler and twisted the head to expose the throat that he, as a Muslim, had to slit before the buck died. He slashed. The buck's head, eyes still open, flopped into a pool of its own blood.

"Do you want the antlers?"

It was Rafiq. He was talking to me.

"What?"

"Do you want the antlers?"

Shaking my head, feeling weak and unable to speak, I looked for a tree trunk to sit on and found one. Closing my eyes to everything and everyone, I propped my elbows on my knees and held my head in my hands, not knowing whether I would cry next, or throw up.

"Are you all right?" Andrew asked. He'd allowed me a reasonable amount of time to sort myself out, but we had to get going.

"I'm fine," I said. "Well, I'm not. Just leave me alone—okay?"

Andrew laid a hand on my shoulder. "It's normal," he said. "The first time out."

"Very consoling."

I let Rafiq drive us into camp.

12

My friends did not have a sleeping tree. They had a camping tree, a sturdy veteran of many visits. Its ambitious canopy guaranteed shade, and its lower branches accepted whatever we draped over them: clothes, towels, ropes— and, Suleiman's necessities: chains with hooks on which game was hung for butchering. Well apart from the tree there was an enormous fire pit surrounded by nature's version of comfort: long fat logs, to sit on or lounge against. Perfect for later, I thought, as the Land Rover nosed into the clearing. But first I had to walk around, swinging my arms to get the stiffness out. I'd have done some exploring, too, if Andrew hadn't called me back.

"Watch out for mambas," he said.

I displayed a calf-high boot. "Mamba proof."

"Well, don't go far," he warned.

Meanwhile, Rafiq had barely pocketed the ignition key before long-established routines had gone into effect. Suleiman with the assistance of Charles was skinning, eviscerating and portioning out the carcasses. What we'd eat. What would accrue to each of us when we headed home, the real reason for the huge supply of ice, since Tanzanian beer drinkers lack the American addiction to cold brew. Malik had the wood-gathering well in hand, though I added an armful, trying to be helpful after Andrew and Rafiq shooed away because I was too slow and clumsy at erecting the tent destined for me. In the main, therefore, I was useless and powerless, a status not much to my taste. I circled the clearing like a minor planet, easily observed, mostly ignored, stumbling sometimes across empty beer bottles and crushed aluminum cans.

Aha! Something to do. I gathered them up and dumped them in a little pile by the Land Rover.

"Yours?" I asked, when Andrew came over to see what I was up to.

"Maybe. Sometimes we miss a few."

"Pack it in, pack it out," I cooed, happy to claim the moral high ground, especially since I was uncomfortably aware that Charles, Suleiman and Malik would be exposed to predators while I slept in a tent.

"Is it fair?" I asked. "We have shelter and they don't."

"Animals hate fires," Andrew replied. "Everyone's perfectly safe."

"But fires go out," I protested.

"Not if they're fed," Andrew replied. "Suleiman's a light sleeper."

"And when he snores, it's Sulieman the Loud," said Rafiq, who'd added the latest empties to my pile of trash. "The lions think he's another lion. They wouldn't dream of invading his territory."

"Suleiman the Protector! I love it!" I glanced toward Rafiq, whose gaze held mine long enough for me to catch my breath. Hazel eyes. Tan. Wavy dark hair falling around his temples. All of which led me to thinking enviously of Agnes and her unconflicted approach to sex. My hunch re Babson had been on the mark. Worries about Martin notwithstanding, she'd slept with Elliot. Her report the next day? Since he did have a fascinating mind, she'd settle for lunch in the future.

But Rafiq wasn't focused on me. He and Suleiman had a banquet to prepare. Andrew and I could pay our way, he said, by preparing skewers for the impala kabobs. Eager to do anything useful, I pulled out my handy dandy Swiss Army knife, which in years to come would be confiscated by TSA operatives maintaining a checkpoint at Washington's Dulles Airport. Seated on one of those nice fat logs, I let wood curls fall around me as I whittled.

I was also trying to decide whether I should be pleased or disgusted with myself for calmly observing the butchers at work. I watched bellies slit open. I watched pinkish intestines tumbling out and glistening in the setting sun. I watched bloody hands carefully extricating floppy, mahogany-colored livers and bloodier hands severing slippery hearts from unwanted lungs that quivered like palmfuls of pale amethyst foam. Hearts as well as livers went directly on the hot grill, to be smoked and seared and served as appetizers, the palate-teasers for ravenous campers.

Twilight had slid into darkness by then. My world had shrunk to six hungry carnivores sitting around a fire. When the impala kebabs were ready, Rafiq passed his special chutney around. "Dip," he said. Less gamey than venison, a little sweeter and very tender, the impala cried out for the chutney's fruity tang. A swallow of warm beer came to the rescue when mouth, tongue and throat caught fire from the little green peppers that only Rafiq could nibble like harmless raisins. Soon everyone was dipping and sipping, including Suleiman, who served up the pilau, which all of us could enjoy, and the hog curry, which he and Malik couldn't.

"Tell me the winch story," I demanded.

"It's Andrew's story," Rafiq said.

"That's because Rafiq was driving—and he'd rather not remember," Andrew retorted. "We were after buffalo and hadn't done very well. Then we startled a small herd, including a bull with horns wide enough to balance a 747—"

"And I knew someone who'd die for those horns," Rafiq said.

"Which is why the driver had his eyes on the herd, not on the ground, unfortunately," Andrew continued. "Pretty soon the wheels were spinning, and the buffalo were out of sight. We were up to our axles in black cotton soil. That's trouble."

"Deep trouble," Rafiq agreed.

Looking around, they'd spotted a tree and had a little debate over who was going to wade through the muck to loop a winch cable around it.

"I lost," Rafiq said.

"You got us into the mess."

The cable had reached around the tree, just barely, but barely's enough, so Andrew activated the winch, his intention being to drag the Land Rover backwards toward the tree and onto solid ground. At first, nothing seemed to be happening.

"I wasn't worried," Andrew said. "It can take a while to break the suction."

Even so, he looked back, over his shoulder, just to check. Rafiq was standing by the tree, arms crossed, staring toward the Land Rover, waiting for it to start moving, which wasn't happening. But there was nothing wrong with the winch. Slowly, slowly, as roots gave way, it was pulling the tree down. Then gravity took over—

Andrew shouted, "Move, Rafiq! Move!"

The tree didn't hit the Land Rover, either.

"So how many trees did you uproot before you got out of there?" I asked.

Andrew and Rafiq laughed.

"That was the only tree around," Andrew said, "and the nearest village was ten miles away. So we dug—"

"And dug—"

"And dug. And the moral of the story is—"

"Obvious," Rafiq conceded. "Do what I say, not what I did,"

Andrew and Rafiq—so different, so sympatico! Their banter could go on forever, but we had drunk prodigiously and eaten very well. It was time to turn in. Malik augmented the pile of wood by the fire. Charles laid out some tarps for the crew to sleep on. Blankets wouldn't be needed. The fire would keep the two young men warm. Suleiman had his coat.

Andrew caught up with me as I was unzipping tent flaps. He insisted that I take his revolver, the one we'd quarreled about so many months ago. If I had to leave the tent during the night, he said, I should take it with me. My flashlight, too. That alone would keep most animals away. And, finally, I should stuff a sock under the zipper when I secured the mosquito netting. "To keep out snakes."

By then Charles had arrived with a basin of steaming hot water.

"Such luxury!" I exclaimed.

"We aim to please," Andrew said. "Sleep well."

Just behind my tent, where no one could see me, I stripped and bathed, having first swept the surrounding vegetation with the beam of my flashlight, which didn't reach very far, a distressing sign of dying batteries. Andrew's revolver lay, easily reachable but safe from splashing, on the roof of the tent, which sagged slightly under its weight. But all that belonged to a world of technology that my imagination had abandoned along with the sweaty grime of the day. I was a sylph, a dryad, a magical forest creature. The air feathered lasciviously over the sensitive, normally hidden places of my—sigh!—all too material body, which wouldn't let me fly, though maybe I could dance. I took a few steps and *ouch! ouch! ouch!* Sharp pebbles. Thorny twigs. Whatever. My bare feet were too tender, and I was a naked woman getting chilly. I reached for my clothes, the ones I would sleep in and wear the next day.

Back to ordinary, pulling on my tee shirt and jeans, I realized there was something else I had to do. Bathing near the tent was fine, but this required a little more distancing. So there I was, several yards away, a two-handed creature with three necessities to juggle. Flashlight. Revolver. TP. This time my imagination ran to lions salivating over my fleshy, comically exposed haunches. All went well, of course, and the evening would have had a perfectly unremarkable ending, if I hadn't succumbed to temptation.

Or got scared. Because maybe I really did misinterpret a noise. A twig snapping? A strange rustling? And maybe I did see, briefly, a suggestive shape passing through the weak beam of my flashlight. And surely, if I'd waited to be certain, it might have been tragically too late.

Actually, I was just plain curious. Never before in my life had I fired a gun of any kind. And there I was, all alone, in a vast dark wilderness. So I did. I pulled the trigger.

Almost immediately, Andrew was calling, "Diana! Diana!"

Seconds later, he appeared, rifle at the ready, followed by Rafiq and Malik, also armed, and Charles and Suleiman, who brandished kabab skewers, no less.

"What happened? Are you all right?" Andrew demanded.

"It's gone," I said, grateful for the darkness that made it impossible for me to look anyone in the eye.

"Thank god! What was it?"

"I don't know," I said, "but I was scared."

And so, with that absurdly lame confection, I was trapped into a masque of fear and fragility. I hated the role. I hated myself. I hated my audience. Steadying me with his rifle-free arm, Andrew led me to the circle of brightness around the fire. Everyone else followed, watching with great concern, as I enacted an emotionally-exhausted collapse onto the nearest log.

"I'm okay," I whispered, giving an appropriately grateful squeeze to the hand that clasped my shoulder protectively. And then I strengthened my voice, but not too much, as if I really were recovering from a truly terrifying experience. "Thank you. Thank you all."

Rafiq nodded and ducked back into his tent. Malik and Charles reclaimed their places on the other side of the fire. Suleiman's head disappeared under the collar of his coat. To all intents and purposes, Andrew and I were alone.

"You promised to bring some Scotch," he said.

"It's in my duffle."

"I'll fetch it," Andrew said. "Will you be okay?"

Feeling like a naughty child, who'd eventually have to confess, I nodded. Being alone, in fact, is exactly what I wanted. I'd been stupid, thoughtless—and a bit petulant, too. The driving had been challenging, worthwhile and fun, but a newly minted chauffeur isn't in charge of anything, and I certainly didn't appreciate my status as supernumerary in camp. So I'd gloried in my little gesture of defiance, my silly assertion of self. Bang! An instant's ego-gratification. Serious damage to be undone.

The Scotch helped, not its fast-acting high-proof alcohol so much as its symbolic value, connecting me, however tenuously, to a familiar world. *Reculer pour mieux sauter*, as Agnes might put it. Fall back in order to leap forward. I savored the smokiness of a single malt, its initial bite, its long smooth finish, and then I seized the bull—or the buffalo—by the horns. "I suppose you know there was nothing there. Do the others suspect?"

"Rafiq might. As for Charles, Malik and Suleiman, they have certain stereotypes. Panicking at phantoms fits the stereotype."

"Will you tell Rafiq?"

"He's my friend. I won't lie, if he asks. I'll also tell him that you know you were stupid and thoughtless and you'll never do it again."

"So I'm not banished?"

"Of course not. But you hate the killing. I don't understand why you want to come."

"I grew up in Colorado. Backpacking can be pretty miserable, but I loved the mountains. It's a trade off. Now I have a question for you."

"Fair enough."

"Supposedly you've given up trophy hunting for photography—but I seldom see you with a camera. Unless we're working, that is."

Andrew sighed. "My kind of wildlife photography is totally boring as a spectator sport. My ordinary clients go home with pix of cute lion cubs and elephants flapping their ears and funny monkeys, but I do my own work when I have photographer clients—or when I'm alone. Or sometimes with old friends, like Rafiq. Or maybe you?"

"I don't need to be amused," I said.

We sat quietly, like old friends, which we were becoming. Andrew and I had evolved a solid, only slightly lopsided power relationship at work, and the reverse would always be true in the bush. So we were equals, more or less. We had some more Scotch and sat companionably, our mood of contentment in no way disturbed by Suleiman's stertorous repertoire of snorts, snuffling and rumbles, until suddenly and unbelievably to me, his notorious snoring was overridden by an even louder, far more sonorous and almost cosmic panting sound. *Heh! Heh! Heh!* It filled my ears. It resonated in my bones. It had my jelly of a brain trembling. And it had to be very very close. *Heh! Heh! Heh!* I grabbed at Andrew's arm, jiggling his Scotch, spilling it over both of us.

Andrew did not reach for his rifle or his revolver. "That's your favorite animal," he said. "It's a lion."

"My god!" I shouted, leaping to my feet. "It's practically on top of us."

Andrew tried not to laugh. "Don't worry. It's miles away."

Heh! Heh! Heh!

"Really?"

"Really. You'll get used to it."

"More Scotch," I said.

Eventually I was too sleepy (or too drunk) to care whether a lion was twenty miles or twenty yards away, although I was glad for someone to walk me to my tent.

Once again the revolver was on offer. "Do you want it?"

"Yes," I said. "You can trust me."

"I know," he said. "Don't forget the sock."

And then the lion chimed in. *Heh! Heh! Heh!*

13

After breakfast Andrew nailed a paper plate to a tree trunk. "Shooting lessons," he said. "Hand gun first." Everyone should be capable of self-protection in the bush, he decreed. Including me.

How could I object? Holding the revolver as instructed, I aimed and shot. The first surprise was the kick that I had failed to notice in the thrill of shooting the night before. Only when my hand jerked back did I remember that even a miniature cannon has to recoil. The greater surprise was me hitting the plate at fifty paces on the third try. Not a bull's eye, but well within the target. Everyone applauded.

"That's enough." I said. Quit while ahead.

But Andrew wasn't done with me. He held out a rifle. "Next lesson," he said.

"Keep the stock pressed against your shoulder," Rafiq warned.

This lesson was tougher, the heaviness of the rifle itself being the hurdle I hadn't expected. My arms quickly felt the strain of positioning it properly as I struggled to get the hang of sighting anything at all through the telephoto lens. By the time I was ready to pull the trigger, my arms were trembling and *ouch!* The lens tube had jammed into my nose, breaking the skin. There was bleeding, too. Before I got home I looked as if I were wearing a black eye patch. The shot, naturally, had missed the plate.

"Once more," I insisted.

The bullet flew wide of the mark, but I managed to cushion the recoil properly, thus preserving my dignity and, perhaps, suggesting promise. In time. With practice. Which wasn't likely, if I could help it.

"Much better," Andrew said.

After that, things went down hill. As if we didn't have plenty of legally butchered hog meat stashed in Andrew's cooler, to say nothing of the illicit impala meat and those impressive impala antlers, we hadn't filled our quota, according to Rafiq. I asked to see the permit, a much folded, pale-to-invisible carbon copy on flimsy tissue. It didn't mention the hog, of course. It did mention a bushbuck, an antelope that's considerably larger than an impala.

"One animal," I argued. "That's all we should have. Plus the hog."

"Andrew has a big freezer," Rafiq was saying.

"Who's talking?" Andrew scoffed. "And Milly likes bush meat."

Bush meat as camp meat had been at the heart of my bargain with Andrew. Taking a legal bush buck as well as the illegal impala was more slaughter than I'd bargained for. Especially since Rafiq was pushing for another hog, too. Feeling betrayed and deceived, I protested. Clive might shrug it off, but Ambassador James Freeman would not take kindly to an IO driving for petty poachers.

"Your choice," Andrew said. "No one's forcing you to take the wheel."

"Good," I said and climbed into the back of the Land Rover.

The unholy haul for the weekend was as follows: two hogs, an impala and a bushbuck, and official connivance made it possible.

The system had two phases: the prep and the payoff. Easy-to-identify elements—heads, hooves and hides—were tossed. Antlers, too, unless they were truly impressive, like the impala rack that wasn't there because it was covered with a blanket. After that, meat was meat, especially if the cache contained the right number of leg bones, since no one was going to measure the length of a femur. Finally, each time we had to stop, Andrew or Rafiq would slide out for a little chat and to offer a packet of bush meat, thereby showing appreciation for the rangers' dedication to such an important job. How generous! How considerate! The same script governed even when the haul was legal, a matter of investment, of insurance, of guaranteeing safe passage to impossible-to-hide trophies. And so, on the day of my disillusionment, the gates rose, the chains fell, and we heard the magic word: "Pass!" Malik, of course, had earned a very hefty allotment for his cooperation.

Even the determination of legality could be tricky. When Andrew shot the bushbuck, it was fair game. But Rafiq had been driving along the edge of the preserve, and the wounded animal had staggered into the park to die—and be collected. Legal? Or illegal? The reverse might also happen. In either case, should the hunter leave the carcass for the lions and jackals? Or make human use of it?

Thanks to the censorious lump in the back seat, there wasn't much joking around on the way home—and oh how happy I was to get out of the car and join the pedestrians on the ferry! When we reached my house, Andrew offered to carry my share of the meat into the kitchen. Milly's, too.

"Just bring Milly's," I said. "Keep the rest."

Andrew did as requested.

As he turned to join Rafiq in the Land Rover, I held him back. "There was no excuse for sulking," I conceded. "But I was angry—and that was justified."

Andrew acknowledged the problem. "I guess we've lost our driver—unless you change your mind."

"Not necessarily," I said.

"No elephants. No lions. No endangered species. Permit details respected. Beyond that, no promises," he replied.

"I'm too tired to think," I said.

As soon as Andrew left, I phoned Milly to let her know of the legal pork and—sigh!—poached bushbuck deposited to her account in my freezer. Withdrawals available at her convenience! Plus I wanted her honest, common sense reaction to my weekend, which looked unlikely to happen, since her phone kept ringing. When finally she did answer, I was more concerned than relieved. Her voice was unusually weak and she spoke very slowly. But nothing could muzzle Milly's irreverence.

"I've had poached eggs and poached salmon," she quipped, "so why not poached bushbuck?"

"Are you all right?" I asked.

"Oh yes! I'm just fine." The heavy sarcasm suggested that she wasn't.

"I'm coming over," I said.

When I beheld Milly, and Milly saw my black eye, we exclaimed in chorus: "Oh my God, what happened to you?"

That being cook's night off, Milly had hobbled to the door, on crutches. Her face was in far worse shape than mine, wholly bruised and swollen, swallowing her cheekbones up, turning her eyes into slits. *Jambo"* she said, sarcastically, drawing me in. "Welcome to Tanzania, where these things don't happen."

By "things" she meant violent crime. Not only had she been burgled, she'd been brutally beaten, as if Dar were Lagos, where crime was incomparably worse—or so we'd been led to believe, since witnesses to crime in the Nigerian capital were seldom allowed to survive. From the way she looked, I suspected that Milly herself had been left for dead.

"I'm lucky to be alive," she confirmed, as we made our way, slowly, to the living room, where she lowered herself painfully into a goose down sofa and told the tale of her Friday night.

Having attended an "amazing" dinner and dance party at the South African embassy, she'd returned home in the wee hours. Parking her car as usual, she'd opened the front door, switched on the lights and revealed a pair of burglars at work. Her TV was already gone. She'd noticed that. She also recalled that the dismantled components of her audio system had been stacked in the middle of the room. And then the punching and knocking around had begun. Next she knew, it was morning. She was lying on the floor and her cook was trying to get her to sit up. Had she been knocked unconscious? Had she slid into a drunken slumber? Or both? She didn't know.

"I hurt like hell," she said. "I also had a terrible hangover."

"Have you seen a doctor?" I asked, as if it could be otherwise.

The doctor had found bruising, contusions, a cracked sternum he couldn't bandage and a torn tendon in her left leg, which accounted for the crutches. "Those bastards cleaned me out," Milly wailed. "My gold chains and bangles. My pearls. My mother's diamond ring—I'd always planned to reset it. They went through every drawer. My silver, too. Not a teaspoon left."

Some small silk carpets had also disappeared. She'd bought them on a trip to Cairo.

"They knew what they were doing," she said.

"What do the police say?"

"They hope I have insurance."

"Do you?"

"I do, but that's not the point."

"No," I agreed. "It never is."

Not only had her body been abused, she'd been deprived of the precious material history of her life. Sitting close, stroking the back of her bruised hand, I tried to share her stab at optimism when she pointed to a pair of precious ivories that the thieves had overlooked. Not the best of the bunch, but better than nothing, she said. Focusing on that tiny bit of good fortune, she pulled herself together, offered me some sherry and asked what on earth had happened to me.

My black eye made for a funny story, but I didn't conceal my deep disappointment with Andrew over the bush buck.

Milly laughed. "You're turning a pimple into Mount Kilimanjaro," she said.

We left it at that.

As I was backing out of Milly's driveway, her Embassy-provided gate guard gave me a smart salute, which slowed me down long enough for a useful chain of thought to get under way. Was there any way the guard could have noticed mischief makers breaking into the rear of the house, if the thieves had kept their intrusion quiet and their lights well shielded ? My conclusion: not without a periscope. Especially since the burglar alarm wouldn't have sounded. Milly had disabled it many months before, after geckos set it off at two in the morning. There's safety and safety she said, and I need my beauty sleep. More useful, from my point of view, I noticed, for the first time, that the wall in front of Milly's house was hardly a meter high, Yet Embassy patrol cars, assuming they'd passed her house once or twice while the burglars were at work, had noticed nothing either. So much for the efficacy of clear sight lines from the street, I thought. I'd found the perfect defense for my flourishing foliage. Driving home, I was very happy.

More bad news—worse news, really—would break on Monday morning. One of our drivers was dead. Not Juma, but Massoud. Mistaken for a thief, he'd been pummeled to death by an angry mob. Although a conscientious shopkeeper had protested that young Massoud wasn't the crook who'd snatched a packet of batteries from a neighboring stall, a rabid posse desperate for a culprit had gone after him.

Massoud wasn't the only innocent victim of vigilantism in those days when policing had become a profit-making enterprise in Dar. Because it wasn't remunerative to investigate petty crime, the police responded lethargically or not at all to most pleas for help, leaving people to pursue justice as best they could, due process be damned. In the office, we took up a collection for Massoud's young widow and twin toddlers.

The Massoud incident gave me a better understanding of Lily's behavior some weeks before. Having invited me over for dinner, she'd been astonished that I accepted and actually showed up, right on time, wine bottle in one hand, a six pack of coke in the other. The soda was for Jack, her son, who was in third grade.

"Diana! You came! Come in! Come in!"

"Of course, I came. Do you have a corkscrew?"

"I'm not *that* hard up," she said laughing.

Offering me a seat in a plush armchair, the velvety look being the favored style of the day, she sank into the matching sofa, and soon the girl talk began. Against her family's wishes, Lily had separated from an unfaithful husband. Since single motherhood wasn't quite respectable in those days, she received neither assistance nor sympathy from her parents in her struggle to support and care for her son, so her greatest challenge was financial, Lily revealed, which led her to apologize for her house. It was tidy, but so tiny that all the furniture seemed oversized. She also apologized for the street on which she lived. Narrow. No street lights. Above all, she apologized for the neighborhood. Dirt poor, but respectable, except for gangs of aimless boys whose behavior verged sometimes on the delinquent, she was sorry to say.

As Lily spoke, Jack sat on the floor, leaning against his mother's knee and putting a little metal airplane through barrel rolls and loop-the-loops. The coffee table was the airstrip.

"Why were you surprised to find me at the door?" I asked. "I said I'd come."

"Experience," Lily said.

She'd issued invitations to other colleagues, including my predecessor, her previous boss, but no one ever came. If it wasn't scheduling conflicts that made acceptance impossible, it was last minute cancellations due to illness or a sudden deluge of work. "But, really, it was fear," she confided. Poverty being stereotypically associated with crime and her neighborhood being anything but affluent, it had finally dawned on her that her area must have been, classified as off limits for Embassy personnel. Not that any one had ever clued her in, whether from misplaced kindness, or pure cowardice or, as Lily thought, a bit of both.

"I was sure the security officer would learn of your plans," she said. "I was sure he'd order you not to come."

"All the more reason to be here," I replied.

Lily's eyes filled with gratitude, and soon I was sharing the circumstances of my own impending divorce. Lily was surprised to learn that my parents weren't much happier about my husband-leaving than hers had been. Embassy gossip was constrained on my side by the delicacies of being a supervisor, but we'd both experienced the complications of being women in a man's world. Nor was there any risk in revealing our castle-building versions of the future.

Eventually Jack relaxed, too. He told me that he wanted to fly around the world in record time when he was a pilot. I said I'd look forward to flying with him one day, as he brought his little plane in for a landing on the coffee table.

For dinner we had some sort of goat stew with rice and vegetables. It was delicious. I asked for the recipe, which required some mysterious greens that spinach might or might not be a good substitute for.

The evening ended as strangely as it had begun. When it was time for me to leave, Jack, gently prompted, thanked me for the coke, after which Lily gave him a hug and told him she'd be right back. She followed me to my car, got into the passenger seat and insisted that I keep the windows rolled up. "Those boys—they'll reach in and steal your earrings," she warned. She planned to accompany me to a major intersection a few blocks away. "You're a white woman and all alone," she explained. "Some of the boys can get obnoxious at night."

"What about you? Walking back. Alone."

"They know me," she said. "They wouldn't dare."

Massoud would be killed in a market not far from Lily's house, and she never invited me to her place again. Maybe, knowing I'd come, she was protecting me. Not from the neighborhood rowdies, I'd guess, but to keep me from getting in trouble with a Security Officer who seemed to be happiest when no one left the office.

As it happened, I was to be the bearer of the bad news about Massoud.

14

When I reached the office that awful Monday morning, the coffee urn was cold but it hadn't burnt out. Since our decrepit old building was absurdly short of electrical outlets, the heating pad tucked behind Milly's sore back had priority.

"What I need is a heating *suit*," Milly said. "Everything hurts."

"Go home," Clive said. "Rest. Take it easy."

Suffering in solitude was worse than suffering in the office, Milly insisted. "Distraction beats self-pity every time." Moreover, she wouldn't object to having her heating pad disconnected from time to time, if we supplied her with regular infusions of steaming hot coffee.

"Coming up!" I called, switching plugs.

With everyone pitching in to succor a stoical but pain-wracked Milly, I volunteered to fetch the predictable batch of unclassified cables from the Embassy.

"Juma can take you," Clive said.

Massoud, it seemed, hadn't shown up for work yet.

At the Embassy I discovered why. The police had phoned to ask the Security Officer to verify the identity of a crime victim whose pockets had yielded U.S. Embassy ID documents. Maybe the papers were stolen, they suggested, delicately. Unfortunately, the over-battered corpse—a shattered skull, broken ribs, bruises, contusions, lacerations and abrasions!—matched the papers. By the time the Ambassador had been apprised of Massoud's murder, I was already in the communications room, plowing through classified traffic. Gina summoned me to the front office, where an unusually humble Ambassador suggested that I might be the right person to convey the tragic news to my colleagues.

"The personal touch," Freeman said. "Easier to take."

Not easy for me, though.

Or for Clive. "Are they absolutely sure?" he asked.

"Yes," I said.

After an immeasurable moment, during which he sat mute and motionless, Clive erupted. He pounded a fist on his desk, overturned his chair as he got to his feet and paced around like a blind creature seeking an exit. When he finally spoke, his words came through gritted teeth. "There are times when I can't stand this place." And then our normally mild, mellow, philosophical PAO buried his face in his hands and wept.

As the details seeped around the office, people froze in horror or collapsed into the nearest chair. At USIS we were proud of an esprit that allowed us to operate more like a cooperative than a hierarchy. Massoud's death was a blow to us all.

Although calls had to be dealt with and library patrons had to be assisted, nobody felt like working. Kiki and Mo were lucky, in a way. They had thoroughly engaging, back-to-back interviews scheduled, to select a fresh batch of Fulbright scholars. Most of us simply sought distractions. Andrew took refuge in the darkroom, perfecting prints from his last shoot. I tried to catch up on some reading, but nothing registered. Hardest hit was Juma, who had to do double duty even as he fumed over the fate of his friend and fellow driver. The Ambassador had already lodged a formal complaint with the authorities, but we knew that no one would ever be prosecuted for Massoud's death. And so it went. A rock rips through the surface of the lake causing great perturbation. Soon the lake is mirror-like again. By the end of the week a new driver had been hired.

Meanwhile, toward afternoon on that black Monday, Lily had finally got around to sorting through the unclassified cable traffic I'd plopped on her desk.

"Oh! Oh!" she said.

She handed the noteworthy item to Milly, who drew a deep breath and delivered more bad news: "Inspection. Next month. Brace yourselves."

Milly directed Lily to place the cable front and center on Clive's desk. Important material often disappeared into the maw of his in-box monster, but this was one cable that he had to see. According to Milly, preparations for the inspection should begin immediately.

I'd been through inspections at other posts. Lily and other long-serving

FSNs knew what we were talking about, but Kiki was mystified.

"What's an inspection?" she asked. "Sounds scary."

"Depends," said Milly.

"It's like an audit," I explained, "a matter of accountability. The inspectors care about three things. Fraud. Impact. And morale—are we a happy post?"

"The worst is the paperwork," Milly sighed. "Inventories. Accounts. Questionnaires. Creating a briefing book."

"What about the cozy little interviews?" I asked. "Are they really confidential?"

"You have to wonder," Milly agreed.

"Back-stabbing, tale-telling, credit-snatching—how do they sort it out?" I continued. "Do they even bother?"

"Sounds like a good time to get the flu," Kiki said.

"A sick out! I love it—ohhh!" Milly's hand flew to her sternum. "It hurts to laugh," she said.

Knowing that the records in the Information Section were reasonably complete, Lily assured me that our share of the paperwork drudgery wouldn't be too onerous. Little did she know that she wasn't relieving me of my real worry: my own black market currency operations. Would I be able to deflect pointed questions convincingly? Lie detector tests could be gamed, I knew, but facing savvy humans was more worrisome. Then I remembered Rafiq's definition of safety: the mutual protection society. "If I go down, he'll go down." Not very comforting. The whole post could go down.

Andrew, I learned, had been through several inspection cycles. The first hadn't gone well. Thinking about it still made him angry. Evidence of a scam involving spare parts for vehicles, purchases far in excess of requirements for a small fleet, had leaped out of the records, as they were being meticulously examined. The finger of accusation had pointed initially at Andrew, because of his association with Rafiq, who'd won a few Embassy contracts for vehicle repair. Fortunately the inspectors had decided to tie up a few loose ends, which led them to irregularities at the Embassy as well. The mastermind turned out to be the General Services Officer, an American who was going through an expensive divorce. He was peddling commissary liquor and cigarettes, too. Andrew had been fully exonerated, but far from mollified. Rafiq ceased bidding on Embassy contracts.

Facing the latest demand for accountability, we dove into our files for proof that *our* Dar-es-Salaam was an exemplary post.

"Not just good," Clive insisted. "Excellent."

Clive set himself to working his grapevine, in hopes of identifying our inspectors. Not to sway them before they arrived. That would be stupid, Clive said. Uncovering their passions and pet peeves, however, would enhance our ability to please them once they'd arrived.

Agnes laughed when I described the intensity of our pre-inspection mobilization. If everyone worked half as hard to satisfy clients as we were working to satisfy the higher ups, the world would be improved beyond recognition, she declared.

It was twilight, the temperature had dropped a few degrees, and we were enjoying ruby-red Campari over ice in her grassy garden. Mamzell gamboled up and dropped a tennis ball at my feet. I tossed it as far as I could. In no time she was back, demanding another round. I obliged and became her slave.

"Here's what to do," Agnes advised. "Keep the inspectors busy. Organize dinners and receptions. If they're into ivory, hold your nose and take them to the best sculptors. If ivory horrifies them, scour the market for quaint *kangas* and exquisite baskets. Or take them to Mikumi. Everyone loves elephants."

"Except you." I laughed.

"I adore elephants," she retorted. "As for sharing their habitat, you can have it."

"Well," I sighed, "my safari days are over, most likely. Too much tightrope walking."

Agnes shrugged.

Having drawn from Agnes that shockingly insufficient dose of empathy re my deeply compromising involvement with petty poachers, I decided to head home. Bad mistake. I spent the rest of the evening brooding over a mission of mercy that I couldn't evade: an expedition to the outdoor market with Milly.

Watching a week's salary blown on ivory travesties would ruin my Saturday, but for Milly it would be much needed therapy. I had been enlisted because none of Milly's usual cadre of merrily amoral ivory collectors was available. Sofia, who worked for a Greek construction company, was visiting family in Athens. Maria, Milly's counterpart at the Brazilian Embassy, was logging overtime. Janice, her closest Tanzanian friend, was recovering from fever. And so on. As for Kiki, she was spending the weekend in Zanzibar with David. That left me to keep Milly from overdoing it physically, whether or not she overspent.

As it turned out, I was the extravagant one.

Milly was knocking on my door fifteen minutes early. I didn't object. Even at seven fifteen Dar's sun was too hot for me, but heat avoidance had nothing to do with Milly's desire to be at the market the minute it opened. Determined to prevent her stolen property from being resold to innocent buyers, she dragged me from stall to stall, demanding to see the ivory carvings in reserve as well as those on display, discussing her sad mission with merchants and artists she knew and those she didn't. All were sympathetic. None appeared to be complicit. Each was ready to console her with replacements. "At a good price, madam, a very good price." Milly recoiled as if she were being offered cute little puppies the day after a long-loved pet had been put down.

"Let's get out of here," she said, sooner than I expected.

"Wait," I said. "I saw something."

Milly had been trying to seduce me for months, extolling this carving, praising that one, urging me to consider investment value. Ivory would maintain, or increase, its value more reliably than the *makonde* carvings to which I so stubbornly gravitated. Rave as she might about her obsession, I preferred the look of burnished ebony, which was not jet black, as I had assumed. It was wine dark and honey-veined with the memory of life, although a dye popularly known as shoe polish was smeared over the cheaper pieces to blacken them in a way that was boring as well as deceptive.

That morning I had my eyes on a *makonde* work that perplexed Milly even more than it repelled her. Made from a gnarly old tree root, it was nearly as tall as I was.

Some gleanings from the forest insist so strongly on being a heron or a giraffe or a damsel that a carver has merely to follow inherent instructions. In the hands of such a plodding craftsman, the root structure that attracted me might have yielded a peaceable kingdom complete with lion and lamb and all that. Or the opposite: nature red in tooth and claw. But this creation was under-determined, a shape-shifter's delight. No sooner did a form with a name present itself than it fell away, like a white cap in a rough sea. I was enchanted. "It's like cloud-watching," I said.

Milly thought I was crazy. "It's grotesque," she declared, meaning ugly, not awesome as Hegel or the Romantics would have put it. "You can't be serious," she said.

"I'm really tempted," I said.

"I don't understand it," she said. "It makes me feel dizzy and confused."

"Yes," I said. "It's fascinating."

Eventually, resigned but loyal, Milly stepped in to stiffen my bargaining. Good friend that she was, she would mitigate my lapse in taste by making it more affordable.

The dealer wouldn't budge. "It's unique," he insisted.

"I'll take it," I said.

"You'll need a truck," Milly warned.

I had an answer for that. "Rafiq has a whole fleet of trucks."

I did another circumambulation, picturing my extraordinary acquisition in the foyer of my house, lending interest to a certain bleak, bare corner.

"Look again, Milly. So dramatic—"

"Did you say traumatic? When guests walk through your door, they'll feel as if they're having drunken hallucinations even before they've had a single drop!"

I'd been rummaging through verbiage to find a way that wasn't silly or pretentious to describe how I felt in the presence of this object I was paying a mint for, but Milly had lit on the single perfect word for its mind-expanding impact as well as my "part and parcel" reaction to a spacious, sun-washed savanna. Emily Dickinson had got close with, "inebriate." Classicists prefer "Dionysian." But I'll stick with Milly's word. "Drunk."

Drunk on nature.

Drunk on beauty.

Drunk on life.

Just plain drunk.

15

A diplomatic receiving line is a guest delivery chute, a courteous way of counting heads, after which guests are free to eat, drink, vie for a VIP's attention, or otherwise exploit the occasion, until checking out, officially, with a "Thank you" and "Good night" for the host. Sounds like a cushy way to make living, doesn't it? Not quite. Cup of tea or glass of wine in hand, not forgetting the proverbial crumpets or canapés, diplomats are working the party, injecting ideas, absorbing information, cementing relations. Condemned to endure yet another reception, I usually did my best to eke out a tolerable mix of pleasure and profit, but often, I confess, I crept away as soon as I could. And, as hostess? Jubilation, always, when the last guest departed. Time to free my feet, drop into a sofa and imagine life on a remote, under-populated island.

Attending cultural programs was another a part of the job. The music might be lovely, the art inspiring, the lecture engaging, the poetry accessible, but when we Americans walked through the doors of the British Council, the Alliance Française, the Goethe Institute or the Gorky Institute, we were also checking on the competition. Was the venue packed with people who mattered? If so, how could we generate bigger and better crowds to report to Washington?

Entrée. Tactics. Impact. The inspectors would examine us from all perspectives, but I'd already conducted my own cost-benefit analysis. Relentlessly as we pushed policy, told America's story, countered Soviet disinformation and made influential friends, it would have been absurd to contend that Clive, Kiki, Milly and I were measurably affecting the course of the Cold War, especially in tangential East Africa. There were, of course, other reasons for working like demons in Dar. Self-advancement, for instance. And self-respect. Both allowed for dollops of just plain pleasure.

That Friday evening at the German Ambassador's house, for instance, I'd given myself wholly to a recital by a respected German violinist accompanied by a sufficiently competent local pianist. The white wine was pretty good for an ordinary diplomatic function, predictably a Riesling, but on the dry side and complex. I sipped as I listened. More quickly than I wished, the artiste completed his program, tacked on a peppy little encore and took a bow.

Timing it perfectly, a waiter appeared. On a hunch that the red might also be worth a try, I was reaching toward a glass of *rotwein*, when someone selected the Riesling and said, "I know what she likes."

It was Dieter, and he didn't. Couldn't, in fact. We'd met mostly at diplomatic events, the first being my welcome-to-Dar party at Clive's, and there had been only one, just one, date-like dinner for two at Nzuri. Greatly to his macho consternation, I'd paid my own way.

Smiling sweetly, I picked up the red.

"Prost!" I said, adding something complimentary about the violinist and his selections.

"Yes, he's one of the very best," Dieter agreed. "I have several tapes." No CDs back then. And certainly no ITunes. "You're welcome to borrow them—or come over some evening. I'll invite some other people, too."

"What a nice idea," I murmured, diplomatically. "But live music's what I really miss, especially the suspense of hoping for a great performance. In Moscow, at least, we had the Bolshoi."

Dieter laughed. "As if there's no suspense to living in Dar! Will we have power today? Or not?"

And then he issued a very tempting invitation. The Germans had hired a private plane—German owned, German piloted—for a weekend trip to the island of Pemba, the northern anchor of the Zanzibar archipelago, and there were seats for a few non-German invitees.

"I've never been there," he said. "But now's the time to go. Before it's discovered by the big tour companies."

Yikes! Not only had I been presented with an opportunity to spend a weekend in paradise, the invitation had been issued by a very presentable specimen. Teutonically handsome. Possessed of the full array of European graces. A Herr

Doktor Professor in linguistics before becoming a diplomat. Not only could I put an end to selfie sex, I could sleep NATO. I was on the verge of saying, "I'd love to," when the German Ambassador approached and inquired, ever so politely, if he might borrow his colleague for a while.

"Excuse me," said Dieter, with his usual little bow.

"Of course," I nodded.

And so, instead of being comfortably committed, I had time to stew. That required another glass of wine, at which point I was rescued from tedious indecision by Kiki. She was breathing a sigh of relief after easing herself away from the Minister of Education, who burdened his conversations with minimally relevant quotes from Shakespeare, Milton and Donne.

"What do you know about Pemba?" I asked.

"Not much," Kiki replied. "It's probably like Zanzibar without Stonetown. Why?"

I told her.

"Lucky you. Try to do some sailing on a dhow," she said. "It's really exciting. David took the tiller one afternoon. He looked like an emir from Oman. Minus the beard and the turban."

"Except an emir wouldn't be handling the boat. He'd be giving orders. And you?"

"I tried it, but a gust of wind came and I didn't know what to do. The boatman took over. Just in time—whoops!—excuse me."

She had spotted the Minister of Culture, who could make her professional life miserable if he felt slighted. Clive, meanwhile, was engaged with the Minister for Information, with whom I'd already exchanged a few words. Grateful that Dieter was still busy with his Ambassador, I hovered in the shadows, nursing the last glass of wine I could safely drink and processing my feelings. Why was I habitually rude to the one eligible male who'd shown an interest in me? Was there anything about my present life that didn't involve compromise? I hadn't rejoined the Foreign Service out of passionate patriotism or a deep commitment to diplomacy. The pay and perks were good—and I needed a job. Tanzania, until dangled before me, had played no role in my alt-life fantasies. Finally, presented with an opportunity to see fabulous fauna outside a zoo, I'd joined up with hunters who weren't above petty poaching, thus violating a whole bunch of principles I'd once held dear. So why shouldn't I spend a weekend on Pemba with this almost perfect companion?

And then I felt it. A spasm of revulsion. His lips on mine? No way. Sometimes life is very simple.

That resolved, I looked around and spotted a top editor from the *News,* a fairly rotund, middle-aged man by the name of Alfred Kibaki, who seemed to be as marooned as I was. He'd just returned from a visit to Moscow, a Soviet-sponsored tour in the company of a dozen other African journalists, the sort of excursion we Americans also arranged, via the International Visitor program administered by Kiki.

Kibaki, despite his immersion in Soviet culture, seemed pleased as I approached. "Ah—Diana," he said.

"Welcome home," I said, as we shook hands. "How was your trip?"

Kibaki laughed. "We got nothing but the best. The lights worked. The water ran. The radiators were hot. We overdosed on caviar and *champansky—*"

"The caviar," I sighed. "I'll miss it for the rest of my life."

I could have predicted the stops on his tour. A call at the Ministry of Information. A session with reporters from *Pravda* and *Izvestia.* Spiels from scientists and economists. Views of massive infrastructure projects. A voyage on the Moscow River. A pilgrimage to Red Square and Lenin's Tomb. An evening at the Bolshoi to watch muscular males leaping around in *Spartacus.* As Kibaki reeled off the itinerary, he reached the stop that had us both laughing, the indispensable genuflection to Communal Farm #1.

Immediately I was remembering my own visit to this showpiece of Soviet social engineering. Its barns were dark and filthy, its cattle scrawny. I'd felt sorry for the cows—and the workers, but our guide described them as extremely fortunate. Above all, he boasted, the workers had free medical care—and free dental services, too, in a clinic through which he proudly led us. The centerpiece was the drill, a far cry (call it a terrified scream) from the painless, high speed devices that were commonplace, by then, even in Third World capitals.

"Maybe you'd enjoy a visit to the U.S.," I said, a serious blunder. It's really stupid to raise expectations before fulfillment is guaranteed. In Kibaki's case, Clive, Kiki and the Ambassador would have to be on board.

"I wouldn't refuse," Kibaki said, but—whew!—he was more interested in sharing his impressions of Soviet journalism. "You're American,' he began, "but you must know something about the British press—"

"Such as it is," I said.

"Well, *Prava* and *Izvestia* make London tabloids look good."

"What! No busty page two girls?" I teased. "But seriously, I wish you'd talk to Andrew about your impressions. Peter's been offered a scholarship to study at Lumumba University, and Andrew's afraid he'll fall for the indoctrination."

"They'll try, but the smart kids see through it."

"Meaning?"

"Lumumba's a ghetto. No one takes it seriously."

"Then why do they get takers?"

"Desperation. Lack of options. Why don't you get Peter into a U.S. university? Nice lad. Deserves a boost. "

"We're trying," I sighed. "Acceptance is likely. Money isn't."

Kibaki frowned. "Andrew's a good man. I'm surprised you don't take better care of your own."

"You've got a point," I said.

The conversation was getting awkward, but Clive rescued me. He clapped Kibaki on the back like a long lost brother. "How's it going, Old Buddy? Long time no see."

Gratefully backing away, I bumped into a French consular officer and giggled. I couldn't help it, and he didn't mind. Everyone knew the story. Intending to jog along the beach one night, he'd parked his car on the road paralleling the shoreline. A few minutes later, three men jumped him, mainly to snatch his car keys, but they also stripped him down to his briefs. Car and money gone, nearly naked, he had a long walk to the French embassy, much of it through the heart of the city, where fortune graciously smiled. Virgilio, driving home after a dinner with friends at Nzuri, was stuck in a traffic jam caused by a minor accident at a particularly busy intersection when his eyes lit on a strange pale creature slinking along in the shadows.

And, speak of the devil, Virgilio, arriving very late, burst through the door. He stopped, looked around and recognized us first. "Yves!" he said. "Diana!"

"My savior," Yves said with a smile.

I greeted Virgilio, but I wanted to hear the end of Yves's story. "Have they found your car?" I asked.

"No. It's probably in Kenya by now."

"The big market for stolen vehicles is Nairobi," Virgilio explained. "What have I missed?"

"Besides the recital?" I asked. "Nothing. As usual."

"Well, you two are the first to know. I am the proud father of a baby girl. I just got the call."

These days Virgilio would have been Skyping with his wife. Encountering friends, he'd have whipped out his smart phone to show us pictures of happy mama and healthy baby. But words were all we had back then—and Virgilio's were full of exuberant delight. "She has blue eyes, I'm told. Like her mother. And dark hair like me. A diplomat from day one!"

"He's a daddy!" I gave Virgilio a congratulatory hug. Yves delivered a playful guy punch to Virgilio's chin, then eased away to join a group of men clustered around Agnes, leaving me to delve for more details. Weight? Eight and a half pounds. Name? Angelica.

"And when will we see them?" I asked.

"In a couple of months. Better safe than sorry." Meaning: newborns are fragile, while Africa is full of bugs, bacteria and viruses.

"Of course,' I murmured. "And, by the way, you never filled me in on your visit to Mikumi. How did it go?"

"Phil and Eileen were terrific," he said. "And, on the Fort Dietrick disinformation front, Diana, you can relax. The operation is totally above board. Best of all, the evil researchers are gone, and the baboons are completely over their trauma. But I'm a city boy through and through," Virgilio shrugged. "I prefer my animals in a zoo."

"You and Agnes." I said, smiling.

A fireball of happiness, Virgilio launched himself into the crowd , spreading the good news.

Virgilio would never know it, but thanks to our little chitchat I'd lit on a gracious way to deflect the Pemba invitation, assuming that Dieter phoned to pursue it, and he'd have to phone because I'd reached my saturation point for post-concert socializing. So, should I have to, I'd cite a prior commitment to visiting Phil and Eileen. There being no phone at the Baboon camp, date shifting would be impossible, allowing me to deploy the best of all white lies. Credible and uncheckable.

And maybe I *would* go to Mikumi, I decided. If Phil and Eileen weren't around, or if others had already been installed in the guest hut, I'd spend a night at the Mikumi Lodge, sleeping in luxury, watching animals from the comfort of the patio.

I made for the door, where the Ambassador's wife was performing the departure ritual on her own. Had her husband requisitioned Dieter for something grave enough to affect the U.S. Embassy as well? If so, I'd find out. Meanwhile, having somehow eluded her usual train of admirers, Agnes was also ready to call it a night.

"Martin is history," she confided. "It's over. I meant to call you, but I've been fiendishly busy."

"Are you saying he's HIV positive?"

"No, he's fine. I'm glad about that, I really am, but I can't forgive him for putting me through hell."

"Smart girl," I said. "And, by the way, do you want to go to Pemba? I know someone who's looking for companionship."

Agnes laughed. "I'll cuddle up with Mamzell, thank you."

Hmmm, I thought, what's happening with Agnes?

16

I was absurdly proud and excited as I planned my first solo expedition. Destination: Mikumi. Departure: after breakfast on Saturday morning. Return: the next day. Although my car could probably manage the ruts between the highway and the Baboon Camp, Mary would sound the alarm if I wasn't home by Sunday evening. Sunday was her usual day off, but quid pro quo: any time she needed leave time, she got it. On Friday I picked up a few bottles of commissary wine, as a gift for Phil and Eileen. I also gave Juma some shillings, asking him to fill a gerry can with gas in between his errands for Clive. I didn't think I'd need it, but a little insurance never hurts. Confused for some reason, Juma approached Andrew for clarification. That's how Andrew learned of my plans.

"I don't suppose you'd like some company," he said.

"That wasn't the original idea," I said.

"Well, this is the dry season, and it's a really good time to see hippos—"

My ears perked up. I'd yet to see a hippo.

"Good time for hippo photos, too. Of course, we'd have to take my Land Rover."

"No hunting. No bush meat," I decreed.

"No shooting," Andrew agreed. "Unless a hippo charges."

My choice. Solo semi-adventure or hippo watching? The hippos won.

To preserve the illusion of control, I took the wheel of Andrew's cranky old Land Rover as we left town. I didn't enjoy it. Shifting took all my strength. But something else bothered me even more. It had bothered me for some time. With no one else around, I could bring it up, at last.

"I always feel so guilty," I said. "You should be home. Running errands.

Helping Lucille. Keeping her company. Doesn't it annoy her—you off in the bush so often? And what about Peter?"

"Peter!" Andrew snorted. "He wants to be with his friends, not his Dad. They worship the boombox."

I laughed. Peter's friends weren't unique. They were typical. Audio tapes and portable cassette players supplied the glue and rhythm of a teenager's life back then. It was global, and woe betide the adult who interfered.

"As for Lucille," Andrew continued, "You must be the only one who doesn't know. I was a widower with two young children. My girls needed a mother. Lucille had been abused. She needed a protector, but no decent man would marry her. Why not help one another? It was my father's idea and, being a preacher, he married us, expecting we'd fall in love, eventually. That didn't happen, but we kept the bargain, with Peter as a bonus. I'm not jealous of Lucille's everyday life; she's not jealous of mine. But we're friends and we're a family."

"So you do care," I said.

"Of course," he said. "But not in the conventional way."

By the time I'd negotiated the serpentine road over the coastal range, my left arm, my shifting arm, wasn't just tired. It hurt. Reaching a straightaway with visibility in both directions, I let the obnoxious vehicle drift onto the shoulder and stopped. "Your turn," I said. "This gear shift is a beast."

Andrew wasn't surprised. "You lasted longer than most," he said. "Even Rafiq complains."

With traffic no longer claiming my attention, I could appreciate the sepia landscape we were driving through. Trees and bushes had dropped all or most of their leaves. Grasses of every kind had gone to seed, then dried into straw. At frequent intervals we passed scorched patches alongside the road.

"Cigarettes," Andrew said. "People toss live butts without thinking."

Dry season fires could also be started by heat lightening, according to Andrew. Vast swathes of vegetation burnt to the ground while panicky animals fled to safety. But many fires weren't accidental. Farmers used the ancient technique of slash-and-burn to maximize yields on fresh crop land. In this case, too, the animals could evade the flames. Poachers' fires were different. Set alight strategically, they forced valuable wildlife to flee toward destruction.

"Perfect!" I said. "Fire behind. Rifles ahead."

"You've got it. Meanwhile, rivers shrink, and water holes dry up. The dry season is a very stressful time for wildlife. "

"Which explains the Great Migration of wildebeest in the Serengeti."

"And makes it easier to find hippos. Fewer places to look."

The track connecting the highway to the Baboon Camp was so dry its potholes were like vats of powder that billowed up and filtered down as we bounced along. We saw no Suzuki as we emerged from the woods, but a peek into the kitchen hut was encouraging: half full mugs of coffee suggested a late breakfast followed by a scurry to reach a sleeping tree before the baboons were dropped down. We peered into the guest hut, too. No evidence of occupation.

"Room for you," Andrew said.

I should have been delighted, but something in me resisted. Suddenly I wasn't in the mood to be grafted onto other peoples' lives. I shook my head. "No," I said. "Room for you."

"Don't be silly," Andrew said.

"What's so silly?" I demanded. Since Mikumi wasn't a tourist magnet like the Serengeti, a suitable vacancy at the Park's guest lodge was all but guaranteed. Andrew could drop me off and return around sunset, I suggested, with Phil and Eileen, for drinks and dinner on the patio, assuming they were free and amenable. "My treat," I added, "in appreciation for all my wonderful weekends at the Baboon Camp." It had to be my treat. Only I could afford the Lodge's inflated, tourist trade rates. But I couldn't say that.

That settled, we set out to inventory water holes. Our score that afternoon? A few puddles and not a single hippo, although we did encounter a small herd of cape buffalo caked in cooling mud, the source of which remained a mystery.

When things got this dry, Andrew told me, elephants dig for water in dried up river beds. They kick holes in the sand, extend their trunks and suck up the seepage.

"I'd love to see that," I said.

"Sorry," said Andrew. "Not here. In the Selous."

Back at the lodge, I bathed, changed, found a well-cushioned rattan chair on the patio and set myself to tallying the creatures seeking a night cap at the pond below. A lone male elephant. A few impala. Lots of birds. Since the pond itself had receded to half its normal size, the surrounding hillocks seemed higher and more imposing.

Andrew arrived at seven, without Phil and Eileen.

"Aren't they coming?" I asked.

"As soon as they can," he said. "The Park office seems to have some issues, so I left them to it." He beckoned to a waiter, who took his order for beer, then looked toward me.

"Want another?" he asked.

"Not yet," I said. "I'm nursing this."

Phil and Eileen were still angry when they finally appeared. The bumbling, baboon-darting researchers had left the country months ago, but repercussions from their stupidity continued, according to Phil, calling for beer even more quickly than Andrew had. The brew appeared, foamy and cold. He gave it a connoisseur's savoring. "Ahhhhh! Just what the doctor ordered," he said—and then, raising his glass to me, he added, "Thank you, Diana. We needed this escape."

Eileen agreed. "I'm so sick of it," she said. "The baboons are fine, thank God, and we've promised to brief the authorities in absurd detail on all future research projects. But every week, it seems, there's a new question, a demand—and they're hassling us about permits again. Thirsty for tea, of course."

"Dangerous stuff," Andrew said. "the more you comply, the more they'll want."

"Virgilio seems to have had a good time," I said. "Except for the bugs!"

Phil laughed. "He wasn't so happy about the Mahoneys climbing all over his car. He did a thorough inspection for scratches. The primitive bathing facilities didn't thrill him either. But Eileen's gourmet goat stew put him in a good mood."

"Plus: beer works every time," Eileen insisted. "And thank you for the wine," she added, turning to me.

Dining on the patio that evening was close to heavenly, no thanks to the bland English-style cuisine. A cloud free sky gradually darkened. The moon found its double in the pond. A breeze kept us cool without inducing shivers. No one wanted to break the spell, and the anecdotes kept flowing.

Phil made sure to warn me about hippos. "Never *never* get between a hippo and his water," he said.

He'd been careless once, strolling along the river, watching out for crocodiles, but paying little attention to roundish footprints sunk deeply into the mud. Too small for elephants, he decided. Hippos? Possibly. That hunch was right, but seeing none, he'd discounted the danger, until the first hippo flattened some bushes, bee-lining for water. Phil, fortunately, was not in its path. Like rapid fire, right behind the first, came five more hippos, each just as single-minded, each unswerving. One brushed ever so slightly against Phil's shirt as it galloped by, two tons at high speed.

"I was petrified," Phil said. "And lucky."

Phil's experience jogged loose a hippo story I'd heard from Agnes. She'd been entertaining some visitors from her home office in Paris, showing them what her unit had accomplished and making sure they had a good time. Their itinerary included a boat ride on Lake Manyara. The Parisians adored the elephants splatting and swirling water with their trunks, rolling in muddy shallows, spraying themselves with dust. But a hippo provided the excitement. Detaching itself from its closely-packed herd, it swam toward the boat, got quite close, then sank out of sight. The passengers ran from larboard to starboard, imagining the worst, which happened. The boat began to tilt. Slowly, slowly the deck's slant approached the vertical, threatening to dump human tidbits into a crocodile-infested lake. And then, abruptly, the boat fell back, and they saw the hippo, mere yards away, wiggling its ears, gazing back. Was it laughing? That boat trip, according to Agnes, was the highlight of the tour.

"Hippos are curious," Andrew said. "They like to check things out."

"They also have a sense of humor," he said.

"How can you tell?" I asked.

"You'll see," he said.

"If we ever find a hippo!"

"We will," said Andrew.

And we did.

I was driving, somewhat reluctantly, so Andrew could focus his infinitely adjustable Nikon on this or that unsuspecting creature as I headed this way or that seeking water according to his hunches. It was a pretty discouraging business. Well known ponds had been reduced to remnants, hardly enough to satisfy the thirst of a few dikdiks, the tiniest antelopes of all, let alone a herd of hippos. Others were full enough, but not with hippos.

By late morning I'd been ready to quit any number of times, but there was always another possibility to check, according to Andrew. And another. And another. Eventually, I urged the Land Rover up a small hill from which the descent was fairly steep. Slowly, slowly, I we rolled downward, toward a gully containing a ribbon of water bordered by thick vegetation. Soon we were leaving tread marks on damp earth as we approached an oasis, open water surrounded by healthy stands of sword-like reeds and papyrus stalks that exploded into flowers like lacy, lime green starbursts. We'd entered a supple, verdant world.

And there they were, packed barrel to barrel and sometimes overlapping, with chins resting on rumps, a herd of hippos, up to their shoulders in water, their wet black backs glistening in the sun. I counted twenty some, and nearly as many water-loving Cape buffalo staring down, like baleful judges in black robes, from a nearby ridge. Following Andrew's recommendation, I parked the Land Rover on some firm dry ground rising a few feet above water level. A modest promontory.

And so I learned to love hippos, especially the way they honked and grunted and sighed, as if they had all kinds of things to say to one another, for they were very responsive to one another. If one moved or merely yawned, a wave of minor adjustments worked its way from hippo to hippo, then onward, as ripples in the water. When neighbors began snorting, shoving or lunging at one another, the herd exerted the opposite effect, absorbing and containing the disturbance. A very sophisticated society. I was impressed.

And Andrew was right: the hippos seemed curious about us, too. Unlike the buffalo, who remained vigilant but motionless, the very essence of aloofness, the resident congregation of hippos delegated a scout to check us out periodically. A broad back would sink out of sight. Soon there would be a darkening of the pond's surface no more than a dozen feet away and a shadowy submarine would be directing its sensors toward the bipeds on the shore: bug eyes, pink-speckled nostrils, twitchy pink-speckled ears. The first scout risked no more than a periscopic view. The next surfaced the whole of its muzzle, exhaling with an endearing "woof". One or two scouts made a pretense of attacking. They surged up, jaws gaping, water sluicing around enormous teeth, staring. I stared back. We might have been playing the blinking game—and I always lost. The sun was too intense for my blue eyes, but its effect on the water was ideal for photography: reflections that caught every whisker on a hippo's muzzle.

Andrew was in his element. As the hippos got bolder, the photo ops got more and more sensational. Ears waggling, nostrils bubbling, snaggle teeth easily countable, they closed the distance between us, surfacing more and more fully.

And then came the joker who ventured too close, lunging as if he meant it. This beast wasn't stopping!

"Charge!" I screamed and ran behind the Land Rover. Crouching out of sight, hoping for the best, I couldn't see anything, but I heard something that didn't seem possible. Andrew was hooting with laughter.

I stood, hands on hips, and saw my nemesis—or its cousin, hovering in the water, watching the funny humans. And I'd run. Humiliating.

"It's not funny," I said.

Andrew made the laughter stop. "I'm sorry," he said, "I should have warned you. Hippos feint. And the ground's too high for a lunge here. We're safe. That's why I chose it."

"Thanks," I said. "Is there anything else I should know—before it's too late?"

"I got some great pictures—"

"Not of me!" I exclaimed.

"One, possibly."

Anger vestigial, but still feeling sheepish, I conceded the possibility of humor. "The ferocious hippo attack!"

If Andrew's camera had been a modern digital model, we might have viewed the shot and I could have requested a deletion. That wasn't possible in those days. Before I could oversee the destruction of print and/or negative, Andrew would have to develop the whole roll of film in the office dark room.

But instant revenge was possible. "Now you," I demanded. "I get to take a ridiculous picture of you."

"I'm running out of film."

"Tough!" I said. "Now face the hippo. Look scared to death."

Andrew mimed a masterpiece of silent movie-style horror. And that's when the fun began. Handing Andrew's fancy Nikon back and forth, we took parody pictures with and without curious hippos. First me, then him, we posed ourselves against the battered old Land Rover as if we were aristocrats with a vintage touring sedan. We took turns stalking a mystery animal through dramatically parted reeds, and we stuck commanding poses, rifle in hand, atop our not so commanding promontory. In the end, not a single negative was destroyed. Everyone one in the office had a good guffaw when we passed the prints around. Me included.

Heading back to Dar, we stopped for a late afternoon snack with the cook pot ladies on the hill. Corn on the cob—tender and delicious, even without butter.

"So what are we going to do next weekend?" Andrew asked.

"Are you kidding?" I exclaimed. "All I can think of right now is the inspection."

Our team had five days to finalize preparations, plus a weekend to relax, assuming we didn't have to work on Saturday and Sunday, too. The inspectors would arrive the following Monday.

"And if everything's ready and the weekend's ours to enjoy?"

"Kilwa," I said. "The Arab ruins. The old Portuguese fort. I'm dying to see them."

Kilwa lay on the coast, well south of the Rufiji and just above the border with Mozambique. I'd never heard of it before I reached Tanzania, but history lingered there, on the mainland and on a small island reachable by dhow, or so I'd read.

"It's a deal," Andrew said, holding out his hand, which I grasped.

"Clive permitting," I said.

17

The final week of inspection prep did not begin well, especially for Andrew. Past accusations sprang back to life when a mandated inventory of the stuff on the shelves failed to match the paper trail. Frazzled from a debilitating case of pre-inspection nerves, Clive leaped to regrettable conclusions.

"Well, at least we've caught it," he said. "Where's Andrew?"

Andrew, as it happened, was out schmoozing with his reporter buddies, so Milly did as she was told and summoned me instead. As I passed her desk, she gave me a warning. "He's furious," she said.

"What do you know about this?" Clive demanded. "You two are thick as thieves."

"What do I know about what?" I asked.

"The missing supplies," Clive said, all but shouting. "And we don't have receipts for all those typewriters you gave away either."

I ran my eyes down the offending inventory, taking it slowly, mostly to get my temper under control. Meeting anger with anger wouldn't help me. There might be some irregularities, I conceded, but supervising vehicle maintenance wasn't in my job description—or Andrew's. "And look at the dates on those donations, Clive. Months before I arrived."

"Well, let's get some receipts. Pronto! And tell Andrew, when he turns up, I want to see him."

Relieved and chuckling to myself, I rang up the relevant editors, who passed me on to the relevant business managers, who all said the same thing. If I wanted receipts for the typewriters, whatever I needed, they'd supply. "No problem. Anything else, Diana?"

"Nothing thanks," I trilled. "Keep up the good work."

Back in those Cold War days there was a universally appreciated joke about the U.S.S.R.'s claim to be a workers' paradise: we pretend to work and they pretend to pay us. Modified to fit the Tanzanian media scene, it would go like this: they pretend to publish a quality product, and we pretend to respect it.

Good old Milly, meanwhile, had discovered another oddity in the inventory. Some items appeared to be overstocked. Asking Lily to hold the fort, she headed for the garage to consult with our maintenance chief, a mechanic who'd been hired at some point since the last inspection. She returned considerably later, and she was smiling.

"Mystery solved," she called, barging into Clive's office. I made sure to be right behind her.

There *was* a problem, she reported. But it wasn't theft. It was sloppiness and F-level math skills. Shipments had been incorrectly labeled, boxes were stacked haphazardly, loose items were all jumbled up, but little or nothing was missing. As for the paperwork itself, no embezzler would have been so inept.

Clive demanded to know why the mess hadn't been caught and cleaned up earlier. To my mind the arrow pointed back to him, but I kept my mouth shut. Milly was carrying the ball very adroitly.

"I did a little guilt tripping," Milly continued. "The Chief admitted to being pretty weak on the numbers. But he had a defense. He'd kept our vehicles running well and that's all that anyone seemed to care about. Wasn't that enough?"

Clive took a deep breath, set his feet on the floor and made for the elevator. "Someone needs a reality check," he said. "He'll shape up or ship out."

"Do you still want to see Andrew?" I asked.

Through closing elevator doors Clive threw me a sour look.

Milly deserved high praise for sleuthing, but our triumphalism was short-circuited. Lily called me to the phone.

"The German Embassy," she said.

That meant Dieter. I took the call in my office. The Pemba expedition hadn't happened, he reported. Sick pilot. But the fellow had recovered, and since everyone else was agreeable, the trip would take place this coming weekend instead. "Maybe you can make it this time?"

I could, of course. And I was tempted. I knew and liked most of the group, and surely I could manage Dieter for a couple of days. But Dieter wasn't the only problem. Being trapped on an island once I'd tolerated a reasonable quota of sun, sand, snorkeling and companionship had negative appeal.

"What a shame!" I said. "We're facing a routine inspection and it's really annoying, but we may have to work overtime this weekend."

Wishing me success on the inspection, Dieter closed the conversation with a gallant reference to some other time. I murmured something equally vague and ritualistic. Bridge burnt. No regrets.

The rest of the day played out in the same cheerless mode. Clive continued to act out his pre-inspection anxiety by finding fault with everything and everyone, including Aisha. Her desk was messy, he growled, when a prowl through the library yielded nothing consequential to rectify. Lily dodged censure by appearing to be single-mindedly absorbed in the delicate task of constructing an impeccable record, although she'd had everything organized by day two. Even Dolly moped. Clive was sniping at her, too.

Then Agnes phoned and blasted my hopes for sharing a relaxing round of sundowners after work. "Come as quickly as you can," she said. "It's Hasina."

I was all ready to sprint down the stairs a few minutes before 3:30, when Lily asked to speak with me, in private.

"Of course," I said. "Come in."

She took the chair usually occupied by petitioners of one kind or another and said, "I'm worried."

Lily was always worried about something. Her rent had gone up. Her philandering husband had decided he couldn't afford to contribute to school fees any longer. Her car was making strange noises. Although her USIS salary was substantial in the Tanzanian context, she was a single mother battling an unforgiving budget—and that afternoon, she feared, there was disaster on the horizon.

"They'll reclassify," she predicted. "They'll reclassify, and you know what that means."

To translate from the bureaucratese, Lily feared that the upcoming inspection would start an administrative chain reaction leading to a determination that our FSNs were paid substantially more than equally skilled Tanzanians in comparable occupational slots in Dar. Or worse: a decision that Dar employees were grossly over-compensated for their meager responsibilities at our poky little post. Either way, our loyal hard-working colleagues would end up with a pay cut—or a pay freeze, making sure their "overly generous" salaries didn't increase, no matter how brilliantly they performed under pressure. Successful squeezing earned bonuses, promotions and commendations for the well-paid Scrooges in DC.

I listened sympathetically to Lily, because I'd seen it all before. Cuts. Cuts. Cuts. And every so often a raise. It was foolish. It was short-sighted. It was cruel. "Well-paid, contented workers are the best possible advertisement for the land of the free and the home of the brave," I'd argued, trying (futilely) to prevent a crushing, cross-the-board pay slash for FSNs at a previous post. That strenuous (aka aggressive, in the sexist language of the times) defense of hard-working, loyal employees had given me a corridor reputation as "not a team player," but I'd happily do it again for good people.

"I'll do my best," I told Lily. "But don't get your hopes up."

Not for the first time since I'd arrived in Dar, I wondered if I done the right thing in seeking reinstatement.

Kiki looked in while I was brooding. "Why so glum?" she asked. I explained and she agreed that downgrading our FSNs wouldn't be fair. Taking the seat that Lily had occupied minutes before, she shared the equivalent injustices she'd suffered in her previous position as a teacher: exploitative pay, condescending treatment, being used as a scapegoat for social ills.

"That's why I left," she said. "No appreciation. No dignity."

"Out of the frying pan into the fire!" I snorted. "Look at the Foreign Service promotion stats."

"Exactly. And how many female career ambassadors are there?" Kiki asked.

"Not many," I admitted.

As we bleakly considered our prospects for juicy follow-on positions, let alone our chances for making it into the Senior Foreign Service, I appreciated the solidity of our gradually-built relationship. Early on, I'd been the experienced colleague sharing tricks of the trade. The equalizer then had been Kiki's greater knowledge of Dar and Tanzania.

That familiarity had led her to suggest that we drive north one Sunday to the old city of Bagamoyo. Its excellent port had been the African terminus of the ancient slave and ivory trade. From there both commodities were shipped to Zanzibar and thence to the rest of the Arab world—along with Zanzibari cloves.

134

We asked Milly to come along, but she declined. Too hot. Too depressing.

Together, that day in Bagamoyo, Kiki and I beheld the appalling remnants of slave-holding cells, and for the first time I wholly grasped the big picture: Arabs as well as Europeans had milked Africa of its healthiest men and women. Was it worse to become a chattel in Mississippi than Oman? Maybe. But in degree only. Enslaving people is wrong. Period.

Our excursion had a happier element. We were fascinated by the extraordinary skills of the dhow builders at work on the beach at Bagamoyo. Some two-masted, some three, all rigged with lanteen sails, dhows had capitalized on strong trade winds to dominate trade between East Africa and Arabia, and India, too, in the centuries before canon-heavy ships from Europe flooded the continent with traders, missionaries and conquerors. Like their ancestors, the master builders on the beach at Bagamoyo relied on hand tools and human muscle to construct their ocean-going vessels.

So far from shooing us away as gawking intruders, the shipwrights welcomed our eagerness to understand their craft for the marvel it was. Keels, we learned, had to come from a single massive piece of wood, often a tree trunk, usually mahogany. Ditto each rib, for which sturdy individual branches might also serve. Every element was meticulously trimmed and planed to fit precisely where it was needed. And so on, until a seaworthy ship rolled down its bed of logs into the surf.

Standing, by invitation, on a keel only half ribbed and below decking already begun, I felt a kind of awe, as if I were standing in the nave of a cathedral. So strong! So graceful! Kiki felt it, too. We ooohed and aaahed—and the boatwrights were delighted. One day this vessel would sail to Oman. If only we might be aboard!

In the end, my only experience of going to sea on a dhow was a little less awesome. The boat itself was a one-master with a single sailor at the rudder. Half way across a narrow strait the sea got choppy, and I blessed the ratty old life preserver I'd almost refused to wear. But that excursion was yet to come when Clive called me into his office as I hurried to reach my rendezvous with Agnes.

"What now?" I thought.

Clive, it turned out, was in a thoroughly good mood. He'd ferreted out the names of the inspectors. Although not personally acquainted with either, he'd learned what he needed to know. "They'll be exacting," he said, "but fair."

"Sounds promising," I said.

He'd discovered something else, which explained his buoyant mood. "They're bird watchers." He chortled.

I had a sense of foreboding. "I don't know anything about birds," I said.

Clive didn't either. "But the Brits are crazy about birds. Call the British High Commission and find a birder who knows where the exotic species congregate. Hopefully not too far from Dar. See if there's someone who'd be willing and able to serve as guide. Tell them how grateful we'll be."

Not convinced that bird watching rose to the High Commissioner level, I phoned the British Council and made arrangements to meet with the director, whom I knew well—and Kiki knew even better. So why didn't she get stuck with scrounging for bird lovers? I'd never know, because my fleeting sense of annoyance was replaced by a more sophisticated insight. Showing them around, I'd get to know them, and they'd get to know me, which might be useful. Meanwhile, I needed to see what kind of trouble Hasina was in.

The little car parked in Agnes's driveway was unmistakably hers. A professor's transport, she called it. The paint had lost its gloss, and it was rusting badly, but it got her where she wanted to go.

Hasina and Agnes were in the garden with Mamzell, who immediately dropped a tennis ball at my feet. I tossed the ball into a thick bush, to keep the sometimes annoying dog occupied as long as possible, embraced Hasina, told Agnes that a glass of white wine would be perfect, then turned back to a very distressed-looking Hasina. Normally resistant to alcohol, in deference to Islam, she had a glass of wine in hand.

"It's Sheik," she said. "He wants a son—"

Agnes looked up from her wine pouring. "Meaning his mother wants a grandson."

"She also wants what she calls a real daughter-in-law," Hasina said bitterly. "Obedient. Deferential. A household slave. But Sheik deserves a son—"

"Don't they know that a child's sex is determined by the father?" I asked.

"Science is poppycock, according to Mama," Hasina said. "And even if I did agree to another child, even if we had twin sons, I'd still have to live with her. At this point I don't care if he divorces me—"

"You do," Agnes said.

"Yes, I do. But there comes a time—and I'm ready, except—" An expression that began in sadness took on a harrowing aspect as Hasina tried to enunciate something her vocal apparatus and trembling jaw resisted. She persisted, and finally it emerged. "Noor. I can't bear to lose her."

And so we brainstormed escape scenarios, our goal being to ensure that Hasina would secure custody of Noor. The biggest obstacle had to do with travel documents. Sheikh kept the family passports locked up in his office. For safety, supposedly, although the arrangement reeked of patriarchal control, according to Hasina, who'd always resented it. With divorce pending, Sheikh would probably relinquish Hasina's passport without a murmur, but Noor's? Probably not. Could Hasina gain access to his office, seize the passports and slip out of the country with Noor before Sheikh caught on? Noor had a U.S. passport, but Hasina would need a visa. Could Virgilio help? And maybe Rafiq could drive Hasina and Noor to the border. Which border? Kenya? Uganda? Mozambique? Would they have to cower under a rug or behind bales of cotton? Didn't matter, so long as no airline ticketing record pointed to a specific destination. Say they made it to the U.S. Then what? Lawyers. Courts. Even if Hasina could find a job, there were laws against kidnapping children in search of a more favorable custodial jurisdiction.

The more we schemed, the more hesitant I became. "How about Noor?" I asked. "What does she want? She loves her father, too, I think."

"She does," Hasina said. She wiped her eyes with a hankie that was already saturated with tears.

We fell into a depressing silence.

I broke it with another question. "Have you spoken to Sheikh about this?"

"I'm afraid to," Hasina said. "I'm afraid of putting him on guard before I get hold of the passports."

"You have to risk it," I said. "He's never seemed like a monster to me."

"It's his mother," Hasina replied. "She says I'm corrupting Noor—and she's got him under her thumb. Respect for elders and all that."

Hasina looked toward Agnes for support, but even Agnes, who'd so enthusiastically embellished the escape scenario, had come around to reality. "You need to talk to Sheikh," she said. "Alone. Without his mother."

In the driveway I held Hasina close. "Be brave," I said.

I watched her drive off, then climbed into my own car, where I sat, for some moments, eyes closed, motionless, exhausted. I'd eat a quick dinner, I decided, crawl into bed and read myself to sleep. But when I got home, I found Andrew's Land Rover in my driveway.

What now? I thought.

18

Andrew had brought good news, an officially stamped letter allowing us to spend a night at a government guest house situated on the beach just north of Kilwa. That—ha! ha!—was the simple part. Permission didn't come with a guarantee of pampering, he warned. And, since the place had no phone, the manager might be surprised to see us and a cook might not be available.

"Bring clean sheets," Andrew advised. "And your sleeping bag."

"And supplies?" I asked. "In case we have to cook?"

"Yes," he said. "I've contacted Suleiman."

"Don't forget the tents," I said.

Andrew laughed.

And so, ready for everything we could imagine, we set off bright and early on Saturday morning, which gave us plenty of time to adjust when our piece of paper turned out to be worthless. The guesthouse had been booked for an assembly of regional Party leaders, whose vehicles, we discovered, left little space in the parking lot for ours. I waited in the Land Rover while Andrew checked things out. Shortly he and a man who turned out to be the manager emerged from the building. Poor fellow! His bland managerial expression turned to horror as he looked up from the letter of introduction and saw, in the flesh, the American diplomat he'd just read about—and a woman diplomat, at that. He might have shrugged off a man, leaving the reject (assuming he/she wasn't an Ambassador) to fate. But a woman? Not so simple.

We rejected the manager's first suggestion: return to Dar and come back another time. His second idea held promise. We might try the International Engineering compound. It was also on the beach and a bit closer to Kilwa. If the manager's memory was correct, IE frequently accommodated outsiders as well as their own officials at a guesthouse on the premises.

"Give me a few minutes," the manager said. He'd arrange for subordinates to dance attendance on the Party dignitaries, then accompany us to the IE compound, where he'd introduce us to the Resident Engineer, a Mr. Briggs. Thus, ever so cleverly, he would transfer all responsibility for the lady.

According to Andrew, International Engineering was one of the many contractors working on the North-South Highway between Somalia and South Africa. Some day, undoubtedly, the name would fit. That morning, however, what we'd driven on beyond the Rufiji River was hardly a road, much less a highway, and the prospects for progress in the foreseeable future looked fanciful. Only occasionally did we find heavy machinery in use. Laborers with picks and shovels weren't much in evidence either. Mostly we raised dust from gravel interrupted occasionally by some few miles of paved surface so smooth we might have been airborne on a hovercraft.

When I puzzled over the on-again/off-again effect, Andrew laughed. "You can tell the districts with the powerful politicians."

"Anyone I know?" I asked.

He named a Party bigwig and our dear friend the Information Minister. "His wife is someone's step-sister," he said.

After more than a few minutes, the manager reappeared. Begging forgiveness for taking so long, he requested that I do him the honor of accepting a little gift, a white metal tray inscribed with the words "Government Guest House, Kilwa." Just like the ones presented to the Party leaders, he assured me. Over the years I've acquired (and disposed of) countless commemorative objects, but I always make the presenter feel good. The manager was smiling as he climbed into the back seat next to Suleiman.

"There's no air conditioning," he warned, as we headed further south on the road that was masquerading as a highway. "But you won't need it. Not with the sea breeze. And there's a nice verandah."

That was good enough for me. My hopes rose even further as we bumped over the transition from gravel to pavement. "We must be approaching the IE compound," I quipped.

Andrew got the joke. The manager didn't, but soon he was directing our eyes toward a well-weathered colonial-style bungalow and several buildings

140

that might have been warehouses. The property faced a broad calm bay. Waves made a white line where they broke on a distant reef. A dock cum jetty extended from the beach into water deep enough for the steamers that, once upon a time, had plied along the coast. Moored to one side I saw a white speedboat, its stern weighed down by a pair of outboard motors. Optimism reigned.

But not for long. The compound was strewn with derelict machinery, giant bald tires, coils of rusty cable, empty cable spools and just plain junk. Nor were the warehouses capacious enough to hold the earth-movers, graders, pavers, rollers, etc., for which the road contract had surely included funding. No wonder the work on the highway was languishing.

"So where's the money going?" I asked.

"How do you think the Wabenzi pay for their cars and villas?" Andrew laughed, using the Swahili term for Tanzanian owners of expensive German vehicles.

The virtual junk yard was protected by a chain link fence and patrolled by a pair of unfriendly-looking German shepherds. They barked in savage chorus as we approached the gate, which was padlocked, and they continued to yelp, growl and launch gate-foiled attacks until finally a human guard emerged from one of the warehouses and walked slowly in our direction.

Our manager guide cleared his throat, as if for an important announcement. "I'll handle this," he said. Shouting to be heard above the canine din, he demanded the presence of Engineer Briggs. As the guard trotted off to fetch his boss, the manager turned to me. "You'll be safe here," he said.

"Only if they lock up the dogs," I said.

Andrew looked at me. I looked at him. We were thinking the same thing. Whatever the noble intentions of the manager or the willingness of the yet to appear Mr. Briggs, we would not be spending the night on those premises.

"You handle this," I said. "I'm going to have a look at the beach."

Following the outer perimeter of the fence, I would have been protected from the dogs even if they hadn't been fixated on the enemy at the gate. Gradually the sound of the surf drowned out the canine clamor, but the beach, close up, did not deliver on the loveliness that had been promised from a distance. The water lapping against the jetty had all the translucence of industrial effluent. Shiny splotches rode the swells, and globs of tar studded with bits of white plastic marked the high waterline. Aged deposits of blackened, drying seaweed weren't exactly beautiful, but at least their ugliness wasn't man-made. The IE compound was paradise ruined, no place for swimming, sun bathing or overnighting. I was very happy when Sulieman, wrapped in his trademark black overcoat, rescued me.

The deal was this: since the IE compound was unattractive, though "safe, madam, safe," we'd drive the manager back to the government guest house, then search for a place to camp. Near the beach, if possible. But only after we stopped at a fish market. The manager had people to feed. So did Suleiman, whose skill with seafood would impress me, Andrew promised.

The fish market was actually a small village of fishermen. Fortunately, not all of the night's catch had been snapped up by the early birds from Kilwa. Given first dibs, Suleiman chose slabs of tuna for kebabs and several flat fish I didn't recognize to fillet and grill. Plus an octopus. The manager drove a hard bargain for everything else. The makings of a mammoth chowder, he told Suleiman.

Andrew, meanwhile, was paying his respects to the village leaders, who were impatient for the completion of the North-South highway. Marketing fish would be easier, they said, and the young men needed better access to jobs in Kilwa. When Andrew explained our dilemma, asking for advice on where we might camp, a place that was safe and clean, not too close to a village, but not too far from people either, the villagers were quicker to grasp our requirements than the obsequious manager had been. A ways down the road we'd find a little cove that might be just right, they said.

With a great sense of relief, we deposited the manager and his burden of fish at the government guest house, expressed our appreciation for his—ahem!— efforts, and in no time at all found ourselves surveying the site recommended by the villagers. Behind us was an enormous cornfield. It made a fine privacy screen and muffled the sound of traffic from the wannabe highway. Before us was an idyllic beach with a broad swathe of clean white sand reaching well above the high tide line. The water itself was as clear as tropical seas are supposed to be. Aquamarine in the shallows. Sapphire further out. Some day a resort chain would discover the place and ruin it, but that evening, squinting right and left, we saw no signs of human life. We had it all to ourselves. Plus we were more or less under the protection of important local leaders. Always a good idea, Andrew said.

As he and Suleiman erected and pegged the tents, I collected driftwood for the fire, thinking how pleasant and easy the camp-making routine had become.

Now that I was an experienced member of the team, I knew exactly what to do without asking, which actually wasn't much that evening on the beach. Having heaped what looked like more than enough firewood where Suleiman had indicated, I had only one desire, to dive into that clean beautiful water and wash off the day's accumulation of sweat, but I had to resist. Our planning hadn't been perfect. We had barely enough water for drinking and cooking, but not enough to rinse the salt from a body that wasn't disgustingly dirty to start with.

Wading through the gentle surf of a receding tide was another matter. While Suleiman removed his coat and got down to the messy business of beating the octopus on a rock to tenderize it, I rolled up my jeans and splashed down the beach. The blue of the water was growing ever darker as the sun set to the west, behind the cornfield. Andrew caught up with me. He pointed toward a black splotch on the horizon.

"That's where we're going tomorrow," he said. "I've made the arrangements."

While I'd been worrying about consuming fish that couldn't be kept on ice during the short time before Suleiman got to cooking it, even as I also knew I should trust local judgment on edibility, Andrew had been inquiring after a dhow as well as a camping site. He'd found one, he said. Owned by the younger brother of one of the elders, it would be waiting for us at the main dock in Kilwa. A message would be sent by motorcycle, and if the brother's boat was unavailable, brother Abu would arrange a seaworthy alternative for us. Andrew had pre-paid for gassing up the motorcycle. Round trip.

"Not a budget buster," I said with a laugh.

By the time we were strolling back to our tents, the sunset was at its most dramatic. To the West there was a baroque composition in vermilion and gold. To the East, over the water, the colors were more subtle. Mauve. Dove gray. A hint of green. The beach itself was fading into darkness, except for the fire that was consuming the wood I'd gathered. Fire meant food. I was famished and ready to eat, but we'd have to be patient, Sulieman said. He needed a little more time to produce the banquet he'd planned: two fish dishes, Arab-influenced pilaf, octopus salad, platter of sliced tomatoes, cucumbers and onions. Old hand that I'd become, I knew that the feast would be worth waiting for.

There was, of course, a way to make the waiting bearable. "Can you stand a little Scotch?" I asked.

"I'll try," Andrew said.

Seated just above the damp high water line, sipping from mugs that sometimes held coffee, we reviewed the day, agreeing that it had turned out quite magnificently. And if more surprises greeted us on Sunday? We could handle anything, we decided.

"If the dhow arrangements fall apart—" I began.

"We'll find another boat."

"If a storm comes up—"

"We'll try again," said Andrew. "And if my mug is empty—"

"I'll refill it." I said quickly.

As we sat there watching the last sliver of pink go black, I thought of my German friends on Pemba. They'd be drinking sundowners on some elegant patio, most likely, but I was watching the very same moon coming up. They'd be chatting and listening to music, live or via someone's radio. I was wrapped in a silence that had its own resonance, a hush that seemed to satisfy Andrew, too. The waves came with the gentlest hint of slishing. The breeze could only be felt.

Of course, there was one sound I wanted to hear: a summons from Sulieman. Which finally came. The fish feast was ready.

Andrew stood. He extended a hand, to pull me up. I took it—and how natural it seemed, at first, to walk hand in hand toward the circle of light around the fire. The closer we got, however, the more I felt a powerful burning from the palm touching mine. Disengagement was imperative Not abruptly. Not rudely.

So how?

"Excuse me," I said, making for the cornfield. Not really to pee. To think. Andrew was married. I was his boss. Talk about poaching! I was on the verge of breaking too many taboos and I wasn't ready.

Suleiman turned out to be a master fish chef. The octopus salad was subtly crunchy. The grilled fillets were sweet and moist, the tuna kebabs tingly with chili. The pilaf and the raw vegetables provided balance and contrast. If I hadn't been so delighted with Mary's cookery, I'd have offered Suleiman a job in my kitchen. With guaranteed time off to cook for Andrew's safaris, of course.

That evening Suleiman ate with us. He was part of the conversation, too, and with Andrew translating, I learned about his family. He mentioned a brother who had died of fever, as had his wife. He lived now with two grown sons, one a laborer, still single, the other married and responsible for the family *shamba* or farm, actually a tiny patch of land near Dar, where he often spent the night, leaving his wife and children in the city with his brother and Suleiman. All of Suleiman's grandchildren were in school. Not merely literate, but educated, they'd have real opportunities in life, he hoped.

And then, with Andrew still translating, albeit uncomfortably, Suleiman turned to me, to commiserate. Poor me. Living alone. No husband. No children. I explained that customs are different and that, really, I was happy. Alone but not lonely. I made the point as emphatically as I could—and not only for Suleiman's benefit. As for Andrew, he spoke of his preacher father and of a mother who had worked herself to death to make the preaching possible, something I'd never heard him say before. Firesides are dangerous, I thought. People talk too much. Too intimately. Too honestly.

"I'm fading," I said. "Time to hit the sack." Making another, truly needed, trip to the cornfield, I crawled into my tent and tried to sleep.

Unsuccessfully.

Zipped up to my chin, my sleeping bag was too hot. Left open, I shivered. Worse, the angling of the tent seemed wrong for the slope of the beach. I repositioned my sleeping bag and the pad it rested on. The improvement was marginal at best. Turning this way, turning that way, I tried to nestle my bones into the soft sand below the tent floor. Nothing worked. Meanwhile, the thunderous pounding of waves bearing a rising tide was driving me crazy. Boom! Boom! Boom! I decided to watch the drama instead. I'd watch the ever-traveling moon, too.

Suleiman, I discovered was already asleep. Covered, as usual, with his overcoat, he was stretched out on a tarp beside a circle of dying embers. Andrew was sitting at some distance from the remnants of the fire, his form dark against the white sand.

"May I?" I asked, as I dropped down beside him. "The fire's going out," I added. "Is that a problem?"

Andrew shook his head. "No animals to bother us here."

"But you have your gun."

"I don't expect visitors, but—" He grinned before delivering the line we knew so well. "It's good to be prepared. And speaking of being prepared, I don't suppose you brought the Scotch."

"I'll get it," I said.

Soon we were sipping again. "I'm really tired," I said, "but I couldn't sleep."

"I can't sleep either," he said.

An on shore breeze was blowing my hair around. It was tickling my nose, stinging my eyes. I reached up to push it back, but Andrew's hand had got there first, brushing it aside, holding it there, caressing my cheek lightly with his thumb. He paused at the edge of the cliff, found he wasn't alone—and we jumped, hand in hand, so to speak, into space. It wasn't wild. It wasn't ecstatic. It was better than either. Comfortable. Natural. Right. Dare I say fated? And then the world was impinging again. The air was chilly. The sand was scratchy. I noticed the moon. I heard the waves—and Sulieman's snoring.

We sat for some time, my head on his shoulder, his arm around me, the surf booming and slishing, wind ever stronger, the air chillier.

"We'll be able to sleep now," he said.

"Together," I said.

146

19

Waking, alone, in a nest of two sleeping bags, I was tempted to blame the night's sex on the Scotch, especially the unsafe part. I wasn't terribly worried. So far as I knew, Andrew was no more promiscuous than I was. But I'd failed to practice what I'd so stridently, so self-righteously been preaching. Not that Agnes, whom I'd scolded mercilessly, would ever know. Nor would any one else. As for Andrew, whether he'd slipped out of the tent without waking me because he was a confirmed early riser—or because he couldn't face me, he would protect my reputation. And his own. Suleiman, too, lived by the wisdom of discretion.

In any event, we'd need to be careful. The smallest gestures have tales to tell. "Thick as thieves," Clive had said.

Meanwhile, eager as I was to get up and get dressed, I was held back by my own fear of facing Andrew in daylight. What could I say? What should I say? What I shouldn't *do*, on the other hand, was crystal clear. Once was stupid enough.

Emerging from deep sleep through anxious musing into relative clear-headedness, however conflicted, I'd become increasingly aware of actual, strange voices. I peeked through the tent flaps. Our quiet beach had been invaded by sea and by land. A half dozen fishing boats had been pulled ashore, and the night's catch had been sorted into baskets, except for the larger species. They'd been laid in a row on the sand. Thanks to the highway lurking just behind the cornfield, buyers were coming and going—and haggling, which is always noisy.

Sitting serenely apart, by a modest breakfast fire, Suleiman was eating, Swahili style, with his fingers. Leftover pilaf probably. Always alert, he watched me step out from the very tent from which he'd probably seen Andrew emerge. This was the moment I'd been dreading, but almost immediately he was offering me a mug of coffee and asking if I'd like some fried fish to go with my eggs. I settled on eggs minus fish—and biscuits, fluffy wonders he'd baked in a skillet. I sat, writing, on a log and looked for Andrew. He was in the midst of collapsing the unused tent. He laid out the canvas, arranged pegs, ropes and poles on top, folded everything together, stowed the bundle in the back of the Land Rover and sauntered over to the fire. Something about his look and posture put me at ease.

"The Head Man promised a quiet night—" he said

"And we got it." I laughed. "But not a quiet morning."

And that was that. While I finished my breakfast, wondering if Abu and the promised dhow would be waiting for us, Andrew took care of the tent we'd slept in and Suleiman scrubbed soot from the grill.

We reached the pier. No Abu. No dhow. Par for the course, I thought.

But boatmen are brothers as well as competitors, and the guys on the dock had a message for us. "Down the beach," they said.

There are dhows—and there are dhows. Compared to the ocean-going vessel Kiki and I had admired in Bagamoyo, the little craft riding at anchor was a toy. Four passengers max, I guessed, plus Abu, who didn't fill me with confidence either. Too young. Still, the mini dhow did have the lanteen look, so my romantic spirit was assuaged. I looked toward the distant island. I looked at the choppy seas. I looked at Abu. I sighed and consigned myself to kismet.

On ivory and slaves the Arabs of Kilwa, like those of Bagamoyo, had prospered, until the Portuguese rounded the Cape of Good Hope and started exploring the Eastern coast of Africa. Having discovered the thriving city of Kilwa, the Europeans built a fort to control trade and traffic along the river whose mouth had called the original settlement into being. Of those early periods, aside from some touching grave markers, no material remains on the mainland much impressed me, but on the island, we were told, we could view the remains of the fort. "You can see the walls from here," Abu said. We could also visit some haunting remnants of the Arab period.

"It's not far," Abu insisted. "Just a mile across the strait." But we'd be sailing against a wind that was brisk enough to speckle the sea with white caps I didn't want to see.

Abandoning on all hope of staying dry, I waded into the water, followed by Andrew, who gave me a boost when the boat rose on an incoming wave just as I was heaving a leg over the side. Being lighter than Andrew, I stationed myself on the forward seat, just a slat, really, with Andrew right behind me. Abu tossed the anchor aboard, gave the bow a shove, jumped in and scrambled to his place in the stern, by the tiller. Shouting something, he yanked a cord. Andrew ducked and pushed my head out of danger, too. A dirty-looking canvas flew up and became a sail. It bellied out immediately. We were underway, all but flying. My respect for our modest little craft soared.

In no time at all, Suleiman was midget-sized. He stood, waving, by an equally shrunken Land Rover, and he'd be there when we got back. His job during the interval was to guard vehicle and contents. I'd given him some tea money and plenty more for a good lunch. Should he want to snooze in the Land Rover, that would be fine, too.

If the strait was indeed just a mile across, we must have sailed more than three, tacking against the wind as, little by little, we approached the fort's intimidating sea wall. Fissured, overgrown with weeds, eroded by centuries of weather, nevertheless it loomed above us on our last tack, making our little dhow seem fragile and helpless indeed. No wonder the Portuguese had prevailed, I thought, hearing my neck crackle as I bent it back to see what was left of classic crenelation. Where cannons had been, I saw mostly empty space, but I shivered anyway. Even the crude gunnery of the day could have blown us to bits.

And then we were gliding over a "lawn" of golden sea grass as the water shallowed and the dhow's prow touched on a gentle beach to one side of the fort. I saw a sickly old mango tree with a kind of bungalow crouching in the shade behind it. Also shielded from the searing sun: a rickety-looking table at which an elderly man was seated. Behind him stood a stocky, middle-aged man. A young man—or was he still a boy?—ran to secure our anchor when it plunked on the sand.

Shoeless, I slid into the water. Not quite disgusting, not exactly delightful, the sea grass ticked my toes, and my jeans were sopping wet again. No matter. We'd had a good crossing. We'd landed safely.

Abu hadn't planned to wait around. "I'll be back in three hours," he told Andrew, who translated.

"No way," I said. With the inspectors due to arrive on Monday, we couldn't afford to be marooned for half a day on a speck of an island just north of Mozambique. Andrew put the critical question to Abu. "How much extra—to wait right here?" Abu's demand was too modest to haggle over.

That settled, we found ourselves back in the land of bureaucracy. There were tickets to buy and rules to read before we could pass through the turnstile behind the rickety table. Once upon a time, no doubt, the turnstile had been the only way through a barbed wire fence, the sole access to a little path leading over the coastal dunes toward the interior of the island, but the fence had long since been trampled into the soft sand. Cows perhaps. Certainly goats—I saw the tell tale droppings. To say nothing of antiquities thieves.

Meanwhile, the old man seated at the table was asking for my name, which he spelled out in pencil on a pad that produced carbon copies as receipts. The date was also required, as was the amount received, which gave me time to study the little bungalow behind the mango tree. Peaked roof. Porch. Gingerbread. A caretaker's cottage, most likely. Had the British built it? Or the Germans? More remnants of conquest.

Andrew, as usual, was taking pictures. He was fascinated by the bungalow, too. It would make a strong contribution to the photo story he had in mind, he explained

"What story?" I asked.

" 'O How the Mighty Are Fallen.' And all that."

"The U.S. being the next?"

"Why not?"

I frowned, mostly because I thought I should.

The middle-aged man looked at our receipts, punched our tickets and handed back the stubs. "Keep them with you," we were told—or Andrew was, and he translated. And so we passed through the mostly symbolic turnstile, young Idris following. He would be our guide, he announced, noting that he was helping his grandfather and uncle, as family duty required. Idris was a student, or so he said, and he dressed accordingly, not in a plaid sarong like his elders, but in a white shirt and creased trousers. His shoes were of black leather, well-polished and fully laced, over bare feet.

"A student of what," I asked, as I usually did in such cases.

"A student of history."

"Wonderful. Then you can tell us about this place."

"It is very old," Idris replied.

"Hmmm—about how old?" I asked, mostly to be polite. I didn't know much about Kilwa, but I was pretty sure its Arab foundations predated the year one thousand.

"Very very old," Idris said, reverently.

So much for local expertise! "What history do you study?" I asked.

"I am a student of British history. 'To be or not to be.' William Shakespeare. 'Blood sweat and tears.' Winston Churchill. I have read about America, too. Abraham Lincoln. Martin Luther King. Ernest Hemingway. I like America very much. Do you have any dollars for me?"

"Not with me," I said. "I'm not allowed to use American money in Tanzania."

"We are very poor," said Idris. "You must help me to go to America. I will do anything—"

My heart sank. Wherever I went, the very same, despair-driven plea was bound to arise, and for the semi-educated, like Idris, there was nothing I or Kiki—or the Brits or the Germans or even the Soviets could do. So long as industry and agriculture shrank under Julius Nyerere's impractical system, their prospects were dismal. But I couldn't tell Idris that. It would be too devastating. At that moment, fortunately, we were climbing the dune along a path so narrow it forced us to go single file. I didn't have to meet his pleading eyes as I delivered an embarrassingly inadequate reply. "But Tanzania needs you," I said. "There's so much to do."

"There is no work," he said.

I sighed. He wasn't making it easy for me.

"I have no money," he continued. "What can I do?"

"Maybe the Party can help."

"They will say join the Party. Pay your dues and join the Party. How can I pay if I have no money and no work?"

"Isn't there a special student membership?"

"I am not in school anymore. My father is gone—but I read books, so I am a student."

"Your uncle's a member of the Party. Can't he help?"

"He is only a little man—and he is paid very little to do this job."

"I see," I said. "But you are helping him. That is very fine."

A compliment—that's all I could give him. "So sad," I whispered to Andrew, who was just behind me, still taking photos. He'd heard everything and nodded.

My experience with reconstructed fortifications elsewhere had given me high expectations. I should have known better. The fort had been sizeable, but its remnants lay about like the shards of a broken egg shell. There'd been little effort to reassemble them, except for a sturdy gun platform supporting two weathered cannons. Apparently original, they'd been positioned to keep enemy ships from passing through the strait. I climbed atop a relatively stable stretch of wall and looked toward the mainland, low, green, vulnerable-looking. Authoritative histories are indispensable, I thought. But the past comes alive only when you see and feel and walk it.

"Don't move," Andrew said.

"I'm a wreck," I said.

"You're beautiful," he said.

And then Idris was at his elbow, offering to take a picture of the two of us together. Andrew showed Idris where to stand and which button to press, then joined me on the wall.

"Closer!" Idris demanded.

I still have that picture, my arm around Andrew's waist, his arm around my shoulders. We look like a couple. We look happy.

But there was to be no lingering. Idris was eager to show us the remains of Old Kilwa, which revealed itself after we'd negotiated another hill—I say hill, not dune, because sand was giving way to soil. A scattering of trees and shrubs seemed to be doing quite nicely, too. Panting, sweaty, we reached the top and stopped.

"The palace," Idris said.

Lintels were still in place over some door and window openings. Here and there a scalloped niche revealed a few square inches of tinted plaster that had been protected from the weather. In one dark little room with a largely intact ceiling I looked up and saw the faded tracery of exquisitely painted flowers and foliage—or was my imagination playing with the consequences of water seepage? Stairways, steep and narrow, dropped off mid flight, a hazard for the unwary. I climbed them anyway, to see what I might from as high as I could get. The mildew-darkened dome of one distant building otherwise obscured by foliage excepted, nothing rose above tree level.

Surveying my domain, I thought of the Arabian Nights—and of Sheherazade, spinning tales to stay alive. The city is under a spell, I decided, to protect it from envious outsiders. The Nubian guards have been enchanted, changed into lizards, their chain mail turned into iridescent scales. Once we have left, though, the turnstile will become a marble gate again. Cooling fountains will plash in the courtyards. Idris will be a page, in silks—

Andrew's reaction was less fanciful. "Slaves and ivory," he said. "Looks like business was booming."

Idris, meanwhile, had something more important to show us, something I'd glimpsed through the trees. That dome—

"The mosque," he said.

Perhaps because the builders had been careful to mix the mortar properly, the structure of the mosque was well preserved. Its dome, though tileless, rose protectively above the prayer hall. Its mihrab pointed toward Mecca. Gazing over sand-dusted floor stones, I visualized the fine carpets that would have been spread to cushion the knees of the faithful. Not a chip remained of the mosaics whose inscriptions would have proclaimed the glory of god, the skill of his artisans, the wealth and good taste of his viceroys, but weather-scoured architectural features kept Andrew clicking away with his Nikon. The intricate brickwork of vaults and arches. The play of light through doorways, lattices and oculi. Me, as human interest, he laughed.

And always there was Idris to call our attention to innumerable little details that we might have missed, for which I always thanked him. He was a sweet boy and thoroughly conscientious. Or should I say mischievously over attentive? Andrew and I were never unescorted for more than a moment or two. Still, by the time we'd trudged back to the ludicrous turnstile, he had earned himself a substantial tip.

"Which he will have to share with his uncle and grandfather, no doubt," I whispered to Andrew.

Andrew snorted. "Share!"

"So he really is stuck," I said.

A consoling arm slid around my shoulder. "There's nothing we can do," Andrew said.

"That doesn't make me feel better," I said.

Abu was waiting—and so was Suleiman. But the jinx hadn't been lifted. When we reached the Rufiji, we discovered that the ferry had mechanical problems. The line of vehicles ahead of us was so long we'd be lucky to make the third crossing once it was back in service. If it was back in service. My instinct was to laugh at the absurdity of it all. Andrew was more practical. "I'll see what's what," he said.

Long before Andrew reappeared I was feeling bored and restless. Leaving Suleiman with the Land Rover, I walked around. Some drivers were sleeping behind the wheel. Others leaned against open doors, smoking, but ready to leap in and get going at the first sign of forward movement in the bumper to bumper chain of vehicles. They greeted me. I greeted them. It was the universal camaraderie of strangers brought randomly together. I thought of Chaucer and his *Canterbury Tales*. Also universal: the food venders making the most of a clientele that couldn't run away. I bought some oranges and bananas.

Andrew's report was encouraging. One of the tugs had developed an engine problem that a local mechanic had been able to diagnose and fix. In fact, the ferry was already bringing a load from the other side. And so we waited and waited and waited for our turn to drive aboard, which came well after dark. Normally, since poor visibility makes hazards hard to spot in time to react, the ferry got a rest between dusk and dawn, but the operators had made an exception that night. Standing in my favorite spot at the bow as we crossed the moonlit Rufiji, I allowed myself to be enchanted by the soft cool air, the silvery river reaching into the forest, the dark trees rising toward a starry sky and, best of all, by the perhaps delusive sense that I belonged.

Slightly before midnight we reached Dar. Suleiman hopped off as close to home as four-wheeled transportation could get him, and soon the Land Rover's headlights were playing on my own dark quiet house. Andrew, as usual, carried my gear into the foyer dominated by the cosmic Makonde, then turned to go, which seemed wrong to me. Surely a night cap was in order.

"You can't leave now," I said.

"No," he said.

I never got around to pouring the cognac.

By the time Mary arrived to prepare my breakfast, Andrew was gone. That was the beginning of a risky double life.

20

A pink envelope lay beside my plate when I sat down to breakfast. "From Mr. Virgilio," Mary said, which told me all I needed to know even before I read its peppy pink contents. A baby shower was in the offing. Wednesday evening, at seven. Plop in the middle of inspection week. Monumentally bad timing for me—and for Kiki and Milly and Clive's wife, all of whom had probably ripped open their own pink envelopes. But how were Nancy and Virgilio to know? And how was I to find an appropriate gift for an American infant in Dar-es-Salaam? I hadn't the slightest idea.

Meanwhile, it was Inspection Day One, which opened predictably with a gathering of Americans and senior FSNs in Clive's office. Once Milly had served us all with coffee, Clive poured on the charm and wit, performing the kick-off round of introductions. Joanna Delphin and Daniel Gilmore were well-seasoned colleagues, he said, with experience at posts large and small. Between them, he continued, they'd racked up sixty-seven years of service on all continents, excepting Antarctica, "which, oddly enough," he noted, "plays no role in the Cold War."

That was worth a chuckle. So was Delphin's clarification. "All those years!" she groaned, before pointing to her male colleague. "Mostly his."

"Meaning I'm wiser," Gilmore grinned.

"Looks like we're in good hands," Clive smiled, eliciting courteous smiles in return.

So much for the humanizing prelude. Next came the administrative boiler plate involving accountability, transparency and the assertion that inspections aren't witch-hunting expeditions. "We're looking for best practices," Gilmore declared. "Ways for all of us to achieve maximum effectiveness."

"And don't worry," Delphin added. "Inspections have nothing to do with your annual performance reviews. We're looking at the post as a whole."

And so on. Doing their best to make a script seem spontaneous, the pair emphasized the utter routineness of their mandated snooping operation, barely mentioning the waste, fraud, graft or incompetence they'd rightly pounce on, should they uncover the least hint thereof. And since inspectors come in twos, Gilmore said, they could keep an eye on one another. That was supposed to be funny, too.

Phoney jolliness aside, Delphin and Gilmore seemed nice enough, and I was pretty sure they didn't suffer from a neurotic compulsion to find gross error wherever they went. But asserting that a bad inspection report was an academic exercise with no blowback implications for the individuals involved was a trifle disingenuous. Word gets around.

All our questions having been more or less answered, the meeting broke up. As we moved to file out of his office, Clive held me back, tasking me to accompany Gilmore and Delphin to the Embassy for a meeting with the Ambassador. Juma was waiting. Off we went. Smiling to myself, I pointed out the landmarks that Clive had shown to his fresh-off-the-plane Information Officer.

As Ambassador James Freeman ushered Delphin and Gilmore into his office, I prepared to join Gina. We'd chat, I assumed, while the discussion proceeded behind closed doors. Not to be. Freeman paused, hand on doorknob. "Won't you join us?" he suggested. A good sign, I hoped, and scampered in.

Ritual inquiries involving travel, accommodations, postings and mutual friends having been disposed of, Freeman needed no prompting to satisfy the inspectors' need for information. He was enormously pleased with his colleagues across town, he said. Coordination and communications were excellent, and the positives built around the words initiative, energy, dedication and creativity rolled on and on. All this from the hyper-critical, super-demanding James Freeman, whose lair I'd been so afraid to enter! And then came the topper: he'd particularly enjoyed working with me.

My face felt so hot it seemed ready to skip the blushing stage and burst into flame. I searched for a strong, modest, credible response. "It's been an honor," I said. "And I've learned so much, working with you."

There was a phone call then, possibly contrived. Freeman apologized for having to take it, and that was that.

As we passed by her desk, I gave Gina a surreptitious thumbs up. She smiled, rose and saw us to the lobby. Our next stop was Clive's house, where the inspectors would be lunching. On the way back to the office, I asked Juma what he thought of Delphin and Gilmore. "They seem nice," he said. He hadn't been hanging around diplomats for nothing.

"Yes," I agreed.

Waiting back in my own cubbyhole, I did a little rehearsing for my post-lunch, private interview. Thanks to James Freeman, it went very well, meaning that, before it was over, it was easy for me to surface the sensitive issue I needed to raise. There wasn't enough work for an IO *and* a PAO to do in Dar-es-Salaam, I confided. That being the case, would the powers- that-be react favorably should I seek to curtail my present assignment in order to apply for a more challenging position?

"It's not our decision, you know," Joanna Delphin reminded me.

"Yes," I said. "But I'd like your advice. I wouldn't like my impatience to reflect badly on Clive."

"Not likely," Gilmore said. "Ambition's not a dirty word."

"Actually," Delphin said, "there's a slot that's going to be listed soon. Something that might interest you. It would be a stretch, but with Freeman's good wishes—"

"You heard him. He might object."

"He's a pro," Delphin said. "He'd understand."

"Besides," said Gilmore, "he'll be packing up in a few months anyway. The word is he doesn't want to extend."

"I'm not surprised," I said. "So where?" I asked, turning to Delphin.

"Keep an eye on the listings," she said. "You'll know it when you see it."

Anxieties laid to rest, I remembered the upcoming baby shower and mentioned it to Delphin. "You'd be welcome," I said.

Pleading jet lag and a heavy schedule, Delphin begged off, while wishing the very best for baby Angelica and her parents.

And so I turned my attention to hunting up a baby gift during a whirlwind visit to the outdoor market, where I snatched up a menagerie of animals carved in sandalwood, each about six inches high. The gift was not entirely successful. My impala, it turned out, had horns like twisted rapiers. My giraffe had long thin legs with sharp hooves. My crocodile was pointy fore and aft, and my elephant, naturally, had tusks. To me the little animals had come across as cute. As Mama Nancy saw it, their pointy parts might put out an eye. And so, one by one, she examined the little animals, pronounced them charming and set them aside.

"I'm awfully sorry," she said.

"I should have known," I said.

"She'll love them when she's a little bigger."

That left the hippo.

"All curves," I pointed out. "Like a lumpy egg."

Nancy nodded. The hippo would pass.

But the hippo was too fat for Anglica to get her little fingers around, so Tubby too found itself relegated to the buffet.

I wasn't the only childless friend who'd turned up with a gift that entailed deferred gratification. Agnes had brought an exquisitely illustrated edition of *Le Petit Prince* in English. Its cover featured the funny-looking baobab trees that I had found so fascinating as a child, never dreaming that I'd live in Africa and see them close up. *Le Petit Prince* joined my animals on the buffet. "She'll love it when she's older," Nancy said.

Most guests—all women, of course, some from our own embassy or from friendly diplomatic missions, others from UN agencies or NGOs, plus a few locals—had chosen their tributes more successfully. The hit of the shower, the ladies agreed, was an eye-catching, handmade crib quilt constructed from bright African cottons by Clive's wife, whose eminently portable hobby had brought her honors in many quilting competitions.

Angelica's favorite, however, was Milly's gift, an ivory bangle carved all over with leaves and flowers resembling orange blossoms. Much to Milly's dismay, the bangle slid off almost as soon as Milly had slipped it onto Angelica's tiny wrist. "I got the smallest size," she said, defensively. However, although Angelica had no interest in personal adornments, she'd just acquired the perfect teething ring. Into her mouth it went. To gum. To chew. To gurgle over.

"This young lady has very good taste," Milly proclaimed.

But Nancy wasn't so sure that ivory was safe. Frowning at her baby daughter, who'd begun to wave the bangle over her head where she could see it, all the while emitting unmistakably happy noises, she attempted to wrest the bangle away, unclamping tiny fingers, one by one. Success for Nancy brought ear-splitting protest from a very frustrated baby. Wailing and more wailing.

"For god's sake, Nancy, do something," pleaded Virgilio, the only man in the room.

"If babies were stereos," one of the mission wives said, laughing, "you could turn down the volume."

"If babies were machines," said another mother, "they'd be boring."

"When babies get what they want," Clive's wife observed, "they stop crying."

Virgilio agreed. "I'm sure it's okay," he said.

So Angelica got her bracelet back. Screeching subsided into contented gurgles.

"This is one little girl who's going to be all right," Milly said.

And she would be, I thought. Insulated with a healthy layer of baby fat, protected by all the recommended injections, nourished on plenty of milk from a healthy mother, sleeping in a fully screened house, with the US. Government ready to fly her off to Frankfurt at the first sign of complications beyond the ability of the Embassy doctor to treat, she'd revel in all the toys and ornaments she wanted and, eventually, go to a first rate university.

I thought of Alice and baby Rose, now a toddler, who'd been so bright and energetic when I been with her most recently. But I'd also seen a dark little face collapsed against a breast that was only a pillow. With Rose too weak to suckle, Alice had been reduced to moistening her lips with a milk-saturated napkin. I could hardly bear to watch. Rose had pulled through that crisis, and several others. Alice was a nurse, after all. She did her best for all the other children in Alipolaka, too, but reliable access to vaccines and antibiotics would have helped a lot more.

My thoughts were interrupted by a call to admire the cake and have a slice—or two. The cake, several layers tall, was iced in pale pink with darker rosettes on each tier, a major production. The wine, appropriately, was a rosé. I cut myself a fat wedge, appropriated a glass of wine and looked about for Agnes, who was already gravitating toward me. Her slice of cake, predictably, was about half the size of mine.

"I used to take babies for granted," I said, as we found adjacent chairs.

"Well, lots of them get born," Agnes conceded. "After that it's a crap shoot."

"What put you in such a foul mood?" I asked.

"Martin."

I gasped. "Oh no!"

"Not that. He has cancer. That's why he was losing weight."

"I'm so sorry."

"Cigarettes," she said. "I told him—and told him."

"And the odds?"

She shook her head. "Not good."

"Bummer," I murmured, feeling stupid because I couldn't think of anything better to say.

"But," said Agnes, rousing herself, "I have good news about Hasina."

"She and Noor are safe in the U.S.?"

"No. Said came to his senses. He told his mother off, after which his father told him off. They're looking for their own house near the university."

"Thank God," I said. "I hated the thought of Hasina and Noor running this way and that to evade immigration authorities."

21

I wasn't surprised to find the Suzuki in the driveway when I got home from Angelica's shower. A yen for civilization overcame the Baboon People from time to time and they knew where to find a simulacrum at least. Rushing in, on the verge of calling out, "So wonderful to see you!" I found myself in a temple of doom. No smiles. No bear hugs. Just morose expressions.

"What's wrong?" I asked.

Mary, who'd come to know and like Phil and Eileen, had seen to their comfort, serving drinks and snacks. Phil had gone for whiskey, a worrisome sign. In my experience, he drank the hard stuff only when bad things happened. The day of the blood-sampling fiasco, for example. The possibility of an unsuccessful grant application sprang immediately to mind. Or a grant renewal so stingy it would entail painful cutbacks in Baboon Camp operations.

"John's been arrested," Phil said.

"For what?" I demanded.

"Hang on tight!" Eileen advised. "For poaching!"

"Or aiding and abetting," Phil said. "The police were pretty vague. When we got back to camp this afternoon, we found a whole bunch of them, armed to the teeth, waiting to pounce."

"John poaching! That's absurd," I said.

"The officers had already ransacked the camp," Eileen said. "Papers scattered. Kitchen door kicked in. The Mahoneys loved it. They got into everything. Including the fridge."

"I tried to reason with them," Phil said. "John's with *us* most of the time. Everyone knows that. If we're poachers, I'm a yellow baboon!"

"So tell me," demanded Eileen. "Just when could John be running around with poachers?"

"At night?" I suggested. "A moonlight rendezvous?"

Elaine looked alarmed and peeved. "It's not funny."

"Where is John now?" I asked.

"In Dar, I think," Phil said. "And the authorities want to talk to us tomorrow. That's why we're here. We need advice. We want to help John, but who can we trust? My hunch is that someone very important wants him out of the way."

"Probably," I said. "He's too honest and he loves elephants."

"So what do we do?" Eileen asked.

"Right now, we call Virgilio," I decided. "He's the expert."

Virgilio, still in recovery from the hen party forced upon him by fatherhood, was willing to hop into his car and drive right over. That wouldn't be necessary, the Cheyneys felt, if they could ply him with questions over the phone. I joined in, on the extension, the best we could do with the simple phone systems of the day.

"Sure, shoot!" Virgilio said.

Question one was basic: would Phil and Eileen be taken into custody? Not unless they'd broken Tanzanian law, Virgilio replied, which they probably hadn't. What's more, he continued, they had lots of influential friends and the Embassy had a list of good lawyers, which meant that false charges wouldn't stick, even though the U.S. Embassy, as such, had limited leverage, thanks to our tiny aid program and stance against socialism. "But it won't come to that," Virgilio said. "I'm pretty sure of it." The worst case scenario for Phil and Eileen—"You won't like this," Virgilio warned—would be having their visas revoked, although an outcry from primatologists around the world would probably prevent the Baboon Camp itself from being closed down. As for John, protests and publicity might work. They might also be counter productive. "That's the gist," Virgilio concluded. "Sleep on it, and we'll talk more tomorrow, if you'd like."

"No comfort for John," Phil observed, once we'd hung up.

"Andrew's a resource," I said. "He's amazingly well connected."

"He's on it," Phil said. "We tracked him down before we came here."

I mentioned Luke Kupinga. He had the clout. But would he be willing to expend the political capital?

Phil poured himself a third Scotch and splashed a bit more into my glass, too. "You know, I've invested most of my career in this country. But Tanzania's not the only place with baboons. Eileen and I will be just fine. John's more vulnerable—"

"He could lose his job," I guessed.

"Then he could work for us," Eileen suggested.

"Maybe not," Phil said. "The camp's on Park Service land. At any rate, we'd need to raise salary money, too."

"So we've got to work a little harder on that fellowship," Eileen said.

"What fellowship?" I asked, thinking that Kiki might help. Might John be eligible for a Fulbright, for example?

"John's aiming for a doctorate," Phil said. "I've tried to talk him out of it. His work here is too important. I never dreamed he'd be in danger."

"He'll be okay," I declared. "We'll make sure of it. Somehow."

But rescuing John wouldn't save the wild elephant population from a likely fate of survival only through semi-domestication, as I saw it. Merely to be partially insulated from the depredations of farmers and ivory hunters they needed preserves and parks. They needed dedicated rangers like John. They needed financial support from the millions of global well-wishers who'd fallen in love with them.

As I had.

My theory was this: we see in elephants our best selves. Smart. Sensitive. Social. Infants are protected. Adolescents are taught to behave. Males make babies not trouble. Savvy old ladies lead. The dead are mourned and perhaps remembered. With all their wrinkles and their ponderous gait, elephants aren't the most graceful or beautiful creatures on the savanna, but they're violent only when provoked. As, rarely, by lions, who seem to know they'll lose nine times out of ten should they try to snatch a delectable-looking baby. Against heavily armed trophy collectors and gangs of poachers, however, the most hulking, most enraged bull elephant hasn't a chance.

Furious and frustrated, I invented an alternative self. Me as Super Jumbo, the pitiless avenger. And oh! what I'd do, if I could. I'd wrap my trunk around the villain. I'd trample him with my big round feet. I'd use my gloriously gleaming tusks to pierce him through and through. His body I'd leave to be pecked and gnawed at, or just to rot, like the tusk-deprived, dead elephant I'd seen in the bush one day with Andrew and Rafiq. Swollen from the heat into a great gray mountain, its wrinkles were so perfectly smoothed out that it might have been a balloon waiting to float down Fifth Avenue on Thanksgiving Day. It smelled like any other corpse, however. Vultures swooped and dived to frighten us away from their dinner.

Meanwhile, back in my living room, I remembered that I'd eaten nothing but cake since lunchtime. "Anyone hungry?" I asked. Mary had already gone home, but I could boil some rice and heat up some leftover stew. Phil and Eileen declined in favor of an early bedtime. They were wiped out, and the day ahead was likely to be daunting.

Abandoned to a solitary supper, I mulled over my own situation. I, too, needed someone trustworthy and sympathetic to talk to. At the baby shower I'd been tempted to confide in Agnes. A dose of Gallic wisdom, please! And yet, with her, as with Phil and Irene, I restrained myself. Of what importance was my emotional comfort compared to Martin's cancer? Or Hasina's mended marriage? Or John's predicament?

I needed to stop worrying about me and start thinking about birds, which I did, reluctantly. On trips with Andrew I'd met so many impressive birds. How many of them could I remember by name? Very few, which was pathetically consistent with my low bird recognition score back home. I always noticed the return of birdsong in spring, but I couldn't name the feathery heralds. Summer days without birds fluttering around would be eerie, but my occasional impulse to learn more about them usually vanished as quickly as it arose.

In short, as I'd explained to my friend at the British Council, I'd been given a task for which I was totally unqualified. He shook his head and said I had the wrong approach. Delphin and Gilbert would identify the birds. My job was only to deliver them to the right spot.

"Which is?" I prodded.

There was, he reminded me, a resort hotel on the beach north of Dar.

"I've been there," I nodded.

"Well," he continued, "on the road to the hotel, shortly before you actually reach it, you'll spot a track going off to the right. It's tricky. No paving. No signs. Turn there, keep going for a while, and pretty soon you'll be circling a marsh. Bird heaven." Easier said than done, I suspected, but I trusted my pal. I also trusted my own navigational skills. How far wrong could I go? On the other hand, the very thought of anything going wrong with two inspectors aboard was harrowing.

"Wish me luck," I said.

"Wait—take this," he said. Lying on his desk, buried til then under a chaos of papers, was a book, *Birds of Africa.* It was heavy. It was glossy. It was full of fabulous photos of beautiful birds. "The Bible," he said. "Not very portable, but complete."

"They probably have a copy," I said. "At home, anyway."

"Take it," he insisted. "It'll make you look good."

I was driving my own car when I picked up Delphin and Gilmore at Clive's house, where they were staying. I'd bought it while I was in Washington preparing for my assignment to Dar, a Subaru station wagon, with four wheel drive and clearance comfortably higher than a normal sedan's. In the snowy mountain West, where I came from, it was a favorite, which suggested that it might also be a good bush vehicle. Once when Andrew's Land Rover was out of commission, we'd used it for some lion-watching. Off road it handled well and its steadiness was mightily appreciated when I had to drive aboard a river ferry via two planks. Best of all that day: an engine so quiet that the lions barely noticed our approach.

Garlanded with the heavy-looking binoculars and cameras of the bird watching clan, the inspectors were ready to go as soon as I pulled up in front of Clive's house. Delphin's face was shaded by a floppy straw hat. Gilmore wore a photographer's vest with pockets for specialized lenses and the many rolls of film required in a pre-digital era. He chose the back seat. Delphin sat up front. Counting on me to make the inspectors happy, Clive waved us off. "Good luck," he called. "Happy shooting!"

The bird book I'd borrowed from the British Council turned out to be unfamiliar to both my charges, who passed it back and forth with audible enthusiasm. "Look at this!' "Oh wow!" On the one hand, their pleasure pleased me. On the other, I feared that the book's gorgeous bird images were setting up expectations that couldn't possibly be met in a single spot on a single day. Figuring that truth is the best defense, I apologized for my lack of expertise and enlisted their assistance in locating our destination. "I've never been there," I confessed, "and the turnoff, I'm told, is fairly obscure. We'll have to keep our eyes peeled."

By then we were on the narrow paved road that led to the hotel. Trees and bushes grew sparsely in the sandy soil to either side of the pavement. There was no ground cover to speak of. All of which, I hoped, would make it easy to spot the little track we were looking for. And so, barely into double digits on the speedometer, we crept along. The land was mostly flat, the road mostly straight—until an unexpected curve brought us face to face with the hotel, whose green lawns were about to surround us. Somehow we'd missed the track.

"Don't worry," Delphin said. "Now we know exactly where to look."

U-turn completed, I drove so deliberately it's a wonder we didn't stall, the perfect word for what my nicely reborn career was about to do, I thought glumly.

Gilmore cleared his throat, probably in pursuit of an intonation that wouldn't sound critical. "Are you sure this is the right road?"

"It must be," I said. "It leads to the only hotel." I was launching into further justification when Delphin interrupted.

"Stop!" she cried. "Look! There!"

We spent the next many minutes in earnest debate. Were we staring at the faint traces of a seldom-used track nearly erased by runoff from a heavy rain? Telltale tread patterns might be lacking, but look! surely there were hints of parallel tire tracks. In retrospect, I believe we were unconsciously colluding to deny what all of us knew: when a tide slowly ebbs, it often carves a multitude of little channels in the sand.

Just to be sure, I got out and walked for a few yards along a surface compacted to a firmness that allowed no footprints. It reminded me of beaches in New Jersey and Florida, where people can drive safely for miles. Only at low tide, of course. Meanwhile, I decided, it was a surface the Subaru could easily handle.

"So?" I ventured.

Delphin looked at Gilmore. Gilmore looked at Delphin. Each and both looked at me. After an extended ritual of eyebrow raising, shoulder shrugging, lip pressing and much frowning, Gilmore took the plunge. "Let's give it a try."

"Nothing ventured nothing gained," Delphin agreed.

"Here we go," I said.

We rolled off the pavement and headed toward bird heaven. Very soon it was clear to me that our margin of safety was narrow indeed. If I veered to the right where the land rose, we'd surely bog down in loose, dune-like sand. Straying leftward would strand us in soggy wet sand. To say that I was tensing up would understate my anxiety.

Meanwhile, where were the damned birds? Delphin surveyed the scrubby woods to the right. Gilmore fixed his eyes toward the marsh, beyond which I saw a forest of mangroves extending along the shoreline between us and open ocean.

166

Their aerial roots were markedly visible, which suggested that the tide was low. But how low? And when would it turn, if it hadn't turned already? Above all, how long before the nice firm sand I was driving on became treacherous? I should have had an answer to that question. I didn't because I hadn't thought to consult the tide charts for the day.

Delphin touched my arm and whispered, "This would be a good place to stop." I couldn't see why, but I complied. Conferring briefly, she and Gilmore decided to head in different directions. Whichever way they went, they might soon be out of sight. "Don't get lost," I pleaded.

"Don't worry." Delphin laughed. "We've got breadcrumbs."

"That's what I'm afraid of," I replied. "Birds eat breadcrumbs. Just shout. I'll hear you."

Then came the boring part, for me. I riffled through the bird book. I got out of the car and walked around a bit. I saw frogs and salamanders as I stood at the edge of the marsh. Also some herons wading and fishing. Or were they cranes? Or egrets? I didn't see any crocodiles, but the marsh water was turgid. An eight-footer could lunge and grab my ankle before I saw it. What I really wanted was a good book. A suspenseful police procedural, maybe. All words. No photos.

After a while I began to realize that I'd been absorbing, subconsciously, signs that the water level was rising. Things sticking out of the water, like twigs or rocks, weren't they sticking out less? And weren't my footprints getting a bit moist? From Sunday excursions to beaches north of the hotel, I knew how fast the tide could rise, which suggested that a strategic retreat might be wise. Much as I hated to be a killjoy, the bird watching expedition was over.

I didn't shout. I reached into the car and leaned on the horn.

Delphin and Gilmore converged from opposite directions and strikingly different habitats, one wet, one dry. They'd found impressive specimens, they reported, some rare. All had been recorded on slide or print film, which would have to be developed before the images could be shared. Such was photography in pre-digital days! Time permitting, however, they would switch paths, giving each an opportunity to lengthen a life list by adding birds only the other had seen so far. Infected as I was by their enthusiasm, "tide rising" was not a message that gave me pleasure. It certainly wasn't a message either Delphin and Gilmore wanted to receive, as I could tell by the facial expressions they allowed me to see.

Disappointment. Frustration. Annoyance. And, finally, happily, something like resignation.

"I guess we have no choice," Delphin sighed.

Gilmore nodded.

"I'll turn the car around," I said.

Rising water meant that the margin for error had shrunk, but my car's turn radius had not. Three-quarters of the way into a very tight maneuver, rear wheels began to spin in place, spitting sand. The car was stuck. Going down, not forward.

"So we push," Gilmore said. But first, he advised, we should gather sticks and leafy branches to stuff under the rear wheels. "For traction," he explained.

That done, I shifted into first gear and pressed lightly on the accelerator. Greenery went flying. Wheels spun uselessly.

"Let me try," Gilmore offered.

How humiliating! A man taking over! I considered a thanks-but-no-thanks, but good sense prevailed.

Gilmore applied the gas. We women pushed. The car rocked back and forth, back and forth, until, at the apex of a push that felt no different from the others, a suspenseful pause was followed by a spurt of traction that propelled the car onto what passed, barely, for terra firma. Sorely tempted to reclaim the wheel, I resisted. Getting out of there as soon as possible trumped pride and dignity.

"I'm so sorry," I said, once we'd shouted with joy and relief at having all four wheels back on pavement.

"Don't be silly," Delphin replied. "What an adventure!"

Thanking Gilmore for his deft driving, I labored through a painful little speech intended to make sure that the whole post didn't get downgraded as a result of my recklessness. "Don't blame Clive," I said. "Don't say we're all a bunch of idiots. It's me. I'm the one who rushes in where fools—"

"—and the timid would fear to go," Delphin said. "And so we had an adventure. It's not the end of the road."

"So relax," Gilmore said. "I bet there's a bar at the hotel."

"On my tab," I declared.

"There you are." Delphin laughed. "Your punishment."

22

It wasn't long before John turned up at the Baboon Camp. The police had released him without apologies or explanations. What his crime was, who'd got him arrested, who'd enabled his release—he had no idea. Phil and Eileen were equally mystified, but Andrew had suspicions that he refused to share, hugely to my annoyance.

"It's better not to know," he said.

"Since when?" I demanded.

"A little knowledge—" he began.

"—is a cliché!" I snapped.

Andrew and I were sharing the guest hut at the Baboon Camp, the first of many such Saturdays, which delighted Eileen, who claimed she'd sensed the chemistry from day one. Meanwhile, by keeping his hunches strictly to himself, Andrew was infuriating Phil.

"John deserves to know," he insisted. "Who are you protecting?"

"You," Andrew replied. "What you don't know—"

"—might hurt us a lot!" Phil declared.

We heard a lion then. *Heh! Heh! Heh!* That resonant assertion of privilege brought us, almost, back to ourselves, good friends who shared more than we didn't. John was free and he'd kept his job, which was terrific, we all agreed. But he wasn't feeling safe, I insisted, so it was still three to one.

"For god's sake, Andrew, spill the beans," Phil demanded.

John spoke up then, defending Andrew. "I have hunches, too," he said. "What I need is proof."

As was right and proper, John had the last word.

The logistics of being together on the following weekend were more complicated. Clive had asked me to represent him at a United Nations-sponsored conference on "Media and Development" in Arusha, an inland town that was evolving into a new capital for Tanzania. Dar wasn't a sophisticated metropolis, but its status as a port and ex-colonial capital made it far more cosmopolitan than Arusha, which also lacked the charm (and ghastly history) of Bagamoyo. Two years in Dar was going to be quite bearable, I'd decided. Two nights in Arusha would be more than enough.

Milly had reserved two hotel rooms, one originally for Clive, which I occupied, and one for Andrew, which was underused. We managed like lovers in a French farce, exercising extreme vigilance to avoid comical hallway encounters with people we knew—the complication being that, between us, we knew most every one at the conference. I was, by then, a familiar face in media, NGO and official Tanzanian circles. Andrew was all that and also on friendly terms with my press attaché counterparts, including Dieter, with whom I hadn't communicated since he'd flown off to Pemba and I'd gone to Kilwa.

Dieter hunted me up during the break following a pompous, vacuous, dragged out welcome by the Minister of Information, who set the tone for dreary days of defining familiar problems, offering predictable solutions and incentivizing (horrible word!) actions already known to be futile. "Do you need a beer as much as I do?" he asked, as we took a breather in preparation for the next onslaught. On the usefulness of beer our colleague at the British High Commission agreed. He joined us, followed by others, minus our habitually stand-offish Soviet counterpart.

And so it went in Arusha. Session after session. Beer after beer. And the hotel food wasn't so hot either. The nights with Andrew were my compensation.

Agnes, at least, had ducked the conference. Declaring "been there, done that," she sent a substitute. Had my only truly intimate friend in Dar been around for the socializing in the evening, she might have teased me for reaching the yawning stage so much earlier than usual. Often I was tempted to tell her about Andrew, but she took sex way too casually. Inevitably, though absolutely guilelessly, she'd blab. Kiki, too, was out of the loop, in her case to prevent ugly rents in the fabric of office life.

Rafiq, however, knew everything. He had to, but he'd never do anything to hurt Andrew. What's more, thoroughly hating a government that marginalized home-grown Asians as if they were foreigners, he minimized contact with bureaucrats and politicians, except for Luke Kupinga, with whom he'd gone to school. As an occasional safari companion, Luke was always good company, but his professional responsibilities required him to interact with influential people I also had to deal with. Titillating allusions from him could hurt me—and Andrew. I'd escape, in due time, to other posts in other countries. Andrew was stuck in Dar. And we were stuck with Luke some weekends.

The Luke conundrum was oppressively on my mind as we caravanned toward the Selous shortly after the Abuja conference. Andrew rode with Luke. Riding shotgun with Rafiq, I chatted about this and that, while debating, within myself, the big question: sleeping arrangements for the weekend. Fess up? Sneak around? Keep it quiet? Meanwhile, I was keenly aware that Suleiman, no longer confined to the roof, was in a position to hear (and pass on) whatever we said on the road. I didn't believe that he was totally ignorant of English, which made his presence in the back seat a bit inhibiting, but my egalitarian heart hated the caste-ridden rituals of traditional safari life.

Once, just for the fun of it, I declared that it was time for me to ride on the roof. Rafiq tried to discourage me. I called him a killjoy.

It was exhilarating at first. Feeling the wind smacking me in the face, I was a powerful jet approaching the lift off moment. Then, spreading my arms like wings, I was an ethereal creature soaring freely above my earth-bound friends. But only while the going was fairly smooth. As soon as things got bouncy-jouncy, my hands were clamped to the carrier rails, which kept me secure, except when I needed them to shield my face from whip-like branches that left blood-oozing scratches on my arms instead. Thereafter, our helpers rode inside, unless game spotters were needed.

And so, as Rafiq and I chatted about inconsequential things, Suleiman sat silently in the back seat, so silently that Rafiq was suddenly opening up as if he and I were alone. "I've had it with Tanzania," he said.

"You *what!*" I exclaimed.

"My father, his father, me—we've worked so damned hard," he said. "We've built what should be a successful company, an honest company, too, except for one thing—all the drones and hacks I have to pay off. That's where the money goes. And I still don't get respect. Or feel secure."

"I hear you," I said.

"But no more," he declared. "Everything's up for sale. The garage. The trucks. The house. We're leaving for the U.K. At least my kids will have a fair shake—"

"You've heard about Pakie bashing, I suppose," I said.

"I've also heard about Pakistani immigrants who became MP's," Rafiq retorted. "Picture that in Tanzania! And some Pakistanis have been knighted, too. Sir Rafiq Ghulam Khan. How does that sound?"

"Magical," I said. "Have you told Andrew? He'll be pretty cut up."

"I know," Rafiq said. "I'm working up to it."

"You're putting me into a pretty awkward position," I said.

"I'm sorry," Rafiq said.

"This weekend—tell him this weekend," I urged.

Rafiq sighed. "I'll try."

"You'd better," I said.

Reaching the Rufiji, we coasted downhill to a gloriously short ferry queue, and joy of joys! The ferry we needed was already approaching our landing. In hardly more than an hour we had crossed the river and, having already collected the ever helpful Charles in Alipolaka, we'd soon be stopping at the Ranger Station to pick up Sylvanus, our warden for the occasion. This weekend there would be no desperate scramble to set up camp and scour the bush for protein before dark.

Nice dream! Wishful thinking!

A fairly ancient police vehicle stood outside the modest ranger station, where I'd never seen a mere car parked before. Its hood was in the "say ahhh" position, and a young man in a uniform that shouted policeman, not game warden, was fiddling with its innards. We'd barely come to a stop when a large, middle-aged man with the appearance and manner of a high ranking officer, burst out of the station. Trailing him was another young policeman, along with the Chief Warden, whom I recognized. Last of all came a man dressed like a villager. He climbed onto a bicycle that had been leaning against a tree and peddled away. Not one of the five looked happy.

The Ranger Station's radio was old and capricious. It had functioned properly, evidently, when the Chief Warden had called for assistance in handling a possible murder brought to his attention by the now vanished cyclist, who'd been persuaded to hang around long enough to brief the investigating party. Since that urgent SOS, however, the ancient radio had decided on a long nap, thus complicating the crisis when the police vehicle sputtered into camp and died. Unable to summon a mechanic, the investigators were stranded miles from the scene of the crime—unless the Chief Inspector was in better physical shape than he looked.

All this Rafiq and I learned from the Chief Warden, who was heartened by the sight of old acquaintances hovering, impatiently, just outside his station. Sylvanus had refused to budge until he assured himself that all was well with his harried boss.

Speaking guardedly, lest he be overheard, the Chief Warden aired his current woes, his long-standing gripes, his deep resentment. "Yeah, the poachers and criminals have the upper hand. So who gets the blame? Me. The bad manager. Our radios go dead. Our guns jam. Our vehicles break down. We have too few men. So what have I got to manage? Not much. But who am I? Nobody. So—sure!—blame me!" he grumbled. "But don't quote me," he added, glancing toward the Chief Inspector, currently confirming the bad news about the cranky radio to his mechanic manqué, who had snapped to attention from a restful squat by the vehicle he couldn't fix.

Rafiq mimed the sealed lips pledge, then pumped the Chief Warden for more information. According to the cyclist, who'd been dispatched by the victim's brother, some young lad chasing runaway chickens had stumbled across the body of a man with a great gash of a wound. Since he had obviously bled to death, his demise couldn't be assigned to not-so-benign natural causes. Like a heart attack. Or a stroke. And the cause of the gash? Most likely a dreadful goring from an angered buffalo, according to the cyclist. The clearing where the body had lain long enough to grow cold was carpeted with buffalo tracks.

"That's all I know," the Chief Warden said. "But I can tell you this: the story doesn't hold water. That man knew his buffalo."

"Sounds suspicious enough to warrant an investigation," Rafiq agreed.

"Who was the victim?" Andrew asked. He and Luke had ambled over from Luke's Land Rover.

"The Headman. A good man. One of the best."

Rafiq grunted as if he'd been punched. Andrew pressed his lips together. They had known and liked the Headman for years—for his humor, for his wisdom, for his hospitality, for his cooperation in the endless war with poachers. I'd met him, too. We had often passed through his village, a hamlet really, stopping sometimes to pay respects and gather information on the availability of game.

The need of the moment, however, was transportation. "Can you help me out?" the Chief Warden asked.

Assuming the posture of authority, Luke stepped up. "I'll drive them," he said.

"We'll be right behind you," Andrew said,

Luke looked hesitant—no, he looked resistant, I thought.

"In an emergency," Andrew insisted, "two cars beat one."

"Better get going," the Head Warden advised.

"Righto!" said Luke.

Luke led the police team to his Land Rover, where he held the door open for the Chief Inspector. Unaware that he was seriously out-ranked by this courteous hunter in khakis, the latter showed no appreciation for the gesture.

Since the Land Rover would be over-crowded with six passengers crammed in, Charles and Sylvanus ignored the new dispensation. Riding on the roof, they missed Andrew's little lecture on the dynamics of village politics. Dissonance and conflict are avoided as much as possible, he told me, but when problems do arise a council of elders can usually settle things more or less to the satisfaction of all. As for unresolved disagreements, they rarely erupt in violence, he said. Not even fist fights, let alone murder. "There's something very strange going on," he concluded.

"Enough of the academics," Rafiq complained. "What about a jealous husband? An angry father?"

"I doubt it," Andrew replied. "I'd say poachers. He'd been threatened."

"The weapon was a panga, not a gun," Rafiq pointed out.

"A grudge-bearing local could have been bought off," I suggested. "To give it the look of a home grown job."

As suppositions flew up and got shot down, I was increasingly convinced that Andrew's cautionary tales of marauders in the bush were neither fictional nor exaggerated. Maybe I should make my peace with guns, I thought. Maybe I should become a decent shot.

Usually when we entered the village the kiddies would converge on us, begging for rides, for sweets, for a better look at the increasingly familiar white woman. Eventually the adults would tell the young ones to mind their manners. That day, however, the entire population of the village seemed to be milling around like a mob in need of an organizing principle that wasn't available until Luke's Land Rover disgorged its contingent of police officers. People crowded around them. Shouting. Asking questions. Demanding answers. Backed up by Luke and aided by a terrific memory for cliché, the Chief Inspector expressed his condolences and asked for everyone's cooperation in the search for those answers.

That slick, but unfeeling address suggested, to my cynical mind, that the investigation was destined—or designed—to go nowhere. For one thing, the scene of the crime, if such it was, had been irreparably contaminated by the removal of the victim. Even as we arrived, the Headman's womenfolk were preparing his body for burial. Nevertheless, in a ostentatious demonstration of thoroughness, one policeman tromped off with the chicken-chaser to examine the spot where the body had been found. The other went to view the body. Also suspicious: not only did interviews with an array of villagers produce no witnesses, not a single person offered to testify to much of anything. To a man, to a woman, no one volunteered the least hint that anyone might have a motive for harming a universally admired man. And so a comforting consensus emerged. The killer could only have been a buffalo charging so fast and slashing so violently that the fatal wound uncannily resembled a gash inflicted by a panga—

Andrew's discreet inquiries were leading him to mirror my thoughts. "I can see where this is going," he said. " 'Sorry for your loss. Case closed.'"

"Won't Luke keep them honest?" I asked.

"We'll see," he shrugged. "Meanwhile, I've got to see that body."

He had thought of a way to view it, too. He would go to the Headman's house. The widow would recognize him and ask him in. He'd share her sorrows, as he genuinely did. He'd say how desolate he was, which truly was the case. And then he'd ask if he might, maybe, just maybe, say good by to his old friend—

All of which he did, and a very considerate widow had left him alone with her husband's lifeless remains. He emerged absolutely certain that no buffalo was responsible for his friend's death. Nor had the Headman fallen on his own— curiously unfound—panga.

"Someone killed him," Andrew reported, but only to me. "That's why they want him underground asap."

By then, however, the investigation was over. The police were ready to announce their findings. Once again the entire population of the village gathered around.

"Buffalo are notoriously nasty creatures," one policeman said.

"True," Andrew muttered.

"And unpredictable," the other policeman said.

"Yes and no," Andrew murmured.

The first policeman continued, "The Headman, poor fellow, was a victim of that terrible unpredictability."

"Gored to death, I'm sorry to say," the second said, with solemn finality.

The Police Commissioner reiterated his condolences to which Luke, now identified as ranking VIP, added further flowery sympathies. The crowd, having lapsed into funereal quietude, began slowly to disperse.

"Why don't you say something?" I whispered to Andrew.

"Luke's seen everything I've seen," Andrew whispered back. "If he won't speak up, no one's going to listen to me.

"Then something really bad is going on," I said.

Andrew took a deep breath, but exhaled wordlessly. Luke was approaching, to let us know he'd be driving the investigating team back to their headquarters. They'd leave the police car behind, he said, to be dealt with later.

"Good idea," Andrew said.

"After that," Luke added, "I'll head back to Dar."

"Too bad," Andrew said, politely.

"That's life," Luke said.

Andrew watched as Luke walked away. I watched Andrew. His expression changed from bland affability to lip-curling scorn. "Bastard," he said.

"Was he the one who squealed on John?" I asked.

"We'll never know," Andrew said.

I didn't believe him. Earlier I had noticed that Rafiq, normally so generous with his services, hadn't volunteered to examine the crippled police car. When I asked him why, he laughed it off. "I told you," he said. "I'm out of business." But things were clicking together in my own mind. Right from the start, Rafiq had evinced doubts about the professionalism of the investigation. And what, I wondered, did he think of his buddy Luke's contributions? As it turned out, he'd missed a lot—or opted out.

Andrew took leave of the elders. One of them would emerge as the new headman. We collected Charles, Sylvanus and Suleiman from various verandahs, then roused Rafiq, who was draped over the steering wheel, napping. Blinking himself back to consciousness, he estimated, groggily, that we'd reach camp well after dark.

Impending darkness wasn't our worst problem. The Headman's demise had diminished everyone's enthusiasm for hunting, although the prospect of going vegetarian didn't appeal either. Creatively, if not ethically, Rafiq resolved our dilemma. Yes, we had only an impala permit. But twilight is such a deceptive time of day! Mindful as we tried to be, we might target the wrong species en route to camp. Mistakes do happen. And wouldn't it be pretty stupid to let the meat go to waste?

Even Sylvanus, our warden, our watcher, couldn't bring himself to disagree.

"No elephants," I decreed.

Everyone laughed, as I'd intended.

Impala it was, in the end. A lone doe. Instead of zig-zagging through bul-let-stopping tree trunks, she sought to outrun us on the track we were following. Quick and graceful as she was, we were faster. Silly doe, I thought. You should have made us work.

Campsite routines kicked in so smoothly that we might have been robots. Tents were set up, the fire was made, Suleiman worked his magic, and soon we were stuffed to super satiety on kabobs augmented by the canned baked beans that had almost became the heart of our meal. Everyone, by then, had con-tributed to a major reduction in our beer supply, including Suleiman, who was stretched out and snoring well before Charles and Sylvanus had spread their own mats by the fire.

I broke out the Scotch—my fail-safe numbing potion. And so we sat, Andrew, Rafiq, me, whiskey in hand, staring glumly into the fire.

"First John," Andrew said. "Now this."

"Not a coincidence," Rafiq said.

"Probably not," I agreed.

"They slashed him in the throat," Andrew said. "Right where the neck meets the shoulder."

"Where the aorta is," I said. "Or the carotid."

"He didn't have a chance," Andrew said. "And what I saw, Luke saw. He knew, Rafiq. He knew."

"It figures." Rafiq grunted. He picked up a stone and hurled it fiercely into the fire. A geyser of sparks flew up and died. "I am so sick of the whole damned hypocritical system," he declared. "That's why I'm leaving."

And then, as I'd hoped, he let his thinking tumble out. His often frustrated devotion to the family business. The incessant humiliations of being Asian. His soul-searching vacillation in the face of such a big decision. His jumble of dreams and fears for the future. And finally, sadly, the weekends in the bush he'd never enjoy again—and the friends, like Andrew, he'd never see again, unless—

Interrupting himself, Rafiq looked directly at Andrew. "Join us," he said. "You could do a lot better."

"Depends on the meaning of better," Andrew said. Picking up a handful of the dirt our boots had scuffed loose, he let it sift through his fingers. I waited for more. It didn't come.

We sat. We drank. Insects chirred. Overheated wood popped from time to time. Darkness seemed darker.

Waiting for Andrew to unbutton and say something—anything—about Rafiq's imminent departure, I tried to imagine what he must be feeling. Something akin to my husband's shocked-into-silence reaction when I announced that I was leaving him perhaps? The unanticipated equivalence distressed me in terribly tangled up ways. Had I left Moscow and a man who was far from despicable for this, to become a Cold War propagandist in bed with petty poachers? But I was on the better side, wasn't I? And I didn't lie, although I was guilty of de-emphasizing the warts when telling my country's story. For the first time I felt the darkness around us as desolation.

Andrew's words, when they came, came slowly, evenly, quietly. "I'm only surprised you waited so long to make the move," he said. "I'll miss you."

I blamed smoke when my eyes got teary, but smoke had nothing to do with it.

23

An early return to Dar. That was our plan. En route we'd stop in Alipolaka to deposit Charles on his mother's doorstep. We'd also visit Alice, whose cheery disposition, we hoped, would disperse the gloom that sharing a whole bottle of Scotch the night before had only reinforced. We'd present her with a haunch of impala and the contents of the safari first aid kit which—Thank goodness for small favors!—we hadn't had to use.

"Drop me off first," I suggested, as we approached Alice's house. "I'll let her know you'll be along in a few minutes."

The front door was closed, yet unlocked, odd for Alice, but within the range of possibility. My knocking unanswered, I risked a peek and found myself staring into emptiness where a comfy little sitting room had been. No sofa. No lamps. No tables. No ashtrays. No curtains, which I hadn't noticed from the outside. No calendars on the walls. The bedrooms were bare, too, and there wasn't a single bunged up pot or forgotten fork in the kitchen. Had there once been a clinic here? You'd never know. All evidence of the beer business was gone, too. Of Alice herself there was only one hint. The rooms were hospital clean, although a film of dust had accumulated since the last sweeping. Ditto for the outhouse, which I used, despite the empty water barrel.

Waiting for Andrew and Rafiq on what should have been Alice's porch, I was furious with Charles. Scatterbrained youth mindlessly plugging into the routine of the safari—that I understood. But mere minutes ago, as Rafiq slowed and stopped in front of Alice's house, Charles should have remembered. He should have spoken up. Had his mind already strayed to irksome chores only postponed by a respite in the bush? Was he haunted by fears that his father might have stumbled home, full of angry defensiveness after another binge? Was a girl friend in the picture? How could he have been so thoughtless?

Fortunately, as soon as Charles had dashed into his mother's house, his mother had rushed out with the awful news. "Something terrible has happened," she said. "Little Rose is dead."

"Fever," Rafiq said.

Andrew clarified. "Not malaria. Typhoid."

"Typhoid! But how?" I demanded. "Alice boiled every drop of drinking water."

"Rose was toddling around the village with her sisters," Andrew said. "Maybe she was thirsty and someone did what anyone would do. 'Here, sweetie, have a drink.'"

"You can't lock them up," Rafiq sighed.

"And the older girls?" I asked. "Sally and Phyllis?"

"In Dar. With Alice," Rafiq said.

"She hadn't the heart to carry on," Andrew explained.

"Who would?" I demanded. My voice felt—and must have sounded—strangled.

Little Rose. I'd had so many hopes for her. And Alice, my heroine! Would she feel guilty, in time, for abandoning Alipolaka? And how would she manage in Dar, with two daughters and jobs so hard to come by. Agnes might be able to help, I thought. She knew doctors, social workers, the vast NGO community.

"Where in Dar?" I asked.

Alice, supposedly, had a husband who worked in the city. Although hazy about his name, Charles's mother had thrown out a couple of possibilities. Where he might live she didn't know.

"We'll find her," I said. "We have to."

"We can try," Andrew said.

"It won't be easy," Rafiq warned.

Rafiq was right. Street names. Street numbers. They petered out toward the edge of town. And, yes, there was a phone book for Dar, but so what! if the husband had no connection. Nowadays Alice would carry a mobile phone. We'd call her right away on our own smart phones, convey our desolation, hear how she was, learn what she needed. Back then it was easier for people to disappear.

Hollowed out, drained of energy, heavy with grief, I hauled myself into the Land Rover.

All the way back to Dar we spoke hardly a word in English or Kiswahili. The murder of the Headman. Its cover up. The looming departure of Rafiq for the UK. The death of baby Rose. The disappearance of Alice. It was too much to assimilate in little more than twenty four hours. If the pummeling from all those blows was hard on me, the pain had to be immeasurably worse for Andrew—and for Rafiq, who drove us to our respective houses and left us to get through the night as best we could. First Suleiman, who'd inherited the haunch of impala intended for Alice. Then Andrew. Lastly me.

I flopped on the sofa, closed my eyes and let my body go limp as a Raggedy Ann on a trash heap. But I wasn't an empty-headed doll. My mind cycled from hurt to hurt to hurt, around and around and around. I couldn't stand it.

Soon Agnes—who else?—was in my kitchen unwrapping wedges of cheese flown in by her latest Air France admirer. She tore a baguette into manageable pieces, and the wine she poured was impressive. A Medoc, as I recall. Serious offerings from a guy who was pretty serious about her, and vice versa, she admitted, but the refinements were going to be wasted on me that night. Elevated tannin levels? Hints of cherry dominating the finish? Spare me!

Wrapping her arms around me, Agnes let me sob until I could stand a few doses of reality. Yes, she said, she'd been happy to collect all manner of supplies for Alice and her admirable clinic in Alipolaka, but clinics, in her experience, failed more often than they thrived. Why? Politics. Personalities. Financial problems. Sooner or later something or another would almost always do them in. As for dear little Rose, she understood my grief. She shared it, in fact. But she'd warned me a thousand times about attachment. The survival rate for babies in sub-Saharan Africa was appalling.

"Learn to celebrate the ones who make it," she said. "It's easier to bear."

Cold comfort, that, but Agnes had also brought some heartwarming news. About Hasina and Sheik. They had rented a house in an excellent location, near the university for Hasina, almost as close to Sheik's hospital, and there was no more talk about leaving Tanzania. "This could be very good for Alice." Agnes said. "Sheik is well connected in the medical world. He can check around."

"Maybe he can hire her!" I proposed.

"I'll drink to that," Agnes said.

Friends are so important. We allowed ourselves to laugh, and soon I felt restored enough to make inroads on the cheese, appreciate that very fine Medoc and learn enough about the pilot to think that this amour might be the right one for Agnes.

At the office, too, there were heartening developments. Since Lily's philandering husband had been doing well in the export/import business—"The polite term for smuggling," Lily had told me—he'd decided to enhance his image by augmenting his support for the child he'd made with his wife. Already young Jack was wearing new shoes of the sort that filled his classmates with envy, and he had a shelf full of new toys, including cars that skittered around the floor under remote control.

Lily was not enthusiastic. "Who'll buy the batteries?" she asked.

Even more problematic, Papa had taken to dropping in with bags of candy and other goodies.

"So I'm the baddie, setting limits," Lily said.

The largesse might not last, however. The woman who'd seduced her husband had presented him, recently, with a child, his second son. "Not legitimate," Lily noted. "But a son's a son. In the long run, I'll be the loser. Again."

"We have a saying," I told her. "Don't look a gift horse in the mouth."

"That doesn't mean I have to like the situation," Lily retorted. "Meanwhile, the traffic's in your in box, including the cable with the jobs, unfortunately. It's on top."

Lily was referring to the latest announcement of USIA job openings worldwide. Where the positions were. When they had to be filled. A minimum of three job bids was expected of each officer nearing the end of a tour. Here's how it worked: each foreign service officer carried a personal rank; all jobs were also ranked; applicant rank was expected to match job rank. The most qualified bidder was supposed to get the job. That wasn't always the case with the popular or prestigious jobs. Meritocracy meet favoritism. Meanwhile, I took Lily's "unfortunately" to mean I'd been a fairly decent boss.

That should have set me up for the day, but the effect didn't last. I couldn't keep my mind on the job list I needed to analyze. My thoughts dwelt instead on Lily, the wronged woman in a painful triangle, while I, her otherwise admirable boss, was playing the less noble role in another triangle.

Self-flagellation is like quicksand. Once you get sucked into it, it's hard to get out. Kiki saved me. She burst in and threw herself into the chair facing me. "It's over," she said.

"What's over?" I asked.

David would soon be leaving for his Fulbright year in the U.S. He'd miss her, he'd said, as they shared a slow, close-clinching dance at their favorite club. He hoped they could part as friends, he murmured, but a long distance romance made no sense. Surely she agreed.

"What could I say?" Kiki wailed. "It's over."

"There's always Dieter," I said.

Kiki giggled. "Poor Dieter! But, seriously," she continued, "was I being used? Did he assume I could order the Fulbright committee around? Which I can't, as you well know, though I wish I could, sometimes."

"You could ask him," I said.

"Sure!" she hooted, and then she sighed. "But how sad! His application was strong. He didn't need to play games—if that's what he was doing."

I was so proud of Kiki. Dar, an unchallenging post for Information Officers, provided terrific training for neophyte cultural specialists. Over the past year and a half Kiki had been responsible for the success of a whole gamut of programs—speakers, exchanges, exhibits, films, performers. All managed with flair on a stingy budget, the supreme test for any USIA officer, I always felt. Her next post would be Casablanca, but first she had to spend a year learning Arabic.

"No problem." She'd laughed, as she mentioned this little complication. "I'll learn belly dancing, too."

Dar was working well for me, too. I'd arrived on the defensive and full of trepidation. Would Ambassador James Freeman find me as unsatisfactory as the officer I was replacing? Quite the contrary. With Clive already lining up a post-retirement appointment to the advisory board of a not entirely obscure think tank, Freeman floated the idea of my remaining in Dar. Not as IO. As PAO. He could make it happen.

I was surprised and flattered, but far from ready to make a commitment. "I'll think very seriously about it," I said.

If I was tempted, the attraction was anything but professional. There was Andrew, first of all, but my sleep was already being invaded by bouts of pre-separation anxiety vis-à-vis the weekend safaris that might soon be disappearing from my life. No more of the savanna's vast open-faced magic, its blue sky, its acacia umbrellas, its baobabs, its herds of grazers, the crazy wildebeest, the sullen buffalo. No more sun-dappled forests offering tender foliage to stately giraffes, tiny dikdiks, graceful impala. No funny hippos. No lurking alligators. No star-canopied nights fraught with shadowy mysteries beyond the firelight. And how would I exist without elephants in my life?

Or lions? I'd miss them, too. Once, in the Selous, Andrew had parked the Land Rover no more than twenty feet from a family of lions. Like well toned young mothers sharing a bench near the sandbox, two females sprawled comfortably on a shady little knoll. Seven or eight hyper-active cubs gamboled around them, kittenish electrons circling the maternal nuclei. The cubs balanced like acrobats on fallen tree trunks, until they slipped off. They wrestled with one another, turning into tawny fur balls that rolled around, then fell apart. They toyed with the tuft of this or that mama's tail, batting, chewing, tugging. Eventually the mama under attack got annoyed, and a thick furry rope lashed back and forth. Enough!

A dark-maned male with a scar on his nose had napped through most of the action. Waking periodically, he got to his feet, stretched, yawned and let out a funny little whining sound. Sensing no threats, not even from Andrew and me, he resumed his nap, which the cubs rarely dared to interrupt. If ever they did, however, he glared and gave a little growl, a patriarch not to be trifled with.

Andrew and I watched that pride for half a morning. Even then I hated to leave. As youtube would eventually demonstrate, humans are suckers for cats. I'd also developed a strong affection for yellow baboons, especially the mischievous Mahoneys, whom I preferred to the non-acculturated troupe. And I would definitely miss Phil and Eileen.

To bolster all the extra-curricular attractions of Tanzania there was only one compelling job-related argument. Clive's PAO position matched his own rank. One. Moving from my office into his would all but guarantee me a promotion. But I already did most of Clive's work, and I was bored more often than not. Even with a promotion and a raise, two more years of manufacturing things to do would be hard to take.

24

For several weeks after that calamitous weekend, I mourned, resisting all safari-promoting blandishments and throwing myself into ordinary diplomatic life. The Dean of the diplomatic corps, a position always filled by the currently accredited ambassador who'd served longest in Dar, decided it was time for a morale-building beach party at the hotel I'd last visited with Delphin and Gilmore. Since he represented Cuba-supported Angola, the affair was attended by a phalanx of Russians easily identified by their sun-deprived, pale skins and unfashionable beach costumes.

Soon after came the American Embassy's annual Fourth of July reception, when a mob trampled the flawless lawns of the Chancery garden. Aside from the requisite high level Tanzanian dignitaries, our most important local contacts and our many diplomatic colleagues, the party was for each and every American in the country. Development experts escaping the boonies. Missionaries of warring confessions. Idealistic teachers. Intrepid researchers. Endangered species protectors. Young backpackers passing through. A handful of business people. Everybody's kids. Once the opening ceremonies devoted to flag raising, anthem singing and formal toasting had been endured, the Americans chowed down on what they'd really come for: classic American picnic food.

"Anything for a hotdog," Phil said, slathering his with mustard.

Eileen disagreed. "Pizza. That's the real all-American dish." But pizza hadn't been on the menu, she complained

Eileen and Phil were still debating that vital issue when we got back to my house, where they were spending the night.

"What do you think?" Phil demanded of me.

"Easy peasy," I replied. "Cheeseburgers rule. With green chili, in my neck of the woods."

What else claimed my attention during those weeks of hyper-conscientiousness? The Ambassador gave a formal dinner to honor a pair of U.S. congressmen on a fact-finding trip. Their issues? Ivory poaching and Julius Nyerere's notorious socialism. For them Milly organized a visit to the outdoor market, where they made a point of buying makonde figures in rosewood as well as Masai beadwork for their wives. Andrew's photos recorded every segment of the visit. Both Clive and I attended the Ambassador's dinner for the congressmen. My presence, I assumed, was calculated to remind me that Freeman was counting on me to pursue Clive's job.

Far more entertainingly, the Alliance Française sponsored a performance of Jean Genet's "The Maids," a low cost dramatic splash that Kiki envied.

"Just two characters," she noted. "Even we could afford a play like that."

Phil had managed to get John admitted into a PhD program on wildlife management at his own university. "It wasn't hard," he said. "John's over qualified." John had already chosen his thesis topic: jaguar protection in the Southwest. One issue remained: John desperately wanted his family to accompany him, but the Embassy was reluctant to issue the necessary visas.

"If the whole family goes," Virgilio explained, "they might not come back."

"They'd make pretty good Americans," I said.

"So would zillions of other people," Virgilio retorted.

Virgilio caved, eventually. Baboon camp hospitality may have swayed him. Or fatherhood, maybe, had made him more compassionate. Phil and Eileen had it harder. Although they could count on the services of a Park Service substitute as they followed baboons around, they were wrestling with mixed emotions about John's good fortune.

"It won't be the same," Eileen moaned.

"I'll miss him, too," I said.

Andrew's son Peter was already in Moscow. He was stumbling over Russian, but doing well in engineering courses at Lumumba University, where he reveled in the creature comforts. Plenty of water, hot and cold. Electricity twenty-four hours a day. Cheap vodka. Andrew was disappointed, but counting on the disillusionment that was inevitable, according to Moscow returnee Kibaki.

"Fatherly pressure. Counter-productive, but normal," Agnes observed. "Tell Andrew he'll get farther with a lighter touch."

"Who me?" I said.

"Who else?"

It was the only bad advice she ever gave me.

As if Peter's absence weren't hard enough on Andrew, it was time for Rafiq to leave for the U.K. His house was soon to be occupied by a black African family. His trucking business and garage had been sold—for a shockingly low price—to a Big Man's nephew, against whom no one else would bid. Since the new owner planned to hire his own crew, Rafiq's expert mechanics and skillful drivers— "Good men," according to Rafiq—were looking for work.

"That was the hardest part," Rafiq said. "I surprised them with severance pay. But it won't last long."

"I wonder if the Embassy is looking for mechanics," I mused. "Or drivers." Massoud's position had long since been filled, and our maintenance man had shaped up sufficiently to keep his job. Milly had seen to it.

"I'll check," Andrew said. "You never know."

Even the Land Rover had been sold, but Rafiq was desperate for a final weekend in the bush before he and his family boarded their flight to London. This farewell safari would have to include the whole gang, he decreed, including me, if I would trust Andrew's rattletrap outside the city.

"I'll trust you to repair it when we break down," I said.

"Free service," Rafiq promised.

And so the Dar contingent, with heavy heart, picked up Charles in Alipolaka and Sylvanus at the ranger station, where the Chief Warden assured us that we were likely to find the hartebeest our permit would allow us to take that weekend. "I've seen several," he said. And then he slapped Rafiq on the back. "Don't worry, my friend. Enjoy yourselves." Everyone got the message, including me. I really was a member of the team.

Making just one adjustment to our usual route, to avoid the pain of traversing the murdered Headman's village, we bounced along until we reached the tidy little clearing that was our headquarters in the bush. The tree with its low branches like welcoming arms; the fat, fanny-pleasing logs around the fire pit full of ashes from previous visits; the ruts from repeated Land Rover parking— everything was just as we'd left it. *We.* Andrew. Rafiq. Suleiman. Sylvanus. And

Charles, who would never know the anguish he'd intensified by not giving us timely warning about Alice and Little Rose. And me, the one who decided he was too young to bear that burden.

I wanted to drive for the hunt that afternoon, but my friends had hatched a little conspiracy. They ganged up on me.

"You're shooting," Rafiq said, handing me his rifle and getting into the driver's seat. "Not if you want to eat," I said, laughing.

"I'll back you up," Andrew said.

"But I don't want to shoot," I protested.

"Just this once," Rafiq said.

"Be a sport," Andrew said.

"Please," said Charles.

How could I refuse?

Rafiq at the wheel, Charles and Sylvanus spotting from the roof, we zigzagged through lightly wooded hartebeest habitat, and soon there was a rapping from Charles. On the right! Rafiq braked without alarming a sturdy young buck gorging on leafage that must have been unusually delicious.

All eyes—dammit!—were on me.

Stock to shoulder, eye squinting through the telephoto sight, which no longer mystified me, since I had done some practicing, aiming at and sometimes hitting trees, I held my breath and pulled the trigger. Bam! The animal bounded away.

Andrew shot. The animal fell.

"See," I said. "You got him."

"You wounded him," Andrew insisted. "I just finished him off."

There were indeed two bullet entry holes, one in the neck, one in the chest. Which wound been made by whose rifle? Impossible to say. Both weapons used the same ammunition. But neither Andrew nor I had fired an instantly fatal shot. Charles delivered the coup de grace with a knife, allowing the poor creature to bleed to death, which meant that Suleiman could join us for the final feast, a curry cooked by Rafiq, to which Suleiman added the appetizer, barely singed bits of hartebeest liver, as meltingly tender as the most decadent fois gras.

And then it was time to raise our beer bottles and belt out a raucous off key version of "For he's a jolly good fellow." A lion did us the honor of roaring.

The next day, after a large, late breakfast and a collaboratively prolonged process of packing up, we set off for Dar, Andrew driving. One by one we said good by to our companions, first Sylvanus, then Charles, then Suleiman—and finally Rafiq, who escaped only after a big long hug—and a kiss—from me.

Since it was Sunday, Mary's day off, Andrew and I had the house to ourselves and all the time we needed to make up, hungrily, for too many weeks of avoiding one another, aside from the shared official responsibilities we couldn't ignore.

"Why?" I asked, as we came up for air. "Why have we been punishing ourselves for things we can't control?"

"Not punishment," Andrew suggested. "Wound licking."

How well he put it! "Yes," I said. "Yes."

But something else had been gnawing at me, something I hated to mention but couldn't avoid any longer. "You know this can't last," I said.

He kissed my forehead. "We've always known that."

And so the fragile, fleeting nature of our relationship found its way into words that were surprisingly liberating. Yes, Andrew and I were star-crossed and futureless. But so what? Let all guilt and all those joy-killing, grasping fantasies dissipate like cumuli after rain. Accept, while you can, the mysterious gift of this unsought, unexpected, profoundly undeniable, core-to-core affinity. This love.

After that quiet kiss of acknowledgment, we came together again, sharing that strange deep tenderness that made our lovemaking what it was.

But my most vivid memory of that night comes from later, as we lay side by side, utterly satisfied, utterly relaxed. We faced a window through whose cast iron security grill a full moon cast patterns of light and shadow across our bodies. My white body wore dark, Maori-like designs. The same design on Andrew's dark skin was as pale as pure light.

"We match," I said.

"We always have," Andrew said.

That morning Mary served us coffee in bed for the first and only time. She seemed to be more delighted than surprised. Who else was playing it cool? I wondered. Had we been fooling no one at all?

25

Stay or go? Bid on Clive's job or move on? Facing a very difficult—and possibly delicate—decision, I decided to speak to Clive about the Ambassador's expectations—and the predictable consequences of disappointing them.

Candor can't always be counted on, but Clive was retiring. He could afford to be honest. And so he was. When I looked into his office, he put down his book. It was a travel guide, about India, which he and his wife planned to visit on their way back to the U.S. They would be enjoying airfare at government expense for the last time. He gestured to the seat in front of his desk and heard me out.

"It all depends on what you want," he said. "If you're feeling really ambitious, you should know that being a stellar PAO in Dar won't make anyone stand up and salute. On the other hand, if at any cost, you want to stay here—"

Oh my god, I thought. He knows, too.

"—if that's what you want, we can probably fix it up."

"Thanks," I said. "I'll have to do some hard thinking."

But Clive wasn't finished. "You've checked the listings, of course. You didn't see anything interesting?"

Actually I had—and the eye-catcher was probably the opening to which Delphin had alluded. The IO position in Lagos had gone vacant. It was rated as a One and it needed to be filled immediately.

Unlike Tanzania, Nigeria was no backwater. It was oil rich, although notoriously corrupt and worse: the vibrant, energetic port city that was Lagos was reputed to be the most violent capital in Africa. On the lesser level of daily irritation, no description of the city failed to bemoan the go-slows, the hard-to-avoid traffic jams that could steal half a day from drivers caught up in them. Not surprisingly, then, most FSOs, especially those with young families, refused to bid on otherwise good openings anywhere in Nigeria. Not in Lagos. Not even in Ibadan in the West or Kaduna in the North, where substantial U.S. consulates were located.

But I was childless and, although divorce proceedings had yet to be launched, any risk I took could harm only me. Colleagues' understandable prudence—or fear—could be my opportunity, a stretch position in a media rich country notorious for its unshackled cacophony of regional and national newspapers, news magazines, radio stations and TV channels. Not only would I snag an exciting job with more responsibility—I'd be supervising Americans as well as FSNs—which would put me on track for a reasonably rapid promotion.

"It's a stretch," I admitted to Clive. "But with the right recommendations—"

"Now you're thinking!" Clive said. "Go for it. Freeman wants you, but he won't get in your way."

The decision was wrenching, yet inevitable, except to Milly, still the mother hen, who drew me aside and said, "You have to be kidding."

"Why?" I asked.

"Name me one good thing about Nigeria," she demanded.

"Its potential," I said.

She laughed and said, "You'll survive."

And so, two weeks later, Andrew and I decided to risk a final safari, our fear being that Rafiq's homesick ghost might haunt us from beginning to end.

In truth, only his venturesome spirit was with us, because nothing terrible had happened to Rafiq or to anyone in his family. They were doing well, he'd written via a series of blue aerograms—no email back then. He'd made contact with long acculturated distant relatives, who'd eased their transition to life in the U.K. His younger kids were happy in school. His wife was adjusting. Since Rafiq himself possessed precious skills in a country where practically everyone had a car—or two, he was already well employed. And what were his long term plans? Another trucking company, of course.

We sought no hunting permits that weekend. We planned to be farmer friendly and go for a pesky warthog. Sylvanus did not object. Within a very few miles after we left the ranger station Charles spotted a boar. Expert driver that I'd become, I positioned the Land Rover. Andrew shot.

The warthog was on his side when we reached him, legs paddling air, not bleeding much, but shrieking in porcine disbelief. A shot from Andrew's revolver ended the squealing. For a few seconds, then, we stood there, observing the motionless creature. The hog's black hide was dusty from the struggle. Its tusks stood out like elephant ivory.

"Two cigarettes," Andrew said. "Do you want them?"

I refused, of course.

Andrew was unsurprised. From my first time in the bush, I'd been declining all kinds of horns and heads. I didn't allow photos of me with dead animals either. Still, he'd asked. Safaris require rituals.

Even before Andrew had shaken off the shame of the bungled kill, Suleiman had begun the skinning and gutting. Sylvanus, though never obliged to, was helping. His reward would be a generous supply of bush meat for his family. My share would go to Milly and Mary. I'd be leaving Dar in a few days.

Standing in the illusion of shade created by the sparse foliage of an acacia tree, I watched Suleiman. He detached the hog's head and set it aside for soup. Next came the portioning. He worked quickly and with such delicacy that his fingers seemed as clean when he finished as when he'd started. I was, as ever, admiring his skill, but my eyes kept straying toward those tusks.

They were unusually long, and there was a sweeping, elegant curve to them. The ivory was a bit yellowish, like a smoker's teeth, but they could be polished up. They could be made to gleam through time and space for me. When memories of Andrew's face begin to grow fuzzy, I thought, when each safari blends into every other, when my own experience gets confused with what I've merely read about Africa, when photos of me look like a stranger's, how else will I connect with the life I've had here?

"I'll take the tusks," I said.

Andrew smiled.

Suleiman reached for the severed head.

www.ingramcontent.com/pod-product-compliance
Lightning Source LLC
Chambersburg PA
CBHW032024050726
47590CB00006B/2297